OF
BEAST
AND
BEAUTY

OF BEAST AND BEAUTY

CHANDA HAHN

Of Beast and Beauty

Copyright © 2019 by Chanda Hahn

Neverwood Press

Editor: Hot Tree Editing

Beta Readers: Laura Martinez & Felicia Thorn

Map Illustration by Hanna Sandvig www.bookcoverbakey.com

978-1950440085 (Hardcover)

978-1950440078 (Paperback)

Also By Chanda Hahn

The Unfortunate Fairy Tales
UnEnchanted
Fairest
Fable
Reign
Forever

The Neverwood Chronicles
Lost Girl
Lost Boy
Lost Shadow

The Underland Duology
Underland
Underlord

The Iron Butterfly Series
The Iron Butterfly
The Steele Wolf
The Silver Siren

PROLOGUE

E veryone dreams of marrying a prince—except for me. I am nothing more than a pawn for my mother's revenge on the seven kingdoms. For she was betrayed by those close to her, scorned by her true love and cast aside like garbage. In return, she raised her adoptive daughters to be as beautiful as diamonds, cold as ice, formidable like the ocean, and as wicked as they come.

Each kingdom needed to be taught a lesson, and I was the chosen tool, her sharpened blade that would cut the deepest into the heart of this particular kingdom—the kingdom of Baist. I would rip their future from them by marrying their prince and future king. But like all deadly weapons, my wedding was a two-edged sword, and cutting them would cut me deeply.

For I am Rosalie, one of the adopted daughters of Lady Eville, and it is my duty—no, my joy to exact revenge on the realms, even if it means entering into a loveless and hate-filled marriage with the narcissistic crown prince of Baist.

CHAPTER ONE

Prince Xander's fingers tightened around my hand painfully, his knuckles turning white, until I realized my own fingernails were digging little moon-shaped divots in his palm and had been for a while. I relaxed my hand; he mirrored my actions, and the pain ceased.

We were pawns in a much larger game, stuck in an unwanted arrangement on both our parts, never having seen the other before meeting at the altar a few moments ago. Once I took his hand, my eyes were glued to the shimmering marble floor and my silk slippers that peeked out from under my too-short dress.

I honestly couldn't tell you what the crown prince looked like. I heard stories he was unpleasant and cold as the blizzards in the northern region, that he was cruel and short-tempered and tolerated very little in the way of women. Handsome, maybe, but I wouldn't know because I refused to look his way or meet his gaze through my thick, imported, white lace wedding veil.

Under my ceremonial dress, the silk slippers had no soles and therefore wouldn't carry me far if I decided to abandon my vow and run off in the middle of the ceremony.

A clearing of a throat drew my gaze to my adopted mother,

Lady Eville, who sat painfully erect in the second row, her dress of ornate silk as black as a South Adder's skin. She made a gesture with her finger, and I couldn't help but follow with my eyes to the beautiful young maiden sitting in the row across from her.

Young Yasmin Nueva from the Busan province had been previously engaged to the prince up until a few hours ago. Today was supposed to be their day. Instead, I was standing in her place, probably wearing a wedding dress custom-made for her, and her shoes. No wonder they pinched. I couldn't help but compare myself to his fiancée. She was petite where I was tall. Her golden hair fell over her shoulder, bedecked with sapphires and jewels that complemented her light blue eyes while my hair was black as a raven's wings. Her elegant ears sparkled as diamonds hung from her dainty lobes; mine were unadorned and had never been pierced. Light streamed in from the stained-glass window, catching her jewels as she sparkled and tried to outdo the bride standing before her. I had owned nothing as expensive as what Yasmin wore on a single finger. All of my jewelry was fake, or glamoured to appear real.

My hand gripped the prince's furiously, my anger needing an outlet at the injustice of my predicament, but I was able to calm my wrath as I imagined the prince's face full of scorn. My lips curled up in a smile as I glanced to King Gerald's puffy red face and then Queen Anya's, her face pale and drawn. Joy flew through me as I witnessed their discomfort at receiving a dose of their own medicine. Vengeance for my mother.

My arm dropped suddenly as the prince released his hold, but our wrists were tied together with elegant strips of lace and ribbon. It was customary for the newlyweds to be bound together the first full day and night—a symbol of their unity and love.

The priest didn't ask us if we would honor or cherish each

4

other; that was removed from the vows. In fact, there was a fair amount missing from the ceremony. It was painfully short, so as not to drag on the procession any longer than it needed to be.

"I now present to you Crown Prince Alexander the third of Baist and his wife," the court crier announced, leaving out my formal name as the crowd clapped slowly, hesitantly. Confused faces and looks covered most of them. The closest court ladies began to weep, and I swore Queen Anya fainted.

Only Lady Eville, my adopted mother, stood to congratulate us. I should have smiled. After all, we had won, and she had gotten her revenge. But the enthusiasm wouldn't come nor reach my lips. I was married to a prince—though maybe not the most cordial of suitors—but this was still my wedding day and a celebration. It was the only one I would have, and I wanted to enjoy the delicacies, the pastries, and the royal food the servants had spent all week cooking. There would be music, light shows displayed upon the marble walls, and dancing. I had never attended a formal dance, and my feet were eagerly moving toward the back of the hall. I was sure the prince would be a phenomenal dancer.

Prince Xander pulled me hastily down the altar steps, and I stumbled over my feet as I tried to keep up. I paused to greet the guests, but he veered left, dragging me out a side door into a darkened hallway. My thick veil made seeing difficult. The ribbon bit into my wrist as he swung me toward the wall and pressed my back to it. When he leaned close to whisper into my ear as if a lover would, my heart picked up and my breath caught in my throat as I waited expectantly.

"These vows do not bind you to me in any way," he growled harshly as he pulled our bound wrists between us. "Do not expect me to be faithful to you, or to care for you, you hideous creature of the night."

I sucked in my breath in outrage. "How dare you address me so? I am—"

"No one," he interrupted. "You are nothing to me, or the crown, and I wish to never lay eyes upon your face. You and your cursed mother. You did this to me." His voice was filled with disdain.

He pulled a bejeweled dagger from his belt and lifted it up to my cheek, running it down the lace. Through the thick veil, I could only make out that he towered over me, the halls still too dark to see any distinguishing features.

The dagger moved between us, and I felt a pressure on my wrist as he sliced through our wedding bindings. I gasped as the blade nicked me and the brightly colored ribbons spiraled to the ground, drops of my dark red blood littering the white tiled floor.

"Leave my sight and never cross paths with me again," the prince warned.

"What about the wedding celebration?" I asked angrily. He couldn't possibly mean for me to not attend.

He dashed my hopes with a scoff. "There will be no celebrating. Go to your rooms and stay there."

Prince Xander stormed down the hall, leaving me furious and alone on what was supposed to be the happiest day of my life. Instead, I felt my mother's words come back to me. *"Love is weak, but your anger makes you strong. Wrap yourself in your anger, and it will shield you from all who wish you harm."*

My fingernails bit into my palms, and I flashed my bloodied wrist into the air.

Fiergo.

My power lit every sconce on the wall and in the palace. I twirled my finger in the air again, and the discarded ribbons along the floor flew up and wrapped around my wrist, creating a bandage.

It wasn't lost on me, the irony of my wedding bindings becoming my bandage, or how I knew this marriage would bring me and the royal family nothing but pain. I could accept that. Pain was a close friend. We got along just fine.

Straightening my shoulders, I looked across to the mirror on the far wall, my curiosity piqued as I wanted to see myself on my wedding day. Lifting my veil, I saw my black hair, flowing loose down my back; eyes so light they looked silver but when angered turned dark. My unsmiling lips were soft and full. They puckered as I recalled the prince's words. *"I hope to never look upon your face."*

Pity, for I *was* beautiful.

A cough came from behind a stone column in the hallway.

"Who's there? Show yourself," I ordered.

Now that my magic had lit the hallways, I saw the rustle of a pink skirt move as a young child peeked around the column. Wide, fear-filled blue eyes looked back at me and didn't move. I waited for the child to decide if she would run or stay.

"They say you are a witch." Her voice was filled with distrust as she stepped out from behind the column but didn't come closer. "I think you're a monster." The tow-headed child stuck her tongue out and turned to run down the hall. Her retreating footsteps mirrored those of hundreds of other children from my village—although the ones from my village usually tossed rotten vegetables and dirt clods at me before scurrying off. There, I was a lowly orphan of Eville's tower who was used to being desecrated by rotting refuse. But today, minutes after marrying one of the princes of the seven kingdoms and becoming a princess, I would again be pelted with rotting hate-filled words.

Pressing my lips together, I ignored the child, like I had ignored the others before her. I didn't blame them for their hatred; they didn't know better. I blamed the adults. Their

7

minds were turned against the daughters of Eville since birth by their ill-informed parents. It was our mantle; their discord fueled us, taught us to ignore empathy and compassion and focus on our dark arts.

Holding my head high, I ignored the sounds of revelry and music coming from the ballroom, squelched the feelings of injustice and desire to dance, and headed toward my designated rooms. A servant had shown them to me a few hours earlier. I couldn't recall the servant's name, but I was impressed by the wide open room with the pale floral rugs and table by a fireplace. Two overstuffed sitting chairs surrounded a bookcase filled with books beside a window that overlooked the garden and woods beyond. I had my own private bathroom with marble bath and vanity. A king-sized four-poster bed covered with white down bedding sat next to a hidden door in the wall, disguised except for the silver handle.

I tried to open the door, but it was locked from the other side. "Where does this room lead to?"

"That is His Highness—uh, I mean your husband's rooms," the servant said.

"Oh?" I replied, unable to keep the blush from my cheeks.

Now that I was once again in my bedroom, I gazed at the locked door, knowing the prince was probably storming around on the other side. He made it clear that he would never grow to love me, his mind poisoned against my family, so he would never step foot into my rooms. I swallowed and bit back the taste of bitterness that crept into my mouth as I looked at my fancy prison.

Here, in these rooms, I would grow old and die unloved.

CHAPTER TWO

He's trying to starve me to death. My stomach growled noisily, and no matter the amount of tossing and turning I engaged in, I couldn't make it stop. Once I stepped off the carriage with my mother, and after our meeting with the king, I was rushed into the side rooms and poked, pricked, and measured by the tailor as they quickly altered a white lace dress to fit me. Then I was banished from my own wedding feast, and no one even thought to bring me a plate of food. It didn't take much to understand that this was probably based on the prince's orders.

Wrapping my arms around my stomach, I pressed against it, trying to concentrate on getting through the night and making it till morning. A loud grumble of protest from my body was the answer.

"I can't take it!" I snapped aloud and threw off the bedding. There was no way I could get back into my wedding dress by myself with how many buttons there were on the back—even though most of them had been ripped off, as I was left to undress myself. So that left me pulling out the same traveling dress I had worn here. Slipping the deep blue dress over my chemise, I dressed hurriedly. I wasn't planning on being out of my room long, only as much time as it took to get a plate of food and then return to my prison.

Opening the door, I peeked into the hallway. There wasn't anyone stationed outside guarding me; they were more than likely enjoying my own wedding feast. Tiptoeing down the hall, I listened at each turn and followed the sounds of music until I came to the foyer, then passed through to the ballroom.

Staying in the shadows, I observed how splendidly it was decorated. Great marble pillars lined the hall, flowers and vines adorning them. A head table had an array of succulent food and roses. The chandeliers sparkled, casting a warm glow around the room filled with people dancing, eating, and joyously celebrating. My mother was predictably absent. She would have left as soon as they married us to go back and attend to my sisters. The king's and queen's thrones on the opposite side of the room sat empty, visibly showing their lack of approval for our nuptials. Though it didn't matter that the bride wasn't his intended—the nobles stayed to revel in the merrymaking and the coming week-long celebrations regardless.

Entranced by the music, I hung back in the shadows and watched jealously as bedecked ladies were spun around on the floor in a twirl of lace, their jewels catching the candlelight. The music was heavenly, played by the fingers of supreme artists. Closing my eyes, I momentarily forgot the pang of hunger as I listened to the dulcimer and viola. I rested my hand upon my chest, feeling my heart beating in contentment, and I opened my eyes and smiled. Maybe I could find happiness here.

Skirting the room, I made my way over to a side table filled with food and glanced up at the head table, hoping to catch a look at Prince Xander in the flesh and not through a haze of thick veils. I wanted to get a glimpse of my husband. Two empty chairs with equally bare gilded plates dressed the table. It looked like he never even came to his own party either. I wondered where he had gone off to. Sighing, I cast a hungry look at the glazed duck, roasted vegetables, and various sides that were awaiting the bride and groom, but I dared not approach the head table.

Get food and get out, I told myself, then carefully maneuvered around the flowing ball gowns. Snatching a filled pastry from a moving tray, I retreated to a dark alcove and watched my wedding celebration from afar.

Taking another step back into the shadows, I snuck a bite of my pastry and sighed in pleasure at the filling of sausage, potatoes, and herbs. When I finished my treat and licked my fingers clean, I debated going back for another. It wasn't until I made to step forward that I realized I wasn't alone in the shadows.

A gentleman leaning against the wall, nursing a glass of wine, addressed me. "Have you come to spy on the witch?" He raised his glass to point toward the empty head table.

I glanced up into the heated eyes of one of the most striking men I had ever seen. His dark copper hair was slicked back, eyes a golden amber that flashed by the light of the chandelier, his chin angular and strong, his jacket cut bringing attention to his broad shoulders and slim waist. My heart raced as I took him in.

"No," I muttered, embarrassed that he had caught me slinking in the shadows, gawking at the head table. "In fact, I'm—"

"Lying," he cut in. His eyes narrowed as he looked critically at me, then let his gaze slowly roam over me, not missing a single detail. "No woman as striking as you would hide amongst the shadows."

"Maybe this woman prefers darkness," I whispered, but my voice sounded husky.

"So you've not come in the hopes of finding a wealthy husband?" His brows drew back in surprise.

"No." I couldn't keep the rare smile from my lips. If only this handsome stranger knew that finding a husband was no longer any of my concern.

He drew closer, raising his arm above my head to rest on the wall behind me. He leaned in, the smell of wine on his breath strong as he whispered, "Then you are here for a clandestine meeting with a lover, perhaps? If not, I'm sure I could help you find one."

"I'm only here for the food," I muttered, then stared up into the animated eyes, a renewed heat rising to my face. A deep rumble came from his chest that I at first thought was a growl until I realized he was laughing—at me. Not one to enjoy being laughed at, I tried to duck under his arm and move away.

"Wait, don't leave," he said, grabbing my elbow and stopping me from escaping. "I find your candor refreshing."

It was odd that, for once, I had a gentleman who was interested in being near me instead of walking to the other side of the road.

I turned and, out of the corner of my eye, caught a servant carrying a tray past our hiding place. Feeling the need to prove my reason for being here was based on hunger and not anything else, I leaned out and snatched two desserts from the inattentive servant, then slipped back into the shadows.

"Like I said, I'm only here for the food." Handing one to my secret confidant, I took a bite and smiled winningly. This treat was a cinnamon and honey scone covered in a sugar glaze. "It's quite excellent."

The gentleman was reluctant to take a bite of the pastry and instead was looking at me like I had grown horns. *Did I do something wrong? Was that not ladylike?* My heart raced as I realized how childish I must have looked. Instead, he signaled to a servant, who immediately appeared with a tray of drinks; he put his empty glass back on and took two, giving one to me. He held up his glass in a salute, and I met his with mine.

We ate our desserts in silence while sipping on our drinks. It was richer than any available from my hometown and had a pleasant aroma. Anything this fine rarely came our way. A warmth and a slight haze filling my body, I didn't feel at all uncomfortable as I sucked the sugary pastry glaze from my thumb, until I saw him watching my lips and fingers avidly. Quickly, I dropped my hand and held it behind my back, knowing he could construe my behavior as wantonness, and that was not how I wanted to behave. I had once again let my childish exuberance take over, and I wanted to hide in a corner.

Wait, I already am, with a very handsome man. I needed to take refuge in a different corner. Looking about, I tried to find a reason to escape and glanced back at the head table.

The man saw where I was looking and grinned. "Did you know?" he whispered like it was a great secret. "The prince married a witch." He gripped a goblet in one hand. "I don't know how he'll survive being married to her." His cheeks were flushed, and the wine kept sloshing out of the cup and over my dress. "She's only after his crown and will surely kill him."

"Is that so?" I answered bitterly. Any infatuation I had gained for him died and blew away in the wind.

His stylish dark copper hair fell into his eyes as he leaned forward to whisper, "He's cursed for all eternity."

"Why are *you* hiding among the shadows?" I asked.

"Because I'm avoiding responsibility for the moment and enjoying my conversation with you." The stranger took both of our glasses and put them on the floor near the wall. He leaned in close, his hand resting on my shoulder. "Who are you?"

"No one of importance. In fact, it would be best if you forgot you ever met me," I said.

13

Again my words made him pause. "There's something about you." His eyes dropped to my lips, and my breath caught. His fingers lifted my chin, and I became ensnared in the web of his amber eyes.

"I—" I was at a loss for words.

"Do you know what else shadows are good for?" I could smell the wine on his breath; he was heavily inebriated.

"What?" I asked, entranced by his nearness and scent— cedar and leather.

"Keeping secrets," he murmured, then pressed his lips to my throat. I gasped in surprise as the tingle of his kisses ran along my neck and up to my jaw, sending a shock of warmth racing through me. My toes curled and my breath caught in my throat. His lips sought mine, and I didn't pull away, my own curiosity dying to experience a kiss. It was everything I had ever dreamed and then more. My knees went weak, and he had to hold me as I almost collapsed.

"You taste amazing," his husky voice drawled as he sought my lips a second time.

"Stop," I breathed out, turning my head and avoiding his kiss. But I clutched his arms to keep myself from falling over. His kisses left me dizzy, and I needed his support to stand, but he was also tipsy and struggling to keep his own balance.

"No, please. Don't deny my last bit of freedom, for I expect to die tonight, murdered by my new wife." He leaned in for another stolen kiss.

"What?" I gasped, pulling away. The fog in my mind quickly cleared as his words hit home. *He's married! Wait,* I'm *married.* This couldn't go on.

Scared at the feelings he was dredging up and over-whelmed by new sensations he was stirring in me, I roughly pushed him away. His back hit the wall, followed by the crack of his head. I winced at the sound.

He stilled when he caught sight of a woman coming down the hall, dropping his hand from my waist and clearing his throat. Not wanting to be caught in the middle, I stepped back behind him as he approached the noble lady.

"Yasmin," he breathed out and straightened his clothing.

"Xander," she replied curtly, and my head snapped up when I heard the prince's name. The drunken lord I had been bantering and sharing a heated kiss with was none other than my husband. How ironic.

Yasmin stopped in front of Xander, her eyes never leaving his face, not even acknowledging my presence. "Is this it, then?" she asked. "The end of us?"

"No," he breathed out. "Despite my circumstances, we can be together."

Her beautiful blue eyes teared up, and she blinked prettily. "Words, my prince. Your words mean nothing to me when you have gone and married another, and I will not be your whore. You have made me look like a fool in front of my family and friends, and I am no fool," she hissed. "You are the fool who has pledged himself to a daughter of Eville. Do you not understand what you've done? Do you not know the ruin you've brought to our kingdom?"

"My kingdom," Xander said stiffly.

Yasmin's eyes widened at being contradicted. "W-What?"

"It is my kingdom, not yours."

"I meant no offense. It was a mere slip of the tongue. For goodness' sake, we were engaged to be married. We had dreams for the kingdom of Baist. It isn't a dream I can so easily give up because you tell me to. I can't give up on you. I won't. Please, tell me you haven't given up on me... on us."

This wasn't a conversation meant for me. I stepped farther back into the shadows and watched as a spectator at what I had stolen.

"Yasmin, I—" He faltered.

"How will you save your kingdom now?" she whispered, tears forming in her eyes as she turned and left down the hallway.

Her rejection seemed to undo him, and he leaned his head against the wall and rubbed his temples. Then he noticed I was still standing in the dark with him.

Frustrated, I turned, but Xander was quick, his arm pulling me back toward him. "Now do you understand my predicament? I will probably be murdered in my sleep tonight."

"Yes, you probably will," I heartedly agreed, plotting all the ways I could murder him without leaving evidence. I had already decided on six different methods when he distracted me by leaning in close, my breath catching.

Xander snatched another glass from a passing tray, raised it in a toast to his almost bride, and downed the whole glass. Here he was, my husband. And though handsome as the stories said, he was drunk, and I couldn't help but let it mar my opinion of him. It was obvious he didn't know who I was.

"Today is your wedding, sir," I said stiffly.

"Don't you think I know this?" Xander snarled at me. "Why do you think I'm here with you, drowning my sorrows in a drink? My one chance to save my kingdom, and I had it stripped from me as they forced me to marry an old hag. Now I'm doomed."

"Do you have no feelings for others at all?" I gasped.

"The only feelings I need to consider are mine." Xander stepped closer and reached for me, and I had a flashback to only a few hours ago, when he was blinded with hatred for me, refused to touch me when he thought I was his wife. Yet now, under no coercion other than alcohol, he had both touched and kissed me, not because he loved me, but because he found me beautiful and mysterious. I couldn't care less what deadline he had or his problems. He would never come near me again. This was not love but lust.

"Do not touch me!" I threatened, turning on my heel and storming away.

He made to follow me, but with a wave of my hands, I made sure his boots stuck to the floor with magic, giving me enough time to flee.

"I will find you," he called out huskily. "And you will be mine."

The more distance I put between us, the greater my fury grew, not daring to stop until I was back in my room and safe—but what could one consider safe from a prince in his own castle? Crossing to the door that adjoined our rooms, I pushed a heavy chair over to it, just in case a drunken Xander entered and preemptively murdered me in my sleep.

Murder, or something else?

My heart thudded in my chest, my mind reeling from the trail of kisses he left on my neck and the desire he had lit within me. I wasn't sure if I should pray that he never come near me again or if he could finish what he started. I had never been kissed, and unfortunately that drunken one was probably the closest I would ever come.

For in the light of day, there would be no hiding who I was. Once he realized it, he would avoid me until I died... or I murdered him.

CHAPTER THREE

Seek
Chase
Kill

I held back the silent scream of horror, my body paralyzed. Unable to breathe or move, I lay in bed as the night terror took over. Blood! There was so much blood. Tears pooled in my eyes painfully, but I couldn't blink, my fear having taken hold of my body so.

They had come back. The dreams. The visions. They had returned with a vengeance, and I struggled to not choke on the taste of iron in my mouth. An illusion or consequence of my gift, as I knew without any doubt that death had come. Not mine, for I never dreamed of me, but someone near me, close by in proximity, and their death was brutal. Never had I tapped into a killer's mind with such clarity, and what I had found filled me with terror.

When the episode passed and I regained control of my muscles, I sat up in bed and pushed the cover off my shaking and sweat-covered body. Slipping out of the bed, I moved to the window and looked out into the night, searching for the source of my nightmare. No other ominous feelings came, and I breathed easier. Maybe my dream was brought on by the stress of traveling, the wedding, and my very odd day, nothing more?

That's a lie.

I knew sleep would come no more until morning, so I sat in my chair by the fireplace and retreated deep into my mind.

When the morning rays filtered through the curtains and across my face, my nightmare seemed so far away, nothing more than a nightmare. A bad dream.

Instead, I faced a different nightmare as my eye-opening realization hit me.

The prince cheated on me on our wedding day—with me!

I sat in front of my mirror, fuming at what had transpired the night before. How dare Prince Xander seek the attention of another woman after we had taken our vows? He immediately promised that he wouldn't ever love me or be faithful, but to see it firsthand sent my blood pressure through the roof.

When I was angry, my sisters said I turned into the ice queen, my fire hidden behind my frozen expression. No one would know what I was thinking. I would go on and play the part they had assigned me to play.

Witch.

I roughly ran my brush through my hair as I glanced to the adjoining room door and the chair that hadn't budged.

Old hag.

I wasn't old. Barely twenty-two winters, and the prince looked about the same, maybe a little older. Maybe by kingdoms' standards, I was considered an old maid, but not to the fey. Still, I searched my face for telltale wrinkles and was pleased to see my face was flawless.

My eyes strayed to the door again.

He hadn't come. Mixed feelings of relief and regret

plagued me, and I pursed my lips in irritation. The day after my wedding and I was still as pure as snow.

Slamming the brush onto the dressing table, I turned to the door and wished I could bore holes into it with my anger and frustration.

Not only were they starving me, but no servants had even come to attend me this morning. At home, our family had a brownie who helped tend the house at night and keep the fireplace stoked. A cranky hob lived in our garden and took care of the animals and plants. I had yet to see any brownies, hobs, or house-elves around the palace. They were usually commonplace, even more so in royal families, but since arriving, I hadn't seen brown hide or furry tail. I would have to see if I could lay out some milk and attract one. With eight women under one roof, we relied heavily on smaller fey's deft fingers to work through the knots of our hair and braids.

Mother was once a lady of nobility from the highest of courts and privately taught by the brightest of tutors. She learned the languages and customs of the known kingdoms, their history, and everything a future monarch would need. Not to mention one of her tutors, Lorn, was an elusive fey of the north. Lady Eville was born and bred to become a queen, but heartache and betrayal befell her, and her family lost her fortune and cast her aside into poverty. Even her true love didn't save her. Heartbroken, she vowed to never love again.

Seeking solace in a lone tower in the town of Nihill, she continued her studies and planned her revenge. Until one fateful night during a storm, Lady Eville left the tower alone and returned three days later with me. I, Rosalie, became the first of her adopted daughters. Over the years, each of my adopted sisters came to our home in various ways. I didn't know my real family or where I came from. Lady Eville said we were the only family each of us would ever need.

I still do not know how my mother could force the hand of King Gerald to break the betrothal to Yasmin. *What magic did my mother do? Who did she poison or torture to get this outcome?*

Either way, I was here.

This was not how a princess should be treated. The beautifully carved wardrobe was filled with dresses too short for my tall and lithe body. My carefully brushed hair now fell in black waves around my shoulders. I fumed as once again I struggled into one of my own dresses from my trunk.

I placed my walking shoes on my feet and threw open my door, letting it slam against the wall. The loud thud brought a smile to my lips, but not to the line of girls cowering outside my door, who shrieked in surprise when they saw me.

"What is going on?" I snapped in irritation. Three of them who appeared not much older than my younger sister Aura were holding on to each other and shaking.

Confused, I stepped into the hall and looked right and left, but I could see no such troll or ogre that would send them into such a fright. The one nearest me pulled back, and I realized *I* was the creature she feared.

"W-We have brought you breakfast," the one with the honey-brown braid said, her voice barely above a whisper.

My stomach growled, and so did I. "Finally."

The short one cried out, and she might have fainted if the third girl hadn't held her up.

Rolling my eyes, I gestured to the tray in the first girl's hand and said, "Bring it in."

They didn't move. Sighing, I stepped far away from the door as they rushed in like mice, tripping over each other to set out the breakfast, make the bed, and tidy the room. In record time, they completed their tasks and headed back toward the door, except I now blocked their hasty exit.

"Names," I snapped, knowing my face was stony. I was irritated, hungry, and still anxious from last night. It couldn't be helped.

"Prudence, but everyone calls me Pru," the girl with the honey braid replied, her eyes glued to her worn shoes.

"Herez," said the second, her hand on the third's elbow.

"Tillie," squeaked the one who almost fainted. She looked ready to do it again.

"Why is my breakfast cold?" It was the first thing I checked after the tray was dropped off. "Is my room that far from the kitchen? Does the prince eat his food cold as well?"

Three heads shook fearfully, their eyes terrified like a young doe's. Answers would not be coming from them.

"Well?" I asked again and stepped forward.

Tillie was in the midst of pouring me tea, and the teacup slipped through her fingers to shatter on the floor. "Please don't turn me into a frog!" She dropped to her knees dramatically.

"W-What?" I stopped short, surprised by her display. "Where on earth did you—"

"We heard you turn the servants who displease you into frogs and then boil and eat their legs for dinner!" Tillie rambled.

"Tillie!" Pru hissed in horror. Herez clapped her hands over her mouth and stood trembling, her knees knocking together.

If I weren't so hungry, I probably would have laughed at the predicament, but I was in a surly mood, miffed once again by the rumors that had spread about me in the last twenty candle marks.

But I could also poke fun at myself. "Yes, and if I ever receive my breakfast cold or have to dress myself again, I will do just that. But not frogs—no, amphibians are overrated. I prefer rabbits. They're sweeter." I smiled demurely, clasping my hands in front of my dress.

"Eep!" Tillie cried out and almost fainted again, had Herez not stepped in and grabbed her by the shoulders.

I enjoyed their reactions a little too much. "Now, Pru, please return in half a mark with the seamstresses. I'm in need of a new wardrobe."

Pru's eyes flickered up and down my old dress and then over the wardrobe, the open door revealing all the frilly and lace pastel dresses hung inside. It was easy to tell from her expression that she thought I was being difficult or overly picky. I didn't feel the need to explain that all of them were at least four inches too short, created with the petite, delicate Yasmin in mind.

"Yes, miss." Pru curtsied.

I hated all forms of formality but decided to let them continue until I had established myself as here to stay. It already seemed like I would struggle.

"You may go," I said, and the girls scattered, tripping over themselves as they tried to escape.

Because I was starving, the cold breakfast hit the spot. I wasn't one to waste food, and it took very little magic to reheat the slice of duck and hash. A quick glance told me I was indeed eating my leftover wedding meal remade into breakfast. A hash was a phenomenal way to use scrap food, and with the guest list dramatically cut in half, I was sure there was plenty left over.

The quiet unnerved me. My sisters were always chattering among themselves, laughing, giggling, and playing pranks. Even now, I could almost imagine Eden pulling Aura's hair and starting a pillow fight. As the oldest, I was the one always charged with keeping the peace and order.

How I would have loved to be the one to throw the first pillow or cast a tangling spell on their hair, but duty came first.

Mother stated it was my duty to care for my sisters. My duty to help them with their lessons. My duty to be the instrument of her revenge. Duty had always been at the forethought of my actions, so much that I feared I may have missed much of my childhood.

A knock came at my door.

"Enter."

Pru opened the door, her head hung low. "I'm sorry, miss, but all the seamstresses are currently needed elsewhere in the castle."

"What of fey? Have you no brownies?" She shook her head. "Hobs? Gnomes? House-elves?"

"No, miss. The fey kind don't come near the palace anymore."

"Why's that?"

"They fear the beast that roams our land," she whispered.

"Beast?" I asked, but Pru looked frightened. The hair on my arm rose, and I looked out the window beyond, wondering if that was what I had dreamed about. "Tell me more," I demanded.

"It isn't safe to be out in the woods at night, is all. People who head into the woods beyond the castle after dark... never return."

"What about last night? Did anyone go out there last night?"

Pru's lip quivered with worry. "Thomas hasn't returned from woodcutting last eve. But it's probably nothing to worry about, miss. I'm sure he'll return in no time, right as rain," she said with gusto, trying to reassure herself.

I didn't believe it, but I wouldn't press the subject anymore. "Well, can you sew?" Her whole body trembled, but I assumed I saw her nod. "Then you will help me. Come in."

Frustrated with my lack of help, I took the cream from my

tea and headed to the fireplace, pouring it into a dish and arranging my offerings. I would try to coax my own fey servant to help me here in the palace, for I feared that any human help I would get would probably all end up abandoning me in the end.

As I was laying out the saucer, I noticed a broken piece of teacup still on the floor and picked it up. I winced when it nicked my finger but ignored it as I arranged the saucer of cream. Only when I was done did I notice the nick was bleeding, and small droplets of blood were on the bowl. I hoped none had dropped in the milk, for that might attract the wrong help.

Pru watched quietly, not daring to interrupt me. When I was finished, I dusted off my hands and turned to her. "Okay, that should do it."

"Do what, miss?"

"Take care of my lack of help." I waved her back into the room.

Pru entered and closed the door but didn't pass farther past the area rug. I went to my one trunk and pulled out my sewing basket, placing it on the table.

"Lay out the dresses, please." I pointed to the wardrobe, and the young girl obeyed.

When she pulled out the first dress, she turned with it still in her hands and her mouth popped open. "Oh, I see. These would never have fit you." She held it up to my neck and saw how far it was from touching the floor.

"Yes," I scolded. "Which is why we will have to alter them." I pulled my shears out of my basket and some white glamoured thread.

Pru cocked her head to the side and separated the dresses by color. "I don't think the pastels would complement your skin tone or hair, being it's such an unusual color."

I glanced up from threading my needle and gave her a

blank stare.

"I mean, your hair is beautiful. You don't find your particular shade this far west." My facial expression didn't change, and she became even more unsettled. "All right. I suggest we use the fabric from these two." She held up two deep emerald green dresses, and I frowned. Even though green looked beautiful on me, I always compared myself to a prickly thorn when wearing it.

"Very well," I sighed, not hiding my disappointment at the only salvageable dresses being my least favorite color. Beggars couldn't be choosers, though I never thought I'd be in this spot where I'd have to beg for help.

We laid out the dresses along the table, and I tried them both on, selecting the one that fit my shoulders the best. Cutting the other dress into pieces, we added flowy sleeves starting from the elbows and more layers to the bottom. I whispered as I sewed, weaving magic into the thread that would hide the seams and create the illusion that the dress was made from one fabric.

Pru kept glancing over at me while I worked, and after two full marks, we had a presentable dress.

We didn't speak much, considering whatever I said could send her running for the hills, but she stayed to help me into the dress.

"You look beautiful, miss."

"Why do you address me so?" I asked, confused that she would forgo my title and name. "I would rather you address me by my name."

"Which is?"

"You really don't know it?" I asked.

Her head shook. "Once it was announced that Prince Xander was no longer marrying Yasmin, the castle was...." She blushed. "They did everything in secrecy. Even the staff are unsure of who you are, other than the attendants for your wedding who helped prepare you."

I sighed and turned, giving the young woman a nod to thank her for her truthfulness. "I'm Rosalie, daughter of Lady Eville from the town of Nihill."

Pru's eyes widened. "Rosalie." She tested the title on her tongue and quickly cleared her throat. "I mean Princess Rosalie. It is a beautiful name."

"Thank you."

As she cleaned up the scraps, I made my way to the door to leave, but Pru caught up. "Princess, wait." I stopped. "You're not allowed to leave your rooms," she whispered. "When I returned, guards were put in place."

My hand was inches away from touching the handle, curled in a fist, but I hid it amongst my skirt. "Not *allowed?* Who gave the order?" I asked coldly.

"The prince again," she mumbled. "He has no wish...." She struggled to speak his order.

"You can relay the message without fear of reprimand," I assured.

She took a deep breath and started again. "The prince has ordered that he never lay eyes on you for fear you will put a spell on him."

"From my ugliness, I dare say." Pursing my lips, I held back a smile. "Is he even still alive? I could have sworn I was supposed to have murdered him in the night," I answered cynically.

Pru paled, her hand going to her chest. "Surely you don't mean—"

"That was a jest." I waved her off. "I, too, hear the things they say about me. Don't fret, the prince told me that one himself."

A smile came to her face, and she relaxed.

"But I can't be expected to stay in this room, despite the prince's orders. I'm not a prisoner, and I'm not afraid of the big bad prince." I opened the door and stepped into the hall. This time, my exit was halted by two guards on either side of the door.

They stepped in front of me. "Miss, please return to your quarters."

"I am," I said, prepared for this outcome now that I had fair warning.

"Excuse me?" the first guard said.

Gently touching my green dress, I quickly glamoured it to mimic Pru's blue servant attire. I'd taken the idea from last night's excursion, and I was counting on the fact that I was sure they had no clue what I looked like.

The guard glanced down at my dress and back up at me, then shook his head in confusion, blinking multiple times. A glamour sometimes gave the effect of déjà vu. "I'm sorry, miss, but I don't know you."

"Why should you?" I countered. "I'm the new princess's personal handmaiden. Were you here when I arrived with her the yesterday? I thought not. Surely, if you will require her to stay in her room, then I must be allowed to run errands for her." My lie counted on Pru's ability to keep a straight face. Luckily her fear of me outweighed her loyalty to the guards. She paled at how easily my lie came.

The guards gave each other unsure looks, and I needed to sell the lie. I leaned in to whisper to the nearest one. "Please? She is such a witch. I really need to get away from her, even for a few hours."

"She's that bad, huh?" the second guard asked, his bushy eyebrows rising in disbelief.

"Terrible," I groaned and rolled my eyes dramatically. "If I don't move fast enough, I get the switch." I made a whipping motion in the air. "If I serve her cold food—the switch. In truth, I call her 'the switch witch' when she's not around."

A chuckle from both guards was my response, and they waved me through, then looked back at the door with concern.

"Don't worry," I assured. "She hasn't recovered from the festivities of last night. I wouldn't expect her to rise until midafternoon. I'll be back to check on her after a while."

"Good, good," the second guard sighed in relief, pulling at the collar of his uniform.

Holding my head high, I carried on down the corridor as if I knew where I was going, then stalled around a corner and waited for Pru.

"Miss," she whispered in awe. "That was simply marvelous. You sure fooled them."

It *was* marvelous, and a thrill ran through me at how easy it was to deceive them. "Of course, I couldn't have done it without you. You could have given me away."

Pru shook her head. "N-No. I wouldn't dare contradict you."

"Good. Then I think we will get along splendidly." This girl kept surprising me with her quick loyalty, and I could use a confidant. "Pru, I would like you to become my personal attendant. Would you consider it?"

Her eyes lit up, and she nodded. "I will ask the steward first thing. Anything else, miss?"

"That will be all, Pru."

I meandered through the halls, memorizing the layout and entrances to the palace. With each servant or guard I passed, I studied his or her expression. Most were grim, fearful, or wary.

Death had indeed come in the night. Was there an investigation being held? Had they found the culprit? My servant glamour would give me access and answers to many questions I wouldn't otherwise know. Taking an abandoned load of laundry, I followed a pregnant servant into the washroom. I knew how to wash clothes, so I tossed the linens into the large stone basin and listened as I took the large wooden spoon and stirred the laundry. The ten ladies there spoke in hushed voices, worry in their eyes.

"Did you hear? Someone's dead. The beast has returned."

"Who?"

"Thomas Buckold."

"No!" An echo of silence filled the circular washroom, hands stilled, and the water in the basins calmed.

"How?"

"Throat mangled."

Gasps.

"Where?"

"Beyond the stables."

"Which ones, the king's or guards' stables?"

"Don't know."

The women tittered and prattled on like sparrows, repeating the same questions with no clear answers. I knew that to get real answers, I would need to look elsewhere, and that was outside near the stables.

Abandoning the wash, I left out a rear exit and into the courtyard. The pressure of holding the glamour on my dress began to build, and I could feel the headache forming at my temples. Releasing the servant glamour, I felt the pain immediately dissipate and breathed a sigh of relief.

A thrill of excitement slowly built again within me, and I made my way through the yard and to the king's stables.

Not caring who saw me, I walked between the white marble pillars and under the king's insignia of a wolf with a crown of thorns.

I was greeted by equine visions of the purest white. They were being groomed and brushed until their manes gleamed, saddles rubbed with oil and buckles polished. The stable hands ignored me as they went about their business, but I was quite taken with a particular white mare. The plaque hanging on her stall door read "Nova."

"Hello, Nova," I whispered and reached out to stroke her nose. At home we only had Jasper, our workhorse, and Bug, our donkey. I grew up trying to ride Jasper, but he did little more than stand there, refusing to move unless there were carrots or apples. All dreams of riding the countryside bareback, hair flying in the wind, were gone, as Jasper was more stubborn than the donkey and only let my mother ride him. We did eventually learn, but I wasn't one that particularly enjoyed riding horses and left that to my younger siblings. When we were younger, we were led to believe a widespread rumor that Bug was an enchanted prince and forced to live out his days in servitude to our mother. We each have tried to kiss him to break the spell, but were only rewarded with blank stares. Thinking back on it, it might have been Aura who had started that rumor.

I could see a host of guards by the far stables, standing beside a wagon. A large canvas covered a bag with what I assumed was a body inside. If I could get close enough, I could find out more.

"What are you doing?" a gruff voice called out. My hand stopped inches from Nova's nose. "No one's allowed to touch the royal horses except for us." The stable master wagged his crooked finger at me as he rushed down the row.

"I'm sorry, I didn't think there would be any harm."

"Of course there's harm. The priest himself blessed them. We are to let no unclean hand touch the horses."

"Don't be so harsh, Master Thomas," a masculine voice chimed in, and I turned to be greeted by one of the royal guards. Unlike the two behemoths at my door, this one was tall, with broad shoulders and a kind smile. He stepped to my rescue and quickly placed himself in front of me. "I'm sure the lady is pure of heart and her intentions were good."

The stable master sputtered, "But... but no one touches the horses."

The kind stranger placed his hand gently on my back and turned to lead me out of the stables. "Well fine, then she can touch my horse." He tossed the comeback over his shoulder in challenge and winked at me.

I couldn't hide the snort that followed. He gave me a cheeky grin, and I quickly settled my face, my mother's words coming back to me: *"A lady never lets her emotions show."*

Outside of the stable, I looked upon the horse whisperer a little closer. His hair was a sun-kissed blond, his eyes a warm brown, his skin tan from hours riding in the sun. The smile came easily to his lips, and I could feel myself falling for his charm.

"I'm Gaven Hostler," he said with a bow, his black-furred cloak billowing out from around his broad shoulders, where I saw a crossbow holstered. "And you, my lady, are...?"

He was obviously waiting for my name, and I panicked. I wasn't sure of his relation to the prince, and I didn't want to have those warm eyes change to a look of disgust.

"Rose," I answered, shortening my name and hoping he wouldn't put two and two together in case he had learned of my full name.

"Rose." Gaven held out his hand for me to place my arm across.

I was proud that I didn't smile or respond, but my hand shook as I gently laid it across his, Gaven's being the second male's hand I had ever touched besides Prince Xander's. My hand rested on his so he could draw his sword to protect me in a moment's notice, but who would protect him from me?

My eyes were drawn to how my fingers brushed ever so

softly across his wrist. Being treated gently and with respect was a new feeling and one that I desperately craved. We walked down farther to the guard's stables and entered.

"Here we are, Rose." He stopped in front of a large roan eighteen hands tall. Unlike the soft beauty of the king's horses, this was a horse made to carry a man in full armor into war. "Meet Wulfbringer, or Wulf for short." He stepped aside and let me confront the animal, and I felt petite next to his hulking frame.

I didn't immediately reach for his forehead, and Gaven stepped in. Grabbing my wrist, he brought it up in front of Wulf's nostrils and let the massive horse sniff and nibble along my palm, learning my scent. His greedy lips moved across my hand the same way Jasper's did. Feeling more confident, I brought my hand up and ran it down his long muzzle.

As I was being friendly with the horse, I saw a gathering of soldiers standing outside a closed-off area. Gaven watched me interacting with his horse with interest. I had never had eyes study me so intently; I dared not look up and meet his gaze for fear a blush would stain my cheeks.

"You haven't been here long, have you?" he asked. "I would have remembered meeting a beauty such as yourself." He cocked his head sideways, and I could see him studying me, a smile at the corner of his lips. Reaching into the saddlebag hung on a peg in the stall, he pulled out a carrot and broke it into three pieces, handing me one to feed Wulf.

Beauty. He'd called me beauty. My cold heart melted at his kindness. "No, I've only been here a few days. I came for the wedding."

"What are your thoughts of the palace so far?"

"It's beautiful, but...." I sighed and answered truthfully. "It's a very lonely place."

He handed me another chunk of carrot. "It *can* be lonely, if you don't stay busy."

"That's true. I guess I'll have to take up a hobby." As the weight of his words and the promise of a lonely future sank in, my spirits dipped and I frowned.

Gaven must have noticed the change, as he asked, "What's wrong?"

"Nothing's wrong. It is how it is. I can't change my class or wish for a different future or outcome."

"You can if you wish."

"I cannot. I am where I'm supposed to be," I said simply, but my inner turmoil was running rampant. I should have been happy. I was fulfilling my mother's wish, and I held a title on paper, but nothing else that came with it. No crown, no duties, and no love in a marriage. The depressing feeling weighed heavily on me, and I was finding it hard to breathe.

My eyes strayed back to the mass of troops that had blocked off the area behind the stables. Gaven saw where my attention had gone.

"You're not here to see the horses, are you?" His demeanor changed, and I heard the accusation. "You just want to see the body, like everyone else."

"No! I mean... yes," I sighed. "I'm here to get answers. I heard rumors of a beast, but what really happened?"

Gaven looked off into the distance and sighed. "Thomas knew the dangers of wandering the woods at night. He thought he was invincible. He was wrong."

"The last I heard, pride nor rumors were enough to rip out a man's throat."

"Maybe if he had betrayed a woman," he chuckled.

"Is that what happened?" I asked.

Gaven cleared his throat and coughed. "No."

"Then let me help."

His eyes met mine warily. "He's dead. There's nothing

more you can do."

"There is, actually, if I can just see the body. I might tell you who really killed him and set the rumors of a beast to rest." I cringed, hearing the words come from my mouth. How did I explain my gifts? His face would fill with revulsion once he learned what I had planned to do.

"No."

"What?" I looked up in surprise, meeting his stern gaze.

"I can't let his spirit wander aimlessly, haunting the palace. The sooner he's put underground, the better."

"What of his family?" I asked.

"He has no family." His face was pale, his lips pinched, and I knew I had hit a nerve. It was best to leave Gaven and the subject of his dead friend alone.

"My condolences," I said and bowed my head. I abandoned Wulfbringer and stepped out of the stables into the yard.

As we were speaking, a commotion had come about as a small retinue of men in red uniforms under the banner of a red rose on black rode in through the gates. Gaven's demeanor changed, and his shoulders stiffened. Those who had been gathered to look at the body ran back inside in fear.

"Who are they?" I asked warily.

Gaven didn't answer right away, and I could see his hesitancy. "Men from Florin."

"That's not good, is it?" I could read the tension in the faces of those nearest us.

"It's no secret that our relationship with Florin is tenuous."

"Why is that?"

"My apologies, but I must alert the king of their presence," Gaven said firmly, his face drawn.

"I will leave, then," I said and bowed my head, turning to go.

"Wait," Gaven called after me. "Please, allow me to escort

you to dinner tonight."

"I don't think it would be wise."

"Either way, you must eat. I must attend the prince, and you will attend me for dinner tonight. Now with our foreign visitors, it will probably be an even bigger spectacle than the wedding was last night. You will not want to miss tonight."

"Very well," I murmured.

"I shall meet you in the library at a quarter mark before seven." He bowed, brushing his lips across my knuckles lightly. Heat went to my cheeks, and I stared at my hand where his lips had left the barest of kisses.

I escaped, my feet dancing across the yard. *Don't look. He wouldn't be watching you, and if he did, you shouldn't care. Nothing will come of this.*

Right as I headed up the stairs to the side door of the palace, I cast a glance over my shoulder at him. He hadn't moved. His eyes met mine, and he tilted his head in a casual goodbye. I spun around, back stiff, and marched inside like I was part of a military parade. A chuckle echoed behind me, and my hands rose to hide the blush that was creeping up.

It took little concentration to change the color and shade of my dress back to that of a servant. I had more freedom in this guise and wasn't done exploring, but I knew to use it sparingly; if I held on to the glamour too long, the headache it caused would return full force. I wandered back inside the palace toward the banquet hall. In daylight, much of the magic had worn off from the night before. There were still lords and ladies sitting on benches talking, a few with croissants and tea, but the musicians had long gone, and the servants were in a flurry, cleaning and resetting for the week-long celebration.

I passed the outer doors to the gardens and paused as a cool breeze ran across my skin, odd for how warm a morning it was. Turning, I changed course and headed down the steps, studying the landscape and gardens beyond. Tall hedgerows and benches created many secluded sections for lovers and couples to sit and talk in privacy, and by the spare ribbon, hairpins, and random shoe, I knew they used the gardens last night during the wedding celebrations.

Even though we were poor and grew up working hard, Mother had always told us to protect our skin, keep it pure as snow, avoid the sun and its blemishes. We even learned charms to reflect the sun's rays, but now I was married. It didn't matter. I doubted a few freckles along my nose would be the end of the world. Sitting upon a bench, I lifted my head and smiled, daring the sun to mark me.

An acorn hit my dress, and I awoke from my daydreaming. Seeing no one, I turned and looked up at the palace doors as another acorn hit me in the back. Spinning, I caught the outline of a young girl laughing and running across the lawn to the hedge maze.

She was waiting for me and waved before running to the right down another path.

"Why, you!" I laughed and grabbed my skirts, lifting them high so I could chase after her.

My longer legs quickly caught up, and I followed her turn after turn. When I thought I lost her, I would backtrack and continue searching. Another pelt of an acorn had me circling and heading back in the right direction. The chilly air filled my lungs and my breath caught. I hadn't run like this in years, but playing with the child made joy fill my lonely heart.

"Come out, come out," I called and then slowed to listen to her steps. She was one row over, and I had enough glances to know it was the same child who confronted me the night before.

Her breathless laugh came through the thick bushes before turning into a shrill scream.

CHAPTER FOUR

My heart thumped in fear as I raced down the row, unable to find the path that would take me to her. I raised my hand, commanding the vines to unfold and the tree to pull back, and a path opened through the hedge for me to pass through. I found her on the ground, her legs pulled up to her and a black-and-white diamond-backed adder raised to strike. Its hood flared in warning, mouth open in a hiss.

"*Incendium,*" I murmured, and the adder burned and turned to ash. I felt the world shift, as if it were pulling away from me, a magical shunning or recoil as it disapproved of my actions to kill so easily.

I kneeled by the young girl. "Are you hurt?"

She shook her head, but I could see the faint scratches from thorns across her arms and skin. With a quick spell, I ran my fingers across the cuts and they healed.

"Can you walk?" Again a headshake. "I'm going to carry you, okay?"

Her eyes went wide; she couldn't look away from the pile of ash that was the remains of the adder. I picked up the girl, but my skirt that I had just spent an hour adding length to was now too long and hindered my steps. Gently, I placed her back on the ground and regretfully tore off the edge of my servant skirt to expose my ankles, knowing I was really ripping my green gown.

She wrapped her wrists around my neck, and I carried her back out of the hedgerows, never making a turn, just whispering to the plants and bushes to move out of my way. Through each row we passed, I heard her squeak of fear as she watched the hedge close up on itself again.

My eyes closed and I bit my lips when I heard her utter the word "witch" again.

"What's your name?" I asked as I stepped through another row of hedges. We had to be nearing the edge soon.

"Ameline."

"That's a beautiful name," I murmured. "I'm—"

"I know who you are," she said impudently, but immediately regretted her tone and cast her eyes down.

After trudging through the next row, we were through the maze, and I came out one hundred feet from the entrance to the palace. Turning, I adjusted my course across the lawn to head to the doors, but none other than Prince Xander was standing at the fountain, scanning the grounds.

"Ameline!" he cried out in alarm. "Are you all right? What happened?"

She began to pout, and even though she had been calm mere moments before, the waterworks turned on for Prince Xander.

The light of day did not diminish his looks but highlighted them, accentuating his tan skin. His brows furrowed and he glared at me, taking her roughly from my arms. "Explain yourself," he snapped. His eyes were bloodshot, and I would dare guess that he was sporting a terrible headache from his drinking last night. It was obvious he remembered me very clearly, based on the heated glance he gave me and the hatred that was now rolling off him in waves.

39

My cheeks burned in embarrassment, but I was able to gather my thoughts. "I was playing with Ameline, and we were startled by a Sion adder."

"You must be mistaken. There are no such adders in our land."

I scowled and snapped. "I can only tell you what I saw, and I don't lie."

"Then show me this creature." He carefully put Ameline down on the stone path and took a step toward the maze.

My heart plummeted and I murmured, "It's gone." There was no way he would look upon a pile of ash and believe I, a young maid, had destroyed this enchanted creature on my own. He would surely call me a liar.

Xander sighed and looked up at the palace; then his face darkened and his voice became bitter. "It must be the curse brought on by the daughter of Eville. Only she could bring forth such a creature."

"Oh really?" I said in disbelief. I balled my hands into fists, ready to summon forth a fire elemental into his trousers, but he wasn't finished with his tirade.

"First my marriage is ruined, then Florin arrives, and now an adder attacks my sister. It's because of *her*." Xander closed his eyes and rubbed the bridge of his nose. "I can only say that the future looks bleak. There will be more deaths before the moon runs a full cycle."

"More deaths?" I asked fearfully.

He ignored my question, looking down upon his sister. "Ameline shouldn't have been left alone," he reprimanded me.

"I didn't, and I'm not a ser—"

"You're not?" He looked down at my servant's dress and shook his head. "You could have fooled me. How dare you pretend to be a lady when in fact you're nothing more than a servant? You should be ashamed."

OF BEAST AND BEAUTY

"I can explain."

"Impersonating someone of higher class is considered a crime."

"I wasn't." He wasn't letting me clarify, but I could see he didn't like being deceived, and his pride was hurt. There would be no amount of rationalization that would satisfy his ego, and I refused to belittle myself and beg for his understanding.

"You were lax in your duties, and in doing so, you endangered the princess. You should be reassigned. You obviously are not suited for nursery duty."

"I beg to differ," I stretched the truth. I loved children, but they generally feared me. I wasn't going to tell that to the prince though.

His dark amber eyes were filled with loathing, and I knew that no matter what I said, he had already formed his opinion of me. I rested my hands on my hips and glared back in challenge. I wasn't going to back down.

A wry grin crept onto his face. "I know. Why don't you go and serve my new wife."

"But, Xan." Ameline pulled on his sleeve as she tried to warn him of his folly.

"Hush, Ameline," he commanded, and the child fell silent. She looked up at me, her eyes twinkling with the secret she seemed inclined to keep. "I've already heard that she's complained about not having servants or seamstresses available at her beck and call, so I will assign you to her from now on."

With the way he was grinning at me, I believed he thought it was going to be a cruel form of punishment.

A page came running out of the palace to greet the prince. His face was red, and he looked out of breath. "Your Highness, the king is about to meet with the emissary from Florin."

"This isn't good. Did they come alone?"

"Just Lord Earlsgaarde and his retinue, sir."

41

Prince Xander stilled and stared off into the distance. "What an auspicious day for them to arrive. Did they say what they want?"

"No, sir."

"Double the guards on the queen and my sister. Have more patrols out until they're gone from the palace. I want all eyes on them. Do you hear?"

The page bowed and ran to obey the prince's orders while questions filled my mind.

"Is there anything I can do?" I asked, forgetting my place.

"Do?" Xander gave me a seething look. "What could you possibly do? Wait. See to it that my wife stays out of my sight and out of the way of the emissary. Her presence will only muddy the waters as I try and navigate this delicate situation."

"But wouldn't you want—" I started, wanting to plead my case to be by his side. It was the wrong thing to say.

Xander snapped at me, his eyes blazing with warning. "Don't ever presume to know what I want. That would be folly on your part." He cocked his head and studied me, silently wondering how much education I probably received as a servant. What he didn't know was that I received plenty of tutelage, and that it was my naivety that was getting me in trouble.

"I'm clever enough to know that you're stupid to believe all this that's befallen your household is because of one woman."

Xander took a threatening step toward me, but I held my ground, my chin rising, my eyes meeting his in challenge. "I can and I do. Much ill has befallen us already because of one woman."

"Xander, please take me inside." Ameline was becoming restless, trying to warn her brother that he shouldn't challenge me. At her level she could see my hands curled into fists. She had seen my power with her own eyes and knew if it came to a fight, I could reduce her brother to a pile of ash. She pulled on his arm with all her might, turning him away from me and toward the castle.

Xander continued to study me like I was an aberration with two heads. "You are so odd." Then he looked at my ruined dress and exposed ankles, frowning in disapproval. "Get your dress fixed. No one should serve my family wearing rags." He turned, pulling Ameline into the palace after him, leaving me shaking.

My earlier joy was shot down like an arrow to the heart as anger took over.

CHAPTER FIVE

L ifting my skirts, I turned to catch up with Pru, who I had seen walking through the hall. In her arms were reams of fabric, and behind her were three women, each holding four or five gowns each. Where she had procured the dresses, or the seamstresses, I didn't know or care to ask. It seemed they weren't as busy as I had been led to believe. I grabbed a few bolts of fabric from Pru to help relieve her burden.

The guards met us at my own door and let us in without much ado. The one from earlier met my eyes and leaned in to whisper confidentially, "I understand now, what you go through. She is a horrible monster of a woman."

"She is?" I asked, confused, before remembering I had led them to believe that I, the horrible witch, was still inside.

"Yes, you should have heard the fuss she was making. Be careful. She may take out her anger on you," he warned.

I stilled at the lies he spurred forth. *Yes, I might take a switch to him.* My eyes narrowed as I prepared to whisper a curse. Pru caught my wild glare and reached back, grabbing my wrist, then pulled me into the room after her and slammed the door behind us.

"How dare he?" I fumed, tossing the bolts of fabric on the

table before I turned to grasp the door handle. Pru had placed herself in front of the door to prevent me.

"My lady," she begged. "Please, do not give Fagen another thought. He is mindless and was only trying to prove he was your friend."

"By spreading lies," I snapped.

"No more than the ones you yourself uttered a few hours earlier." She winced as if she expected my hand to follow her outburst. But it didn't. Her gaze flickered to the women standing still in the middle of the room, their mouths open as they no doubt realized I wasn't some servant but the lady they were to serve.

Closing my eyes, I released the glamour and sighed. Releasing a glamour was like breathing after holding your breath too long. It wasn't a comfortable spell, unless you possessed an item from that person or you were my talented sister Eden, who could fall asleep maintaining a glamour.

The ladies gasped when they saw my servant dress transform into my emerald-green gown with missing trimming. I banished my anger and tried to recover my composure. Once I was sure I had my mask of indifference in place, I looked over the women and the fabrics and said, "Let's begin."

Under my supervision, we were able to get quite a few dresses altered to fit me, and I was pleased with the color and cut of most of them. For dinner, I had chosen a deep purple velvet dress that accented my dark hair, which was curled and pinned with long tendrils flowing down my back. The seam-stresses learned my bark was far worse than my bite, because after an hour of intense silence, they relaxed and began to talk amicably amongst themselves.

I did, however, notice the milk in my saucer was gone. Which meant a fey had taken my offering and agreed to serve me. With all the hustle and bustle of the ladies in the room, I had yet to see what kind of fey it was, and none presented themselves for introduction. I wouldn't fret; some only came out at night, and I knew I would just have to be patient.

When it came time for my meeting with Gaven, I felt nervous and sick to my stomach. It was the lying that was bothering me. I didn't like to lie or deceive anyone, but it was clear that most of the palace had already come to their first impressions of me without having even spoken to me.

My head was already throbbing from my overuse of glamour, which meant I would be paying for my choice dearly later on. Pru and the seamstresses had excused themselves, taking their work with them and leaving me to await the dinner hour by myself.

Taking no chances in case of a changing of the guard, I touched my beautiful dress and glamoured it into the blue of the servant attire, then yelled, "Get out, you miserable girl! Leave me alone. I don't want to see your face!" For good measure, I tossed a heavy book at the wall.

Stomping my feet, I rushed to the door, threw it open and slammed it behind me, playing on the fact that I had just been banished from the new princess's room.

Sure enough, there were new guards. "I heard from the other guard that she's bad news," the short one said.

Not daring to speak, I just nodded and walked away, keeping my smile at bay. This was proving to be entertaining. Once out of their sight, I released my glamour and let a renewed confidence overtake me.

I had learned that the morning and noon meals were served buffet style, the food kept warm with charms for the guests and late risers. The royals usually took meals in their rooms, with only dinner as a set time and formal occasion.

Passing through the formal sitting room, I made my way

into the library. As I waited for Gaven, I reminisced about my sisters and home.

Closing my eyes, I dreamed of my room in my tower. It wasn't much, but it made me happy. The old guard tower had been abandoned years ago and had undergone multiple additions by various owners, with little thought to architectural design. It was a hodgepodge of style with a large yard, stable, and gated vegetable garden. It was outside of town a ways, near the woods, and we were usually left alone, unless someone was coming for us to heal a cow, gain good fortune, or acquire a love potion or two.

Our bedrooms were on three separate floors of the tower itself. I shared the upper floor with Aura and Eden, my younger sisters took the second floor, and Mother Eville lived on the main level. Our room had two small paned windows with wooden shutters, one of which was frequently left open for Maeve to come and go as she pleased. I hadn't spoken to my sisters in days; before, when we lived together, we hardly went hours without communicating with each other. It was easy to imagine Mother Eville sitting in her high-back chair, knitting and instructing the others in their needlework and spells. In the evenings, we would sing in the language of the old fey, because she said it was easier to learn if sung than spoken.

Maeve, a shapeshifter from birth, would swoop in over dinner and tell us all the gossip she had learned while in fowl form. Usually it was about the boys in town and whom they were courting. A smile fell upon my face as I imagined her frown at the thought of yet another eligible suitor being off the market.

Off the market. Despite being told to never love, for it made us weak, each of us dreamed of being loved, marrying, and settling down. But who could ever love us? Scorned, cursed, and ostracized, we were doomed to carry out spinsterhood. I was still uncertain how I ended up being married to a prince.

I had heard the marriage banns go out, announcing Prince Xander's engagement to Yasmin, and all of my sisters began to discuss who the lucky lady could be.

"I bet she's beautiful," Aura said with a sigh.

"No, she'll be shallow," Maeve answered. "All of the pretty ones are. Probably doesn't have a lick of sense to her."

"That's rude," Aura said.

"Not if it's the truth," Meri countered.

Lady Eville had read the wedding announcement aloud, then crumpled up the paper and tossed it into the fire. She patted her dark hair in place, straightened her shoulders and looked among her seven daughters carefully, her piercing green eyes finally resting upon me. "Come, Rosalie. Pack your trunk."

"Where are we going?" I asked, confused.

"You're going to meet your future husband."

The room erupted into squeals of delight from my sisters as they all began to talk at once and ponder who the lucky lad could be. Me, my hands trembled as I walked up the narrow and uneven steps to the top floor of the tower and began to pack my few belongings.

A husband.

I had never in a million years dreamed I would marry, and so suddenly too. Once the fear and trepidation faded, excitement took its place. Opening my wardrobe, I assessed my best clothes, or lack thereof. Nothing that would do for marrying, but maybe I could alter one of my newer dresses and it would be good enough. I carefully folded my three least-worn dresses and laid them inside.

Next, I moved to pull out my sewing kit from under my bed, along with my bag of medicines. Under my slightly sloping bed, I had quite the collection of books on charms, spells, dead languages, herbology and, of course, a fey tale or too, but I couldn't take them all. What if my future husband didn't want a wife who could read? Running my fingers over the leather-bound beauties, I picked out my herbology text and left the others, although it pained me to do so. I felt like I was saying goodbye to my children. Who knew after I was gone if my sisters would care for them the way I did? Probably not, for none loved to read as much as I did, and none loved flowers like me.

When I had finished packing my trunk and changed into a traveling outfit with skirt and cloak, I cast a charm to make my trunk lighter. It floated down the stairs after me like a kite on a string. I was ready. Mother had sent for a carriage, and her trunk was already loaded. She had only packed one traveling bag, which meant she wasn't planning on staying long, wherever we were going.

After my trunk was secured, I turned to say goodbye to my sisters. The departure felt sudden and unnatural, more like a dream. I would wake up and everything would have been a mistake.

"Where are you going, Rosalie?" Aura asked.

"I'm not sure, but don't you worry. I can take care of myself."

"Who will take care of us?"

"You will, of course," I chastised.

Aura pouted, her bottom lip sticking out. "Ugh, that's too much work." But her pout wasn't real and was followed by a wink. "What if you marry an ugly man?"

"Then I pray he has a beautiful heart," I said.

"What if he has a beastly heart?"

"Then I pray he is handsome on the outside." I pinched her in response. "'Cause I'm not sure anyone could ever really love a beast."

I hugged each of my sisters goodbye, and though tears fell from their eyes, none fell from mine. I was cold inside, not one to let my feelings show, other than my anger.

I sat silently next to Lady Eville as we sped along the dirt road. The streets of Nihill weren't cobbled or paved, and there were a few potholes big enough to swallow a small child and injure horses. I used to sneak out in the middle of the night and use my power to fill the holes back in so no one would be injured. I wondered if anyone would do it once I was gone.

After an hour on the road, I gathered enough courage to ask her, "Where are we traveling to?" I knew better than to ask who my future husband was.

"Baist" came her curt reply.

One of the seven kingdoms that had scorned her years ago. I knew then that this had nothing to do with a marriage of convenience and everything to do with her revenge. My heart sank a little at the thought, but I quickly pushed it aside and wondered how my marriage could possibly affect the kingdom.

Baist, from what I remembered of my studies with Lorn, our fey tutor, was antiquated in their views and behind the other kingdoms in magic use and scientific advancements. They had driven out much of what they didn't understand, or shunned what scared them. The streets were not lit by mage lights but by oil, and their crops were grown by the sun and rain, not magically modified. Their produce was highly sought after by those who had developed reactions to the other six kingdoms' MMPs—magically modified produce.

There were a few healers in the land—after all, the royal family needed to be protected—but medicine was outlandish. Magic mirrors, steam engines, and moving picture boxes were unheard of, and foreigners were unwelcome. The whole country was pure in its views, untainted by outside influences of magic, for magic was bad, used for manipulation and deceit, and nothing good could come of it.

"It's essentially trapped within the past." Lorn had drawn a circle around the country of Baist, and I shivered at the thought of having to live in a country without magical necessities.

"Why is that so?" Aura had asked.

"Because there are no key ley lines of power under the country." Lorn had pulled down an enchanted map of the seven kingdoms. Glowing lines spread out along the different kingdoms, except none passed through Baist. This meant magic would be harder to use, with nothing to tap into or draw from but nature and ourselves; whereas in some kingdoms, whole cities were built around a cross section of ley lines and they flourished. Even the weakest of those in magic could call flame, water, or air, for ley lines amplified their gifts.

"Who in their right mind would even consider living there?" Maeve had huffed. "Do you realize how strong a magic user would need to be to even cast the simplest of spells?"

Lorn had ignored Maeve and looked right at me. "Only the strongest of you could survive there."

And now here I was. Had he known this was my destiny? That pulling off what I did in this forsaken kingdom took more energy and toll on myself than I was used to? He must have known.

I smiled as I thought of Lorn, our handsome tutor. Each one of us, at one time or another, had a crush on the ageless elf, who more than likely viewed us as children. Our years, all less than twenty-two, would be mere babes to his two hundred. His hair was long, black as coal, his eyes as gray as ash, and his ears pointed, the only real giveaway to his fey heritage—that and his magic.

He was the one who evaluated each of Lady Eville's daughters and chose our course of study. He would show up on the very first day of winter and leave once the first flower bloomed in spring. Where he traveled the rest of the year was a secret, one we had tried to wrench from him, but he always smiled mysteriously and gave us a vague answer.

"I must go travel the ley lines and keep watch over the kingdoms," Lorn would say. Why or how the handsome fey came to be included in our reclusive family, I wasn't sure I would ever know.

I knew my mother had placed a traveling charm on the road, for Baist was more than a three-day trip but we made it in one. When we came to the city, I was enthralled with the quaint and beautiful scenery. Unlike Nihill, the town's shops and cottages were decorated with brightly painted windows and trellises with wildflowers. A sweet aroma of baked goods hung in the air, and I leaned out of the carriage and breathed in the fragrant scent. A sigh escaped my lips as I fell in love with the city. Even the girls selling their wares in the streets had ribbons wound through their braids and stitched into their aprons and skirts. Such a simple design but present on every door, window, building, and article of clothing.

Looking down at my own dress, I wished there were an array of colors on my skirt as well but knew Mother would call it foolishness. My dress was fine the way it was. A decoration would not hide the heavily worn and thinning fabric—only magic could.

The city was at the base of the mountains, the palace farther up the trail surrounded by woods and a mountain range. The farther from the lively city we traveled, the heavier my heart became. The path was dark and gloomy as we traveled up the mountain until I could behold the palace.

Palace was a misnomer, as it was more like a stronghold. Tall walls surrounded it, but beyond the walls were woods filled with mists, and I wondered what creatures lived within. I shivered, pulling my cloak closer to my chin as we waited at the gates for the guards to let us pass. They weren't going to until Mother used her compulsion on them to open the gates and we entered. I turned in the carriage and watched the iron gates close behind me, wondering if it was to keep people out or in. Thankfully, once we were inside the courtyard, the morning sun began to rise and the mists dissipated, showing the beautiful landscaping and gardens.

Our arrival at the palace came with much grief. When we stepped out of the carriage, we were quickly swept inside and out of sight. Pity, for I had wanted to spend more time looking around. When it was made known that we were here to speak with King Gerald, we were first laughed at, but then my mother held up a letter sealed in wax with the king's signet and the laughing stopped.

We were ushered into the sitting room off the library and made to wait for close to a full mark. Feeling restless, I made my way around the room, trailing my fingers across the pianoforte and then looking out of the high windows into the garden beyond. Through adjoining double doors, I wandered into the library, my heart racing at the beautiful leather-bound books. Knowing it may well be another mark or two before the king came, I settled into a chair with a book to read, but traveling through the night had exhausted me and I fell asleep.

An angry voice awoke me from my slumber, and the book slid from my lap onto the carpeted floor. Picking up the volume, I placed it on a side table and tiptoed close to the double doors, peeking through their slight opening and listening to the conversation coming from the sitting room.

"How dare you show your face here, Lorelai?" I assumed it to be King Gerald. The king had copper hair that fared toward red into his beard. His cheeks were flushed with anger, and he only had a little paunch in his stomach. He was still attractive, for his age. "After what you did to us?"

"You needed my help—begged for it, you might recall—and I gave it to you."

"What do you want, witch?"

"Witch? Do you so easily forget that, once upon a time, you begged for my hand in marriage?" She laughed heartily. King Gerald's jaw twitched. "I've heard the rumors about Florin and have come to help you."

"I will not accept help from you. Your price is too steep, and I cannot afford to pay it again."

"Fine, then I am here to collect on our first deal. Imagine my surprise when I received news of Prince Alexander's upcoming nuptials. That is not what was promised to me, King Gerald. You promised me your firstborn, and I find you go behind my back and arrange a marriage."

"It's been years and nothing. You never came. I thought you had changed your mind, forgotten our deal or didn't care anymore."

"I never forget a promise. I just had no use for him yet. But now I do."

"N-No, not Xander," King Gerald cried out, and I heard the agony in his voice.

I gasped, covering my mouth and pressing my ear closer to the door. Never had I suspected my mother to be so conniving that she dealt in children. What deal had they made? What curse were they referring to?

"Yes, Alexander. You will stop this wedding this moment, and you will honor our deal." I leaned forward just enough to see her hold out a scroll and unroll it. "Or does a deal in blood not mean the same thing as it used to?"

King Gerald sighed and sat down in a plush chair. "What would you have me do? I have no other male heirs to the throne, and Ameline is too young to ascend. If you take my son, you leave our kingdom in a predicament that could very well lead to war. You know we're not on good terms with Florin. If they see we're vulnerable, we will be attacked. Which is why the alliance with the Nueva family is essential for our country. We gain their armies."

"Silly fool," she snapped. "Why do you think I'm here? I have not come to demand your son's life. I'm here to bring him his wife."

"W-What?" the king stuttered, and I gripped the wall to keep from falling over.

"You will keep your son, he will ascend as king when you pass, and he will not marry this Yasmin girl but my daughter. She will be all you need to protect your precious kingdom."

"I would never agree to this. I would rather he die than marry someone raised by you. You're the epitome of evil." King Gerald slammed his hand on the table, his face flushed a deep red, before grasping the chair for stability.

"If that is your wish, so be it." Her voice was somber. "But be careful who you call evil."

"I could have you cut down right here," he threatened. "My guards will kill you, dispose of your body to be eaten by dogs, and no one will ever know."

"Yes, you could, but that would not put an end to your problems." She held up three fingers and smiled callously at the red-faced king. "I'll give you three days to say goodbye, and then he will be gone." She snapped, then made a *poof* motion with her hands.

"No, no, wait." King Gerald's face crumpled. "You win. He will marry your daughter."

"Excellent." Mother smiled, and I shivered. I'd learned early on that her smile did not necessarily mean good things.

"When shall we arrange the wedding? Next spring?" he

asked, pulling over a spare piece of parchment and inkwell, preparing to write down the new date.

Mother walked over to a table set with a vase of dark red roses. "Why waste a perfectly good celebration? After all, the guests are already here." She turned and raised a dark eyebrow. "Why not tonight?"

The king sat down roughly on the cushioned chair, the legs scratching against the floor. I heard his low groan, followed by my mother's twinkling laughter and I cringed.

Less than six marks later, I was married.

I sighed and wandered the library's shelves, looking for a romance book I could sneak back to my room, when I heard the door open in the front room. Thinking it to be Gaven, I peeked out to find Xander had entered, King Gerald on his heels.

"What are we to do?" King Gerald hissed angrily at him and closed the door to the hall, cutting off my escape.

"I did not murder that man, Father," Xander growled out.

"Then who did? What other explanation do we have?"

"There's something out there, hunting beyond the wards, taunting me to find it. I can smell its stench."

"It's because of the daughter, isn't it? She probably did this, and now Florin is here. What do we do?" King Gerald groaned.

"Keep them occupied," Xander said. "Distract them from finding out the truth."

"This is all my fault. I did this to you." King Gerald waved his arms in the air.

"I swear on my crown and my life that if there's a way to undo what's been done, I will find it. Even if it means making another deal with the witch."

Xander shook his head. "You did what you needed to save my life. I'm the one who will live with those consequences. This should be my decision, but the question is how do we protect the queen and our country from Florin's emissary? I swear that man is like a hound dog. He'll find out all of our secrets."

"If the hound dog wants a scent trail, then give him something to hunt. Take him beyond the wards and fin—"

"No," Xander cut him off. "I will find a way to solve all of our problems without resorting to violence."

King Gerald's voice deepened in warning. "Violence is the only way Florin knows how to solve their problems. If you don't strike first, they will—with a knife to your gut. You have a gift."

"It's a curse," Xander growled. "And a prison sentence."

"Not if you go beyond the wards." King Gerald walked up to his son and poked him in the chest.

The doors opened.

"Apologies, Your Majesty, Your Highness. I did not know you were here," a deep voice interrupted them. Peeking around the corner, I saw Gaven had entered and stumbled upon their argument. "You haven't seen a most rare beauty pass through here, have you?"

Xander shook his head. "There's no one here."

King Gerald turned back to Xander, his voice low and threatening. "You *will* take care of this inconvenience. I will figure out the rest."

Xander and his father left and headed down to dinner, and I stood alone in my hiding spot, angry at what I'd overheard.

Am I the inconvenience?

"Rose?" Gaven called softly into the library. His footsteps came up behind me, and I felt myself stiffen. "Here you are. Are you ready?"

Smoothing my dress, I gave him a forced smile. "Yes."

CHAPTER SIX

On Gaven's arm, I felt like a glittering diamond as we walked side by side, but my heart was as bitter and burnt as coal. Was it only yesterday that the prince was kissing me in the darkness? I dared not face Xander for fear my burning anger and hatred would give me away.

Thankfully, the tables were spread out among the main hall, and Gaven took me to the lower table below the prince. Taking a seat, I couldn't help but look up at the high table where I should have been sitting to see a surly Prince Xander. His face was a mask of pain as he reclined in his chair, his boots crossed and sitting on the tabletop, directly in the spot where my own plate would be. His eyes were buried in his hand as if he had a headache, and he gave very little care to the rest of the room.

Trumpets announced the arrival of the king and queen, and everyone in the room stood, chairs scraping across the floor as we watched the double doors swing open, but only the king entered, Queen Anya absent from his side. His normally flustered color was gone; instead he was pale as he moved to stand next to the high-back chair beside his son. King Gerald signaled the servants to bring out the first course.

I glanced over at Yasmin, who was sitting at a separate table directly across from me, and couldn't help but watch the pitiful looks she kept casting the prince, her bottom lip quivering. Her father, Yassa, placed his hand over hers, giving it a reassuring pat. He didn't cast such sad looks; his gaze was heated and filled with anger.

Lord Verner, a portly gentleman seated on my right, tapped my elbow, gave me a wink, and lifted his glass in a salute. I shuddered at the rosy tinge of his cheeks and his very inebriated state. "It's a pity what happened to him, being forced to marry the witch. If it were me, I would've run for the hills."

"Even if she were beautiful?" Gaven asked.

"Yes, but she won't be. I heard her carriage was pulled by three demons," Lord Verner added salaciously. His thinning hair was wet with sweat, his eyes bloodshot as he leaned forward to whisper as if relaying a deep secret, "It's very scandalous. Not to have the woman he desires and trapped in a marriage with the one he despises." He took another drink.

"How can he despise someone he's never met?" I asked.

"Easy. Just imagine someone taking your prized stallion away and replacing it with a donkey, then ordering you to be happy with your donkey."

"I hardly think the bride and donkey are the same," I corrected.

"Are they not? It's all very tragic. I bet you they'll write stories about it," Gaven added, jumping on the bandwagon.

"Oh, you think so?" I asked, momentarily wondering how I would be portrayed—a forlorn love lost, or the abandoned princess.

"Yes, horror stories," Lord Verner chuckled.

All the men within earshot laughed aloud.

"So it is true, then, the rumors?" a weaselly voice asked Gaven. "The prince married one of Lady Eville's daughters. Do you happen to know which one?"

I had been taking a drink of honey wine and began to choke. Being so awkward with all of the attention, I only just noticed the three other gentlemen from Florin on Gaven's left, also dressed in matching deep red uniforms trimmed in gold. One of them had a white sash across his coat. The mouse-like man with a mustache that twitched erratically was named Earlsgaarde. The rest of his retinue did not speak to any of the guests on their side, and from the way they kept staring at the king and prince, there was no love lost between the countries.

Gaven laughed. "No, there's a whole brood of them, and we haven't seen her yet other than the wedding."

"Pity, because I hear the oldest is as strong as the stepmother." Earlsgaarde rubbed his chin. He seemed to know more about my family than anyone else here. "But it sounds like this is not a happy arrangement for all involved." He pointed to the prince, then the empty plate and seat next to him.

"No," Gaven admitted. "The king and prince both regret the circumstances by which the marriage came about. As for the witch, we're all hoping for the day she turns into a bird and flies away."

"Interesting, very interesting. Then I may need to speak with them," Earlsgaarde pondered aloud.

Gaven leaned forward, eager to continue his conversation with Earlsgaarde, even though he had previously shown his disdain for the men from Florin. Not wanting to hear any more, I tried to tune them out and focus on my meal.

The food was delicious, but after the first few bites, and with the way the conversation turned, everything began to taste the same. I couldn't help but feel miserable for the prince. He neither ate nor drank. He would only rarely look up, but then his eyes would alight on Yasmin; then he'd glance to Earlsgaarde, and his face would turn sour and he would go back to sulking.

Even though I tried to pay attention to Gaven's conversation regarding boyhood stories of growing up in the palace with the prince and his vast hunting expeditions, I was only listening with half an ear.

"Then I chased the animal into Sion and killed it, but not before it left me a token." Gaven rolled up his sleeve to show off the ragged scar from the beast's claws. "But I killed the creature, skinned it, and wear its fur to remind myself that I am stronger than any man or beast."

I glanced back at the dark black fur of Gaven's decorative cloak, surprised he had not left it in his room and gone with something more formal for the evening. But I chalked it up as maybe a prized possession he couldn't go without. Men were odd that way. I could tell from the size that it was probably a fey creature, and my heart was saddened by its death.

Earlsgaarde was quite taken with Gaven's story and asked many questions about the hunt, and the way in which Gaven had taken his trophy.

Not in the least interested in the details of its gory death, I found myself studying the head table, drawn to Xander's plight and pain.

When there was a lull in the conversation, and Earlsgaarde had gotten up from the table, I leaned to my left. "Why is there tension between Florin and Baist?" I whispered so only Gaven could hear.

"Do you not know the story?" he asked, wiping his mouth on a napkin and looking at me curiously.

"No, I don't. I don't get out much," I said softly.

Gaven placed his hand on the back of my chair and leaned in to whisper in my ear like a lover would. "The queen of Florin and her child disappeared in the middle of the night. There were rumors, of course—they were kidnapped by pucas, eaten by trolls, or turned to dust by a witch. But the one that wouldn't go away was that they were murdered at King Gerald's command. The king of Florin has blamed Baist ever since, even though he can't prove it. There's no evidence of their death or kidnapping, so they've been at a delicate peace ever since." He looked over at Earlsgaarde warily. "They've been sniffing around, trying to find a reason to break the treaty and declare war."

"War would be awful."

Gaven nodded. "Yes, Florin's army is far greater than ours. The prince's marriage to Yasmin Nueva would have strengthened our borders and kept Florin at bay, but now?" He shrugged. "Our small country could not withstand another war. We've barely recovered from the last one."

I shook my head, knowing the advances Florin and the other kingdoms had over Baist. All of the magical weapons and artillery that were easily accessible but lacking in this kingdom. "Why are they here now?"

"Today is the eighteen-year anniversary of their disappearance."

"How horrible," I said, feeling a moment's pity for the cruel prince.

Glancing up, I swallowed nervously when I met Xander's angry glare. He was staring right at me, his brows furrowed in confusion. The angry tic in his jaw made me nervous. *Uh-oh! Does he recognize me in my finery? Or is he staring at his enemies on my left?*

My mouth went dry, and I became uncomfortable under his intense scrutiny. I turned my head and tried to focus on Gaven, but I became increasingly aware of Xander. I could feel his gaze like a hot knife slicing along my skin, leaving me shivering. Out of the corner of my eye, I saw he hadn't moved or shifted. I kept my back straight, refusing to look directly at him.

In a stalemate, the prince picked up his goblet, stood up,

and dropped it. It clattered loudly on the stone floor, and every single head, including the emissaries', turned to look at the prince—except for me. I took a sip of my own glass and kept my eyes forward. I was a coward. Nothing short of a fire would compel me to meet those heat-filled eyes.

Gaven seemed to notice Xander's stare, as he asked me, "Do you know the prince?"

"We've met," I answered.

"He hasn't stopped staring at you for the last quarter mark. Have you done something to anger him?"

"I'm sure my very existence is enough to anger him, but as I said, he hardly knows me."

"It seems you've caught his attention."

"That does not bode well for me," I grumbled.

The rest of dinner went relatively the same. After the meal, we were escorted into the ballroom, and I couldn't help but feel a thrill at getting a second chance to partake in the festivities, as long as no one guessed my real identity. I was just one of the ladies, as far as anyone was concerned.

A fire breather caught me off guard, the heat of his breath brushing past my cheek. Laughing, I stepped around him, giving him a wide berth, and became enthralled with the jugglers and acrobats. As beautiful and elegant as the royal wedding was, the celebration tonight was far more wild and up-tempo in an attempt to impress the emissaries' tastes from Florin. Clapping to the beat from the musicians, I joined in a line of women, and we weaved in among the dancers. Creating bridges with our hands, I smiled and pirouetted under them. My skirts swirling, my laughter filling the air, my joy was immeasurable as I counted this as the happiest day of my life. Who knew all it took for me to find happiness was for the country's enemy to come pounding on their door?

No one in this room knew me as a daughter of Eville and a

person to be feared. Here, I was nameless, one of them, and I belonged. Oh, how I'd always wanted to belong.

The music came to a halt and the crowd parted as Prince Xander strolled down the middle of the room toward me. His face was stony, and he seemed displeased with my presence.

Does he know it's me—his wife? Did he find out I escaped my room? Or is he mad at me, the servant?

My hands covered my heart to stop its frantic thudding as I told myself to calm down.

The emissary stepped in front of him and bowed. "Prince Xander, I am Lord Earlsgaarde from Florin. It seems we have come at a most inopportune time. What we wish to discuss with you will wait until the morrow, but until then, will you honor us with a wedding dance?"

Xander's face turned even darker, and he replied stiffly, "I fear I cannot."

"Ah, are you hiding your new wife from us, then? I hear her beauty is that of legends," Earlsgaarde teased, but I could hear the underlying challenge, knew he wanted to satisfy his curiosity and see which daughter the prince was married to.

"It is?" Xander said, obviously surprised, but then regained his composure. "As I said, I cannot, for my *wife*," he said with derision, "has taken ill."

"That's too bad," the emissary muttered, then brightened up. "Then choose a lady as proxy for her, and we will dance and toast to her quick recovery."

Xander turned to walk away, but he caught my eye, and a cruel smile crept up into his lips. Then he nodded and turned back to the crowd. "Very well, I will celebrate my union by dancing with one of the ladies of the court."

Squeals of laughter came from the crowd as a mob of women surged forward to present themselves as partners. That seemed to incite the multitude, and Gaven was briefly pushed from my side. Xander stepped up onto the musician's platform and looked out among the ladies—searching, I'd bet, for a particular petite blonde.

With the current of women and onlookers rushing forth, it created a gap around me, and I stood out in the room alone, with little competition. Except I saw Yasmin, a sparkling jewel among the crowd. Her hair was perfectly coiffed, her dress pressed and unwrinkled; she must have had her ladies ironing and styling since before lunch.

Yasmin was parting the ladies and making her way toward him, her smile a little too confident. My blood boiled.

No, this dance was rightfully mine, not hers. And I would take it.

I raised my chin, smiled coldly and sent a whisper of command his way. It wasn't much of a persuasion, as that wasn't my true gift, but it was enough to get his attention.

Look at me!

Xander's head snapped up from the throng of women around him, and we made eye contact. I dared not smile. I was not inviting him to dance, or to choose me, only to acknowledge my beauty. For this time I was not in a servant's dress, nor was he drunk. Though maybe he was—I saw Prince Xander inhale and stumble as he took a step backward and bumped into the flutist.

Did I hit him with the command too hard? Now I worried what I had done. Magic was not a trivial thing to be throwing about, especially when I was angry. And Earlsgaarde seemed to have been hit with the command as well, because his head snapped up in unison with Xander's, and he was watching me with intense eyes.

Yasmin was almost to Xander, her once smiling face turned down into a frown as she waved up at him from among the ladies, striving to stand on her tiptoes. This was one time her petite height was not working in her advantage.

When I had Xander's full attention, I did the one thing I knew would drive him mad. I turned my back on him and began counting, a lesson I had learned from my mother: *"Show a man your beauty, let him think you're his, and then become unattainable, and they will cross heaven and earth to claim you."*

With my back to the crowd and prince, I couldn't see anyone's reaction. Couldn't tell if what I had done was mad or genius. Would he call for me? Would he pursue me? My nerves were becoming frayed, thinking I had done the wrong thing and made a fool of myself. Steeling myself, I began to retreat, consciously putting one foot in front of another.

I was a fool. Dropping my eyes to the marble floor, I buried my hands in my skirt. Now he had seen me, and I was once again being rejected.

My chest burning, I raised a finger to wipe away a tear when a hand grabbed my wrist.

I looked up and was startled to see Gaven's hopeful face, my heart dropping when I realized it wasn't the prince. "Will you dance with me?" he asked.

"I... uh—"

"Excuse me, but this one is mine," Xander said coldly, possessively, as he took my other arm. But Gaven didn't let go, and the air became tense as two men were claiming me.

Eventually, Gaven released my arm, a fake smile masking his emotions as he bowed. "Certainly, Prince Xander." He stepped back, and I felt the safety of Gaven's presence disappear as a cold whisper of danger drew close. Nothing about Xander told me I was safe. I wanted to run. Run very far away —or right into his arms. I wasn't sure where I wanted to be in that moment, my heart beating too frantically for me to focus on anything else.

Prince Xander stood before me, his eyes searching mine. From the glow of the chandeliers, I could see his eyes smoldering like a burning ember, and he hadn't shaved since yesterday. He looked rugged and dangerous, his power and authority over-whelming, but there was also an underlying wildness about him.

My hesitation must've angered him, because he pulled my wrist and dragged me into the center of the crowd. His left hand moved around my waist, and he waited for the music to start.

"I never agreed—" I began, but the music started and he took two steps. I followed, unsure if I knew the steps to the song, but I quickly realized it was very similar to the Dredilly dance and I could indeed keep up.

"You do not need to. I am your prince," he stated, as if that were the only answer he needed.

"Not my prince," I mumbled angrily.

He turned to search my eyes, and I glared back. My jaw clenched in irritation at his demeanor, I looked over his shoulder at the spinning faces. That was something else I was greatly aware of—my height put me at only a few inches shorter than him, and I fit perfectly within his arms. Neither one of us had to go on tiptoe or lean down to dance.

As we spun, I kept catching glimpses of Earlsgaarde staring at me intently. I wondered if he had received a backlash of my compulsion, for he wouldn't look away.

"You clean up nicely. In fact, I dare say you are quite pretty when not frolicking in the garden," Xander murmured, then leaned down to lift me into the air for the jump the dance required. My feet left the earth and my breath caught in my throat, but I hid my joy from him.

"And you're vain," I added.

Prince Xander didn't seem used to my insolence. My feet touched the ground roughly as he dropped me, frowning as he spun me away from him. When the spin returned, he pulled me to his chest and growled, "I am your future king. Why do you loathe me?"

"That's not true. I barely know you. How can I possibly loathe someone I don't know?" I countered angrily, still on edge from my conversation with Lord Verner.

"What tales are you spinning, woman? Why are you being so trying?" His voice rose in pitch, and I decided to leave it be. It wouldn't do to cross swords or tongues with someone not prepared for battle. Was it fair? No. But venting my anger on him when he didn't understand the reason would do little to end my pain.

When no more biting words came forth, he relaxed and we danced. It was beginning to become quite pleasant, and I was equally aware of every touch as his hand adjusted on my waist. The music faded to the background as the heat of his hand felt like it was burning right through to my skin. When he brushed a stray strand of hair out of my face, I flinched at the contact.

"I wanted to apologize for my behavior earlier," he said as he studied my profile.

I stared at the crowd around us, not wanting to make eye contact. Every second I was in his embrace was unnerving and brought us closer to the truth of who I really was, and I wasn't prepared for his reaction.

He shook his head. "I usually have more control over my temper. Thank you for helping my sister."

"You're welcome."

"And serving my, uh... wife. Has it been taxing?"

"I believe I told you before, I am not a servant. Nor am I a lady," I said, finally meeting his gaze.

"Then what, pray tell, are you, if not a lady nor a servant?"

I smiled in challenge. "An illusion. For I will vanish before your eyes, and even though I'm close to you, you'll never see me. Never know me."

"I could if you let me." His voice lowered and his eyes flickered to my lips. I knew exactly what he was insinuating. "In fact, I would like to know you a little better."

He had complete disregard for his marriage vows, and it infuriated me all the more.

"What of your wife?" I asked coldly.

"What of her?" he responded irritably. "I'm married in name only. There will never be love lost between us."

"Everyone deserves a chance at love," I remarked. "Especially your future princess."

"Yasmin?" He glanced up and around as if searching for his ex-fiancée.

Missing the beat on purpose, I stepped on his toe. "No, your wife, Princess Rosalie."

"I... is that her name?" He paused and his face went still, his expression unreadable.

I was aghast that he didn't even know her—*my* name. Was it as rushed and confusing for him as me? It must have been.

"Yes," I said softly, looking down at my feet.

He became quiet, then shot any further discussion down, saying, "Never mind. These are private matters."

The song came to an end and I pulled away, more than ready to disappear into the crowd. He gripped my wrist and led me to the side of the room. Ladies had surged forward to try and claim the next dance, and his guards were forced to come up and encircle him, forming a ring of protection.

"For you." Xander unclasped a gold rose pin from his cloak, wincing as it pricked his finger before handing it to me. "A gift for the dance."

He held it out in front of me, and I studied the golden petals that were opened.

"Thank you." I took the rose, pricking my finger on the clasp as well.

Prince Xander smiled. "Flowers have special meaning to the queen."

"Really?" I said, surprised he would call her "the queen" and not "Mother." I was even more surprised that he was content to stay by my side and not run off or see to his royal duties.

"The rose especially, because it is one of the most beautiful and also protects itself, hence the thorns. I can tell by the tongue lashing you gave me that you're not afraid to fight, or protect yourself. Not to mention your personality is as prickly as the thorn," he added. "Keep it to remember this night."

Just when I was about to thank him again, Yasmin stepped between us. "If you are giving dances away, I believe you owe me the next one," she purred. "Since ours was stolen on our wedding day."

Xander's eyes met mine, and I swore there might have been a look of displeasure at being interrupted. Or it may have been my imagination, for he bowed his head and took her hand, leading her back onto the floor for a dance.

I didn't want to watch, but I was drawn to them as they moved perfectly together, like ceramic dancers in a music box. Xander stood tall, his shoulders back as he took her hands in his. Yasmin was petite and a flurry of lace and golden curls as they spun. Her feet were light, and she didn't stumble over the steps but floated across the floor as if on a cloud, her jewels gleaming. Her porcelain smile drew crowds, and I could see her flashing it like a weapon at Prince Xander. He rested one hand at the small of her back and leaned in close to whisper into her ear.

"So which daughter are you?" Earlsgaarde had come up behind me, sipping a cup of tea.

"I don't think I understand." I began to panic at being so easily found out—and by the foreign emissary, no less.

"You can't throw a compulsion spell around in a country not prone to magic and not know it will attract unwanted attention. And based on the force with which you conjured, you must be one of Lady Eville's girls. Hmm, my bet is Aura or Eden, am I right?"

Ignoring him and pretending indifference seemed the best course of action as I craned my head and watched Yasmin run her fingers up Xander's neck. My hands clenched, giving me away enough that Earlsgaarde noticed my jealousy.

"I thought maybe there were two sisters here, but not with the way you're reacting to the prince dancing with another woman. I've seen that angry look before, on your mother."

"You know nothing about me," I said firmly.

"You couldn't actually be her—his wife, now could you?" He chuckled crudely, and I took a few steps away, but he followed after me like a kite on a string. "Ah, you're hiding by using glamour, then, so you must be Eden."

I couldn't get over how familiar this strange man was with my family, and it made me very uncomfortable. "I'm sorry, I must go." I turned to leave, but he grabbed my wrist.

"Let me go!" I hissed and tried to yank free from Earlsgaarde's grip, but he wouldn't release me, making my anger only rise further. If he wanted to know which sister I was, I was about to let him know.

"Relax, no harm will come from me. Just abating my curiosity is all," he said.

The air crackled with intensity as I gathered power. With no ley lines, I had to dig deep into the earth and into myself.

The hair on his arm rose at my power, and a low growl came from my throat.

"Ah, yes, the oldest. Of course she would send you. No harm. See?" One by one his fingers released from my wrist. He raised his teacup to me in salute and backed away into the crowd.

Yasmin tittered, her laugh meant to carry and draw attention to her. She succeeded. I watched, my heart sinking at how happy she seemed in his arms, pulling him closer as he leaned close to whisper into her ear.

I sighed in resignation. I may have his title, but I would never have his heart. Why was that thought so troubling to me? I knew my duty, had accepted my mother's wishes and married him, knowing I would never find happiness. What more could I expect?

Nothing.

There was nothing for me here, and there never would be. I would be alone forever.

It was obvious that he would never give the daughter of Eville a chance. He would keep her locked away from sight, imprisoned until she died, and then he would be free to love Yasmin or any other woman who took his fancy.

I was done with this night and didn't want to see him dance with his true love, but still I stayed, watching every single moment they had together, judging their interaction, searching and reading into each glance and caress. Was there love there? Did I come between their happily ever after? Part of my heart delighted in being the one to tear them apart, but the other half mourned at what I had done.

When the dance was over, Xander let Yasmin go with a bow and began to search the room. Earlsgaarde headed toward King Gerald, and I feared he would reveal my ruse. As if he had sensed my thoughts, Earlsgaarde turned and gave me a congenial wave, and I frowned. King Gerald did not seem thrilled at Earlsgaarde's approach, but after a few minutes, the two of them headed out of the ballroom.

That made me uneasy, seeing the two of them together, but Gaven distracted me by coming up behind me and sweeping me onto the dance floor. With each turn I could see the prince's glare, feel it burning across my skin; he didn't seem pleased with my partner. Gaven's hand dropped lower on my waist with a slight pressure as he gave me a confident smile. My cheeks reddened in response.

I knew Xander didn't care for me, but it seemed like he didn't want anyone else to either, for the prince stormed through the dancers, like a ship cutting through a calm sea. His approach and the heat in his eyes worried me. He was angry, and I had a feeling I would be on the receiving end of his sharp tongue.

"Gaven," I said calmly, trying to pull away, but his hand on my back was like an iron band imprisoning me. "Please, I need to leave," I whispered urgently. I needed a place to retreat. To get away from those amber eyes that were hunting me down from across the room. "Take me somewhere else, anywhere but here."

Gaven seemed surprised at my earnestness, but he quickly conceded. Not letting go of my wrist, he pulled me into the hall and out the double doors into the garden.

I shouldn't have looked back, but I did, seeing Xander stop his pursuit and watch us leave warily.

The cool night air felt good on my overly warm skin, and I was glad to be away from Xander and the feelings he was stirring within me. From the steps leading down into the gardens, I could see various couples already walking hand in hand into the maze.

Gaven was eagerly leading me into the tall hedge maze, and

I realized I may have given him the wrong impression. As soon as we were alone, he reached for me, his mouth pressing hard on mine, our teeth knocking together painfully.

"Mmmph," I mumbled in surprise, pushing him away. "Stop, I insist!"

Gaven's breath was ragged, his pupils were dilated, and his cheeks were flushed from the chill air. "But I thought this is what you wanted. You asked to leave, and I assumed—"

"I'm sorry," I said, "but I'm promised to another."

His face darkened, his grip on my arms tightened, and I winced. "Who?"

"I... I, uh...." Unsure how to answer him, I ultimately decided on the truth. "The prince."

His nose crinkled in disgust and his hands dropped. "You would rather become the prince's whore than be with me?"

"I don't have a choice," I retorted, angry he had called me a whore.

"You do. You can choose me!" His fist pounded his chest, and I could see the pain of rejection written across his face.

"You don't understand." I reached for him, but he shrugged me off.

"Yes, I do. It's not the first time someone has chosen him over me. I just thought that once he was married, it would stop." He shook his head and looked at me in disbelief. "I had hoped you were different, but you're not. You're just like all the others," he sneered, then took off into the dark, leaving me alone in the maze.

Alone and confused.

My thoughts were so filled with questions and very few answers that I almost walked right past the beautiful deep red rosebush that had caught my attention the other day. A white stone bed surrounded the bush, with a golden dedication plaque on a column:

To my little flower
May you ever rest in peace.

It was a memorial, but for whom?

There was something comforting about the exotic flowers, though up close, I could see the roses were browning and dying while every plant around them was flourishing. Wondering if there was a disease or sickness, I reached closer to inspect the flower, hoping my knowledge of herbology would help me identify the threat.

Before I could lay a finger on the flower, a branch snaked out and wrapped around my wrist. The thorns, like teeth, sank painfully into my skin.

CHAPTER SEVEN

Hissing in pain, I tried to pull away from the thorns, but they only wrapped tighter around my wrist and dug in deeper. Just when I was about to burn the whole bush to ash with a spell, the thorny branch released me from its painful hold and slinked back into the bush. Seconds later, the bush shimmered and the flowers regained their color, turning deep red. The previously closed buds opened wide, and I swore the whole plant grew before my eyes.

"What magic is this?" I whispered, then reached out to stroke the rose. I could almost feel it stretch and reach for more of my blood, but I recoiled from the bloodthirsty plant. Never before in my studies had I come across a species like this; not even the Venus flytrap could compare. I ran two fingers along my injured wrist and healed the small bloody pinpricks left by the rosebush, sighing as the healing warmth filled my body.

"Interesting, isn't it, that this particular rosebush grows here?" a voice said from behind me. I spun around on my heel and was face-to-face with Lord Earlsgaarde once again. It seemed he had an interest in following me, but I had no desire to answer any of his questions.

His mustache twitched, reminding me once again of a

mouse. He moved forward to inspect the flower, and I wondered if he had seen the rose drink from my blood.

I turned slightly, giving him my shoulder, signaling that I did not want to continue this conversation.

"You can tell by the blood-red color of the blooms and the thorns speckled with a red hue that this is the imperial rose and is only able to bloom in Florin. Until now. Odd, don't you think, that the imperial rose would be planted with such care in the royal garden of Baist, and is not only growing but thriving? Now how could that happen?" he asked suspiciously.

"I wouldn't know," I answered coldly, moving away from him.

He stood with his hands clasped behind his back as he studied me slyly, then gave me a grin. "I'm sorry, but I must know—why does the prince not recognize you? It's obvious to me, at least, that you're the new wife."

It seemed I wouldn't be able to appease him until I gave him an answer, and it felt good to finally tell the truth. "Because he has never set eyes on his wife. I was covered with veils on our wedding day, and he has bidden that I stay locked away in my rooms and guarded forever."

"Ah, but a guard is no match for Lorelai's daughter. Do you want to know why the prince refuses to look upon you?"

My quick inhale made Lord Earlsgaarde smile knowingly. "It's fear. The king has as much told the prince that if he so much as looks at you, he will be forever under your spell." Earlsgaarde came to stand next to me and whisper in my ear. "The same happened with your mother, and now everyone is scared of your beauty. Which is a shame, because beauty should be looked at, not hidden away. Am I right, Rosalie?" He said my name as a test, his eyes glittering as if he'd just uncovered a deep and buried secret.

"I'm sure it's only a rumor." My heart fluttering, I dared not react.

"Rest assured, it is no rumor. There is a witch and beast in residence here, but the question remains, which one murders in cold blood?"

"Why are you here?" I demanded.

His mustache twitched, and Earlsgaarde scratched his neck. "Much was taken from us that fateful night eighteen years ago. The king was heartbroken at the death of his queen. War is inevitable. Unless you can give us something we want?"

"What is that?"

"I think we have an idea, but the question is whether you're willing to pay the price for peace." His rubbed his mustache, and it wavered out of focus. No, it was a twitch. He was always twitching his mustache like it itched. "Peace is never free."

"They're dead," I stated matter-of-factly. "And it happened eighteen years ago."

"Time does not lessen the loss for the king. In fact, over time the pain can become septic. He wants retribution."

"You won't get it," I said, astounded by the absurdity of his request.

"Yes, we will. For I am very, very patient," Lord Earlsgaarde warned as he stepped back and then turned, heading back out of the maze.

I knew I should leave as well, but my eyes were once again drawn to the imperial rosebush. The plaque itself was old, faded over many winters and summers, the unnamed child long forgotten. Did my mother know who might lie below the earth?

I acted rashly, breaking off one of the roses and taking it with me. I would make cuttings and plant it in my room to study on my own time.

When I strayed too close to the edge of the gardens, I felt compulsion magic hit me hard.

Go away!

I paused. Spinning in a slow circle, I searched for the source, the caster, the witch, but I was alone. When I took another step, the compulsion came again.

Go back!

This time I knew there wasn't a caster. Kneeling, I carefully brushed the gravel away and saw the glowing gold sigil on the ground. A ward to compel people to leave the area when they walked across them. I wondered what other spells and traps I might come across if I continued my journey. Each sigil left a signature of their caster, and even though it was old and fading, having been cast long ago, I could easily recognize the creator.

Mother.

Covering the glowing sigil back up, my curiosity was thoroughly piqued. What had my mother done here long ago? Was this why she had returned and brought me with her? Or was there another secret as to why I was suddenly married to a horrid prince?

The farther I moved from the protection wards, the lighter my mind felt. I couldn't believe how strong the spell was after all of these years, though it was definitely weakening. She was a powerful enchantress indeed.

I would have to ask her about this—or maybe it was the reason I was sent here, to finish her work.

Go away! The compulsion came again.

"Yes, Mother," I murmured aloud. "I'll leave for now, but I will be back."

When I returned to my room, I noticed the saucer I had left out to entice a fey now lay shattered on the floor as the moonlight shone through the curtains. I had forgotten to refill the milk or biscuit tray, and someone wasn't happy.

Muffled cussing filled the air, but to those who didn't know better, it would sound like twigs breaking. I knew the sound of fey, however, and followed the noises back to my wardrobe.

Casting a mage light above my head, I opened the door, clearing my throat loudly.

I was expecting a gentle hob, elf, brownie, or even a pixie, despite their penchant for tricks—not the spindly green-hued goblin before me, not much bigger than a toddler, with a sharp nose and long pointy ears, wearing an overly large white silk dress and my satin slippers. He grinned at me, his mouth filled with needlelike teeth, and didn't seem to be ashamed in the least at wearing my nightdress.

Being careless and leaving an offering of milk smeared with blood, I had accidentally indentured a goblin. *Great.*

"I'd much appreciate it if you would put the dress back," I said, trying to keep a straight face at my cross-dressing goblin.

"Furfmuggin," he said loudly in complaint, and I snorted at the foul fey word he was dropping in my presence. He did sashay out of the wardrobe and toss my dress on the floor in a fit, but he was more hesitant about giving up my slippers.

When I held out my hand, he stuck his red tongue out at me and dropped another curse. Well, now I understood why no one wanted to have an indentured fey here, if this was the only kind the land of Baist attracted. It would have to be a hearty and strong fey to survive this magic-starved land.

"Do you have a name?" I asked as he took off my slippers and proceeded to pull my new gown off the hanger and make a bed within the wardrobe. It seemed this foulmouthed goblin was here to stay.

"Gobber. Gobbersnot," he mumbled. Before any other words came out of his mouth, he flicked his hand at me, signaling a very inappropriate gesture, and closed himself back inside the wardrobe.

I couldn't help laughing at my newfound companion. Gritty, tough, and rough around the edges, just like me. He would do.

The two of us would find our way in this magic-barren land together.

CHAPTER EIGHT

Her fear smelled oh so sweet as she ran from me. Slipping on the grass, she fell into a puddle, the mud obscuring her face. Crying, she wiped it away and desperately scrambled to her feet, her blue shoe abandoned in the grass behind her.

Oh, little girl, why did you stray out at night into my territory? Were you looking for me? You must have known I was here. That I was waiting for you.

A grumble came from my chest, and she turned to look at me and screamed.

I fell out of my bed, a tangle of sheets and quilt wrapped around me as I hit the floor. The cool press of the stone against my cheek made me aware of where I was. I was here. Safe.

Sitting up, I tried to unwind my legs from the sheets and saw it—the mud that splattered my legs, the grass stains on my feet.

Hearing a thump from my wardrobe, I opened it and saw Gobbersnot snoring peacefully. His mouth was covered with fresh blood, and on his head as a hat was a familiar blue shoe from my dream.

An anguished cry fell from my lips, and I turned and flung myself back onto my bed, burying my head under the pillow. Then I screamed, releasing my grief, sorrow, and fear into the mattress.

The wolfsbane tea wasn't keeping the visions and the blackouts away. Why? Why now? What reason would I have for them to come back?

Wiping my eyes, I knew I needed to find out what happened. I dressed quickly and used my magic to bespell the guards into a deep sleep so I could slip out of my room. Right before I closed the door, I heard my wardrobe open and the pitter-patter of goblin feet as he slipped out the door after me. I couldn't see Gobbersnot but knew he would be hiding in the shadows—my small rabid protector.

Making my way out the servants' entrance of the palace, I headed toward the woods and felt the intense pressure in my head resume.

Go away!

Leave here!

But the compulsion was weaker, not as strong as before.

Kneeling, I brushed the leaves aside and saw the great stone with the engraved sigils of protection. I mentally traced the location of the wards in the garden to my location out by the woods and realized it was a giant circle. A protection spell. More of my mother's handiwork that was safeguarding the palace against magical beings. This constant thrum of power would also drive most fey away; to them it would be like wearing a bee's nest over their head.

But there was another symbol hidden within the ward. Translated roughly in fey, it was the word "shift."

The farther I traveled, the closer I came to the woods. I turned to look back up at the palace on the hill. Lights shone from a few windows, casting a glow around the area. Even in the middle of the night, it looked like a signal shining far into the valley and the woods beyond.

The woods. That was what drew me. The dreams and feelings were coming from here. Having to use the land drained me, and a mage light would take too much power, so instead I pulled out a glass marble and used it to amplify the moon's light, lighting my path like a torch.

There, in the tall grass at the edge of the woods, I saw her.

Her face was turned down, her legs sprawled at awkward angles with one blue shoe still on her small foot. I couldn't breathe. The world started spinning, and I collapsed next to the girl. It was Herez.

Gobbersnot moved over to the girl and picked up her hand, about to take a bite out of her finger.

"No!" I shooed him away. "Don't!"

"Furfmuggin," he grumbled angrily at me, then moved down by her feet. Giving me his back, he proceeded to try and pry off her other shoe to add to his collection.

"Gobber, no!" I chastised my goblin, but his hand came up, sending me a signal of his disdain. If he couldn't have meat, then he wanted the shoe.

Sighing in resignation, I reached out to touch her cool skin, and her death washed over me like a raging river. I felt her fear, her terror rising up inside my own stomach. She had snuck out to meet a boy and had run into something much more dangerous. Herez knew she was being hunted but was cut off from the palace, so she ran for the woods instead. The beast chased her down, and she slipped in the mud. When she looked up, all she saw were teeth, dark fur, and claws. Then it was over.

I shuddered and gasped, trying not to throw up what was left in my stomach.

Poor Herez.

A loud crack echoed around me. My head snapped up as I stared into the darkness.

I wasn't alone.

Rising to my feet, I caught a glimpse of a large shadow moving through the trees and heard a threatening growl.

Before I could attack, Gobbersnot let out a war cry and ran into the woods. The silky dress he wore made him look like a screaming will-o'-the-wisp as he ran.

A soft groan came from Herez then, and I cried out in relief. She wasn't dead—yet. There was still a chance I could save her. Scanning the woods, I searched for the beast, but both he and Gobbersnot were gone and the night was still. Sensing no other immediate threat, I collapsed next to the injured girl.

"Stay with me, Herez," I commanded as I ran my hands over her wounds and tried my best to heal the damage I could see. Her skin was still cold as ice, but her breathing was stronger.

A shadow fell over me, and I looked up in fear. A strange man leaned down next to me until our faces almost touched as he leaned forward to inspect Herez.

It was Xander. Had he seen me heal her?

I froze as the moonlight shone off his copper hair. The sleeves of his shirt were rolled up as he checked her pulse. His hands were gentle even as his jaw clenched, and I could see the silent fury he was hiding.

"What happened?

"I don't know," I lied. How could I explain that I dreamed of her death and then rushed out in the middle of the night to know exactly where she was?

"Did you see anything?" he asked.

"I thought I saw something." I turned toward the woods but again wasn't sure how to explain the shadow I had seen. "Maybe I imagined it." I didn't dare say any more.

A sharp whistle cut through the silent night, and I heard someone calling Xander's name.

"Over here!" he yelled out and then waited for the group to find us.

The night was lit by torchlight as a group of ten men surrounded me, crossbows aimed, swords drawn, and torches held high. I drew Herez closer to me, my arms wrapped around her protectively. In the dark, the light blinded me and it was hard to see. One of the shadows separated from the pack, and I recognized Gaven with his dark bearskin cloak as he leaned down to check her pulse.

"What are *you* doing here?" Gaven asked accusingly.

He thought I was the servant girl, Rose.

Before I could respond, Herez's eyes flickered open, landing on Gaven's furred cloak looming over her, brushing against her face, and she began to scream and flail. Her fingernails clawed at me as she struggled to get away, her terror making her ten times stronger and my face bearing the brunt of her attack.

Gaven held her arms down as she continued to kick and scream. "Calm down!" he growled out. "You're safe!

Herez stilled, her eyes wild in fright as they darted around at the hunters, her body shaking like a twig in a storm. She saw me like I was the devil in the flesh, and I remembered that she knew I was a daughter of Eville. She looked at me and began pleading. "Please don't harm me. I didn't mean to. I—"

Panicking that she would reveal my real identity to the prince, I reached out and touched her forehead, whispering, "*Somnus.*"

Herez fell into a deep enchanted sleep, and I pretended to be surprised. "She must have fainted."

Xander gave me an odd look, then lifted Herez out of my

lap and handed her to a soldier. "Did she say anything at all? Who it was or what it was?" His voice was stern.

I shook my head, grateful Gobbersnot had disappeared into woods, though I was fearful that he was hurt or injured.

Gaven frowned and looked at the surrounding woods. "I will find this beast if it's the last thing I do." He waved his men on and they barged into the woods, creating enough ruckus that if the beast were there, it would hear them coming a mile away.

Xander reached out and offered me a hand up from the ground. "Come, let me make sure you get back safely."

Nodding, I walked beside him as he led me out of the woods. One of the men brought over his horse. I recognized Nova and smiled when I saw her. Reaching out to touch her muzzle, I saw how dirty my hands were and curled them into fists, hiding them within my skirts.

"Why were you out here in the middle of the night?" His voice was soft. Not accusing, just curious. "Were you meeting someone?"

Ah, there it is. A hint of jealousy. "No." I looked away and smiled. "Why are you out here?"

Xander held Nova's reins and we walked slowly. "Because each night I hunt the beast that roams our lands."

"I heard the servants talking about a beast. They said that's why the fey don't come here," I said, pretending ignorance of the protection spell and wards or lack of ley lines.

"There are many reasons the fey stay away from our lands. The rumor of the beast is just one of them."

"Why have you not been able to find it?"

Xander's jaw clenched and his eyes narrowed. "Do you think I'm not trying hard enough? Do you think I want my people to be murdered in the night? I know there are rumors about me, that I'm cruel, cold, and as unfeeling as the beast itself, but I promise I protect my people."

I was unprepared for his anger that was now directed at me. "That was not my meaning at all."

I was now inches away from him. My breathing was ragged from the cold, and I shivered. He cursed under his breath before reaching up and pulling a blanket from his saddlebag, wrapping it around my shoulders. He rubbed his palms up and down my arms to warm me, but I refused to meet his gaze.

"I'm sorry," he apologized. "The truth is I haven't been sleeping well the last few nights, for whenever I sleep, my people are murdered by a creature."

"Sounds like a rogue wolf," I said, thinking back to our town and how, during lean hunting season, the predators would try their hand at larger animals.

"And that's what I thought too." Xander sighed. "But this is something else. Something I've never come across before. It's smart, knows how to hide its tracks, and lose the hounds by going into the river. I fear we will only find it after more of my people are killed."

My mouth went dry and I looked away into the woods, hoping he didn't see the fear on my face.

Xander grabbed my chin and lifted it up so my lips were inches from his. "Don't worry, I won't let anything happen to you," he promised. "Just stay inside the palace where it's safe. And don't go past the wards. I can't guarantee your safety if you pass the wards."

My eyes narrowed and I pulled away from his grasp. Who did he think he was to try and protect me? I didn't need protection. If anything, he needed protection from me.

We walked in silence back to the palace. When he led Nova to the stables, I removed the blanket and handed it back to him.

We stood there in the stables awkwardly. I didn't want to leave but knew I should; the longer I stayed with him, the easier it was to wish he would kiss me again. I reminded myself that the only reason he kissed me the first night was because he was inebriated. He wouldn't dare again—or would he?

"How's my wife?" he asked warily.

It was the wrong thing to say to me, because that innocent question set me off. "Maybe you should ask her yourself," I snapped. "Instead of asking me, her servant. But no, instead you avoid her and keep her locked in her room like some prisoner in a fairy tale."

Xander took a step back in surprise. "I-I never thought—" he stuttered.

I continued to approach him, wagging my finger. "Of course you didn't. I couldn't care less if you want to avoid her, but you should at least have the common courtesy to treat her as a human being. Let her out of the room, because right now she is the princess in a locked tower, and you, Prince, are nothing more than a dragon—no, an evil ogre."

I had backed Xander right into the stable wall, and he slipped before catching himself.

"And ogres don't live long in fairy tales," I warned.

Xander said nothing, just blinked at me in surprise as if I had grown horns. I was so angry at my feelings for him; even now, I wanted to both kiss him and slap him.

I regained my composure and calmed myself. "I will take my leave now and expect you to keep me up to date on Herez's health." Spinning, I walked out of the stable quickly, too scared to look back. Once I turned the corner, I covered my mouth, surprised that I had just reamed out the prince. I briefly wondered what repercussions would rain down on me for it. Who would bear the brunt of my harsh words—Rose, the servant, or Rosalie, his wife?

CHAPTER NINE

I made it back to my bed and collapsed. Seconds later, I heard the sound of my wardrobe opening and shutting as Gobbersnot snuck back in. My head was pounding, and I pulled the pillow over my eyes to try and soothe the oncoming migraine from using so much energy to recharge the wards.

Lorn was right. I constantly felt depleted and exhausted living in this kingdom, but it was a good ache, one that came from overworking muscles. Whereas my other sisters would complain, I knew the more I learned to draw from the earth and myself and not the ley lines, the stronger I would become. If I could just battle the headaches.

Thankfully, less than a mark later, I was asleep.

A loud, painful shriek startled me awake, but the room was dark. Pitch black. *No, not black.* I removed the pillow from my face and saw Pru standing next to the open wardrobe.

I had forgotten to warn Pru of my new friend, Gobbersnot, who at that moment was wearing dangly earrings I was pretty sure I'd seen in Yasmin's lobes, his head and the tops of his ears wrapped up in a silk scarf like a turban. Pru's shriek of surprise was mirrored by that of Gobbersnot, who quickly cussed her out and slammed the door closed.

"Th-that's a... a...." She couldn't finish.

"A goblin." I smiled.

"What kind?"

"Not sure."

"He doesn't seem to have any manners."

"I like him," I said, and meant it. He amused me. "Although I wouldn't trust him to braid my hair or help me get dressed in the morning," I added.

I was careful to not bring up Herez's attack. It seemed most of the servants had been told the girl had taken ill and was being sent home to recover. I knew it was probably to hide the presence of the beast. Why did they feel the need to protect it, or was it to prevent mass hysteria? Either way, I kept my mouth shut.

A mark later, a package was delivered to my room by way of royal page. He laid a jeweled box upon the table and announced, "Your ban has been lifted, granted as long as you have this." He tapped the box, gave Pru a shy smile, and left.

"Who's it from?" I asked, running my hands over the pearl-encrusted box. The silver latch was decorated with topaz. Never before had something so beautiful been in my presence.

"It must be from His Highness," she replied.

A slow thump came from my chest. A present from the prince? Maybe my harsh words had gotten through to him.

My hands shook as I opened the box and took out the crisp white note card. His penmanship was fluid and neat.

So I never have to look upon your face
Wear this veil or leave this place.
I will not have you put me under a spell
And damn my soul straight to hell.
~Prince Xander

There was no admission of please or thank you, only a direct order—which rhymed, no less. Underneath the card was a thick white veil, this time with a headband full of combs instead of a tiara.

Those scripted words made each breath painful. My hand trembled as a tear fell from my eye onto the card, blurring the prince's name. *How dare he make me cry?* Crumpling the card in my hand, I tossed it into the fireplace and watched as the note caught fire and burned, wishing I had tossed Prince Xander's heart in the fire instead.

"My lady?" Pru stepped forward, her eyes going to the jeweled box. My head began to pound, and I rubbed my forehead, trying to ease the throbbing that was coming.

"I'm fine," I answered. "Please bring me more silk and black dye."

We spent the next hour dying the veil black.

"Did someone die?" Pru asked, holding the newly dyed veil in the air.

"I am," I said. "A little each day that I'm here." I placed the black veil over my head and adjusted the combs, then looked in the mirror and silently mourned my identity.

I donned a long black silk dress with matching lace sleeves. Gobbersnot didn't seem to care for the dark colors and had left this dress fairly untouched. The veil fell to my waist, and I hid my anger behind the dark shroud. It was my new armor.

A soft knock came to my door. I opened it, expecting to see one of the servants, but instead it was young Ameline. Her hands were clasped together in nervousness, and when she looked up and saw me in my black shroud, she gasped and stepped back.

Darn the prince's order. Quickly I lifted the veil and

showed the child I was not to be feared. "It's okay, sweetie," I murmured, kneeling on the stone floor. "I'm not going to harm you."

Her brave little shoulders straightened and her chin rose. "I know," she said with false bravado. "My mother needs you. She's ill. You must help her," she demanded, then pulled on my hand to presumably lead me to her mother.

"I don't think it would be wise for me to be near her."

"Xander is wrong. They're all wrong. The healers don't know what's wrong with her, but they're not like you. You're magic. You can fix her."

I bit my lip in worry. Yes, I wanted to aid Xander's mother, but any help I offered could be misconstrued, and I would pay the price. But I couldn't stand idly by. Grabbing my small box of herbs from the bottom drawer of the wardrobe, I stood up.

"Okay," I said, giving her my hand.

Her smile grew so bright with hope, and I prayed to the stars that I could do something to help her mother. Hand in hand, we left my room, and when the guard went to stop me, she put him in his place.

"Don't stop me, Fagen. I'm on a mission."

"But Your Highness isn't allowed to associate with her." Fagen moved to stop us.

"*Obey.*" I sent a whisper of compulsion his way. As soon as it hit him, he went back to his post.

We were quite the pair as we made our way through the palace to the main staircase and headed up one floor—a tall shadowy figure being guided by a joyous and pastel-colored child.

Ameline marched right up to her mother's suite and barged through the double doors. The queen's room was dark and stuffy, the long cobalt ornamental curtains pulled closed, keeping back the light. Strong incense assailed my nose,

93

causing my eyes to blink involuntarily in protest. The queen looked like a child in the stately bed, propped up by at least six down pillows. Her eyes closed, her head crooked to the side, I was unsure if she breathed.

A strange man in green healer's robes was sitting on a stool by her side, a bowl and knife in his hands. On the bedside table sat a jar of leeches, most already plump and full from feeding on the queen's blood. An antiquated practice used against blood curses that could do more harm than good—and all of it wrong.

"Stop!" I called out, rushing to the queen's side. Pulling the man back by his shoulder, I could see the bowls and bloody towels littering the floor. "How long have you been doing this?" I hissed.

The healer glared at me. His olive skin was exotic, eyes darker still, and in the room it was hard to make out his country of origin. "I've been curing blood curses for twenty years, child."

"And how many of those with blood curses died?" I snapped, quickly calculating the amount of blood on the floor in regards to the queen's sallowness. He had drained her almost to the point of no return. "And how many have you saved?"

"Many with the blood curse say death is also salvation," he answered stoically.

"Is this true, Allemar?" King Gerald said as he stepped out of the shadows.

In my rush to stop the healer, I had not taken full stock of the room, nor seen King Gerald sitting in a chair in the corner. From the redness of his eyes, it seemed he had been crying.

"Have you been hurting her all this time?" the king asked.

"I've been releasing her."

"Get out!" I yelled, my voice rising in fury. "Leave here!"

"But His Majesty has called for me to treat—"

"You heard her, Allemar. Leave and don't return," King Gerald ordered, snapping his fingers. Guards came in the room and physically removed the eccentric healer while he screamed his allegiance and swore he was only doing his duty.

Once the strange man was gone, I attended the queen. Grabbing her wrist, I ran my finger over the cut and quickly healed the open wound. King Gerald stood by my side, and I heard him curse as he watched my magic at work.

"Please send for liquids, preferably a thick broth," I said as I gently laid the queen's hand across her bedspread. The king rushed to the hall to do as I asked.

The healer had been using a rotation of leeches and blood-letting to cure the queen. Lifting the bowl of blood from the floor, I leaned forward and sniffed the contents; a tangy aroma hit my sinuses.

Yes, there was a blood curse on the family, but something else.

"Poison," I said.

"What?" King Gerald rushed to my side. "How can you be certain?"

"I can smell it in the blood."

"That's impossible."

"For most, yes, but I'm not like the others. I am trained in herbology and the magical arts, and I'm quite familiar with this poison. It's wolfsbane, which should have killed her. I'm not at all certain why she's still alive, but she wouldn't have been for much longer if your healer kept going."

"Can you do something? Please, save her," King Gerald begged. "I will give you anything, even up to half of my kingdom."

The tables were turned. He couldn't see me beneath my dark veil. He didn't know I was a daughter of Eville. What half would he possibly give me? I already had his son. Was this how

95

the bargain had been made years ago with my mother? Was this how he had lost his firstborn son?

"I don't think it's yours to give," a deep voice said from the door, and I knew without looking it was Xander. Keeping my back still, I put the bowl down and continued to clean up the mess the horrid healer had made.

"I'm still king, son, and this is my decision."

"No, it's not," Xander said. "You have no right to give our lands away. Not now, not when we have Florin at our gates."

"It's okay," I replied softly. "I ask for no payment."

"That's right, because you already have everything you want, don't you?" Xander sneered at me.

"What do you mean?" King Gerald asked in confusion, looking between the two of us.

"Don't let the veil fool you, Father. It's a daughter of Eville who is sitting beside you. Through your previous deals, she has already gained a title."

Xander stormed over to me, and I stood to meet him.

"There will be no deal, nor payment," he seethed. "If you can help, I order you to do so."

"I had already agreed. I came not to gain favor with the crown or you, but because Ameline asked me to."

Ameline had retreated to the far side of the bed and was watching us with eyes the size of saucers, her hands covering her mouth in worry.

A servant entered with a bowl of broth, and I took it and carefully tended the queen by trying to get her sip from the bowl.

"I know you're tired, Your Majesty, but you need to drink," I murmured. "You need to replace the blood you lost."

Her eyes fluttered open and her lips quivered as she asked, "Have you come to take me to the afterlife?"

"No, you are strong. You can fight this."

"It's all my fault," she whispered so softly that only I could hear her, her tears pooling at the corner of her eyes. Queen Anya obviously thought I was death come to claim her soul. "If only I hadn't run. If only I had held on tighter, I wouldn't have lost...." She sighed and lost her train of thought. "He shouldn't have been forced to marry her. It's because of me that we're cursed."

My hand stilled on the cup as I realized the queen didn't know who I was. If only she knew who was helping her.

"No, he shouldn't have," I whispered just as softly, then held the cup to her lips and watched carefully as she took a few sips. "A few more," I coaxed. "You can do it."

Her neck wobbled as she struggled to lift her head, but I wouldn't let her fall nor a single drop mar her dress. I would make sure she kept her dignity. Her pillows were stained dark from her hair dye, and I wondered if it was vanity or something else that made her change her color. Her head dropped back onto the pillow, and I saw her wince in pain as her breathing slowed, her lungs not fully expanding as the poison took hold of her muscles.

My stomach pitched like water in a barrel when I reached for the ceremonial knife the healer had already used on the queen.

"Stop! What are you doing?" King Gerald roared.

Keeping the blade in my lap, I turned to both of them. "I'm very sorry, but the poison is still in her blood, and I need to draw it out with magic."

"No!" Xander snapped at me, knocking the knife from my grasp and onto the floor. "Don't go near her."

King Gerald's shoulders shook, his face wrought with regret. "I never thought I would ask one of you to help my kingdom a second time, but please, do what you must."

"Father!" Xander pleaded. "Don't make a deal with the devil again. Think of who you're hurting."

His words infuriated me, and as much as I was taught to ignore them, they stung like a rock being flung at my back. Just like all of the stones flung at me in our village. Persecution was unjust and hurt.

"If you won't stop this, I will." Xander unsheathed his sword and made to raise it against me.

This would not do. I flung my arm up and he was frozen to the ground, his sword arm pinned.

"I am not the devil! Though I can introduce you two if you'd like." I turned toward the king. "I will not proceed without your blessing, but take note—the longer we delay, the closer to death's door she walks."

King Gerald's face had turned white; his hand went to his heart as he looked at his frozen son. I tried to not glance at Xander's immobile expression, my anger seething at his attempt to murder me in front of the king.

"Do what you can... please," the king begged.

It was the "please" that convinced me of my course of actions. It was a risky procedure, one I had only read about in a book, but one that would surely haunt me.

"Very well." I looked around for the knife, and a slim green arm slipped out from under the queen's bed and handed it to me. Lifting the coverlet, I saw Gobbersnot looking back at me. His jet-black eyes were filled with hunger, and his tongue ran over his razor-sharp teeth. He glanced at the bowl of blood and back up at me, silently asking for permission. Since poison didn't have any negative effects on goblins, I could see no reason to let it go to waste.

Being very careful that no one saw what I was doing, I nudged the bowl of blood under the bed and heard his greedy slurps like a dog at a bowl of porridge. Taking the silver knife in my hands, I looked at the queen.

Mother would not approve of my recklessness, but I had to help her.

Sighing, I ran the silver blade along her palm, then did it again along mine. Pressing our hands together, I called to her blood, called to the poison within, and pulled.

Come to me, I coaxed and immediately felt light-headed and dizzy as I drew the poison into myself. My blood burned and I wanted to drop our hands, stop the transfer, but I gritted my teeth and held on, pressing our palms together.

Standing became impossible, and I crumpled to my knees as my vision blurred. King Gerald moved to stop me, but I held up my hand.

"No!" I said aloud. "Don't interfere. Not yet." When I felt that I had pulled all of the poison out of her system, I let go, keeping enough strength to run my finger along her palm to seal the wound.

I was going to be sick. The bitter poison was rushing through my own veins, and I knew I couldn't hold on to it without repercussions myself. I grasped for the table as I tried to pull myself up. During the transfer, Xander had been released from my spell, his sword sheathed, his face unreadable.

"Move," I commanded and rushed out of the room into the hall. Looking for one of the bathing rooms, I pushed on the closest door and stumbled into a sink. I let the dry heaves start, and soon I was vomiting up blood, with it the remains of the poison.

I clung to the sink as my body became heavy and I struggled to stand. My forehead was coated with sweat, and I shook uncontrollably. "Mercy daughter and light," I pleaded as I fought the poison. Even though I was using magic to contain it and try to keep it from affecting me, I would still have the symptoms of being poisoned.

"Ugh," I groaned when the vomiting, shakes, and sweating finally stopped.

The door to the bathing room swung open, and I saw Ameline peeking through at me. "Thank you," she whispered.

"You're welcome," I said softly as the door closed.

No one would come for me. I knew that. Xander and his father would be doing what they could to tend the queen. But it was successful. The poison was gone from her system.

But with her being so close to death, I had seen something she had not meant for anyone to see. A secret.

My eyes were closing when I heard the door open a second time and Gobbersnot's cussing as he carefully leaned over me. I saw his sharp, grinning teeth just as I lost consciousness.

CHAPTER TEN

I awoke back in my bed and could tell from the pile of dresses now outside of my wardrobe and on the floor that Gobbersnot had been the one to take me back to my room. Goblins, for their size, were strong and capable of carrying ten times their weight. He was now sleeping away the daylight hours with a tummy full of royal blood.

A cut on my hand would heal faster than most people's, but not with self-inflicted wounds. That was our own problem. Healing magic could work on others but not the caster, which meant I was still in need of getting medicine for myself and now for the queen. I was determined to make her a tea that would strengthen her body and mind, and I needed more wolfsbane for my own tea to keep my dreams at bay.

After spending most of the day in bed, I finally felt well enough to attend to my errands, and I sent Pru with a message for the prince.

After I had saved the queen's life, Xander seemed a bit more generous to me and agreed to my request to travel to town, even arranging the trip for me. It seemed we were allowed to go to a local herbalist as long as guards escorted us.

I was surprised to see Gaven outside on the front steps waiting for me on a horse. I never expected he would personally escort me, my cheeks warming as Pru and I climbed into a carriage. It didn't matter as long as I got what I needed.

The trip didn't take long, maybe half a mark by carriage to get down the mountain and into town. When we stopped and exited the carriage to walk down the back alleys, I noticed children and dogs went silent at my passing. Clothed in darkness, surrounded by guards in royal blue, I was an enigma, a bad omen.

When we entered a small shop with a mistletoe branch on the sign, I thought we would receive privacy, but it wasn't so. Gaven had apparently followed me and was right on my heels. An earthy scent tickled my nose, followed by a hint of sandalwood. Two long tables ran down the middle of the shop, filled with jars and butcher paper, twine, and potted fungi and plants. The rafters were covered with drying flowers and herbs. Light streamed in through a skylight in the ceiling. A sweet liquid was boiling in a pot over the fire, giving off a pleasant aroma. I stroked the soft leaves of a lavender plant as I inspected it for disease.

A petite elderly woman in her seventies waddled over to us, a red kerchief covering her hair, her warm smile exposing missing teeth.

"Hello, Auntie," I said, bowing my head in greeting.

Her smile widened, revealing a third missing tooth. "Greetings, niece," the old woman replied. I noticed the confused look that Prudence gave Gaven at our familiarity.

The elderly woman surveyed my companions carefully before reaching out for a hug. I obliged and leaned in close to whisper into her ear. "The sun and moon stood still."

"Yes, yes," she muttered and rubbed my back reassuringly. "What can Auntie Agress do for you fine folk?"

"I need these items," I announced, handing her my handwritten list.

Auntie Agress's yellowed eyes scanned the list, and her white overgrown eyebrows arched up at me in question.

I nodded slowly, confirming my order.

"Let's see that." Gaven stepped forward and snatched the sheet from her hand, flipping it over and then back before turning it around. "What language is this?" he asked.

"The language of Fey," I replied coolly as I snatched the paper back and handed it to Auntie Agress. "Why are you here?" I asked Gaven.

"I'm here to make sure you're not buying any black magic stuff. After all, word has spread that the queen was poisoned."

"I know that," I said stiffly.

I moved away from the fresh lavender and over to the rows of plants. Picking a leaf off a hyssop, I crushed it between my fingers and smelled the aroma. It had a thick, pleasant mint scent, which meant it would make a strong tea. "Auntie, I would also like a stone's worth of feverfew."

Auntie Agress mumbled, her head bobbing up and down as she moved farther down the aisle toward the fireplace, where she pulled a rope that lowered the drying rack down from the ceiling. With a few snips of her shears, she quickly trimmed the stems of various herbs and plants. Raising the drying rack once more, she then motioned for us to stay as she wandered into the back room.

"Auntie?" Gaven asked, stepping forward to pull the crushed leaf out of my fingers and sniffed himself. "I was led to believe you had no blood relatives."

It took control to not snap at him. "I am adopted, yes, but among the hedge witches, it is courteous to call our elders 'aunt.'"

"So you *are* a witch?" His eyes gleamed with distrust and he stepped back, his hand dropping to his sword hilt.

If he could only see my ugly glare under my veil. "What is

103

a witch? A woman who brews a tea to relieve a headache? Someone who understands the ancient arts of pressure points, who can relieve a pregnant woman's pain, or even a woman of faith who prays for healing? All have been cast out of villages and deemed witches whenever results are not understood. I believe a witch is nothing more than what people are afraid of and do not comprehend."

During my speech, I had moved to the other side of the table and began to point to different plants. "This plant right here, cardix, if steeped for two minutes can relieve a fever, but if steeped for five becomes a poison. Mellinon, if harvested in the spring, causes welts to break out among the skin, but if harvested in autumn cures rashes. Do you understand the difference between each of these outcomes?"

Gaven and Pru shook their heads.

"Patience. Waiting is the tipping point between life and death, a cure or an ailment. And women are known to be very patient," I said slyly.

"I see no reason that you couldn't have sent along the list with your servant," Gaven chastised, obviously uncomfortable with my quiet threat.

"For my medicine to work, I need to know that the herbalist knows their plants, knows what they're doing, and that they keep a clean and orderly shop. Otherwise, how can you trust them?"

I pointed between the two tables and two very similar plants, one on each.

"Can you tell me the name of this plant?" I gestured to the plant on my right.

"Hellion's kiss."

"Are you sure?" I challenged.

"Yes?" He wasn't.

"What about this one?" I pointed to the plant on my left.

"It's the same," Gaven said confidently.

"Actually it's not," I corrected. "All of the plants on the right table are poisonous; the ones on the left are not. You're lucky we have come to a very organized auntie, or she may give you a few leaves of this, and you would be dead by morning."

Auntie Agress came out with a small bag from the back room and began to wrap some of my items in pieces of silk, others in paper, and a few bottles.

"Excuse me, Auntie," Gaven mimicked me. The hedge witch's eyes filled with barely controlled laughter. "What would cause, um... someone to change drastically?"

Her shrewd eyes narrowed. "Their mind, body, or temperament?"

Gaven shifted his weight from foot to foot and leaned in close. "How about all of the above?"

"It's probably a curse," she said solemnly and beckoned him closer. He leaned in, clearly eager for the answer. "It's called the moon cycle. Give her a week and she'll be back to normal." Auntie Agress cackled, elbowing him in the stomach.

Pru sputtered, and I covered my mouth to muffle the laughter, thankful my veil still hid my expression.

Gaven's face burned red; he obviously didn't appreciate the joke. "What about a girl who likes you and then doesn't?" He looked off in the distance and then frowned. His shoulders slumped in dejection. "Never mind, you wouldn't understand."

"It could be a curse," she said again, seriously this time. "Of course, one brought on by a powerful sorcerer or enchantress. Anger any of those lately?"

Gaven looked directly at me. "Yes."

"Then you're doomed." She guffawed again and slapped his arm. After a few minutes of embarrassing him, she settled down and gave him a warning. "Listen, you might just need to woo her, or you can try this." She handed him a small bottle, and he opened it and took a sniff.

"It smells nice. Is it a love potion?"

"Might as well be," she chuckled. "It's perfume, a special blend. Sure to make the ladies fall for you if you give it to them."

He nodded and clutched the bottle to his chest protectively, and I wondered who he was thinking of the gift for. I became uncomfortable in the store and was grateful for my veil to disguise my true identity.

Auntie Agress grabbed my elbow and pulled me over to the corner of the room, urgently whispering, "I've been watching the stars, following their paths, and you're surrounded by death. Be on your guard, young one."

I gasped, remembering Xander's words: *"There will be more deaths before the moon runs a full cycle."* I feared I was the cause.

"Thank you." I squeezed her arm back.

When it was time to pay, I pulled out my purse, looked inside at the few meager coins and sighed. I didn't have enough for the price she was asking for all of the ingredients on my list, but that wouldn't stop someone as smart as me.

"Maybe just the dried monkshood root and the feverfew."

Gaven opened his own pouch and placed two gold coins on the table. "For the perfume and anything else she might need." He looked distracted and left the store deep in thought.

Auntie Agress's head bobbed, and she greedily bit one of his coins. Deeming it pure, she snatched the coins and disappeared into the back.

"I guess that means we're done," Pru said.

My hands were clutched tightly around my purse, trembling with anger. *How dare he embarrass me!* I turned and stormed into the street, catching Pru's reflection in the front window as she swooped in to gather my packages. I had my own money. It wasn't enough, but he didn't need to know that. Part of the trade was knowing when to haggle with a hedge witch; it kept them honest and true. My mother taught me that. He didn't need to step in and save the day. I didn't need saving. Suddenly I was thankful for the dark veil that hid my red burning cheeks the whole ride back to the palace.

We were in a long receiving line of carriages waiting to disembark, while others were being loaded as nobles and guests were saying their farewells.

When our carriage pulled up, I stepped out and saw Prince Xander standing on the top step, head low, his fingers rubbing his temples. It seemed he needed to be here to see them off, though he obviously didn't want to be. Rumors of the beast may have sent them packing.

Prince Xander finally noticed me, his body going rigid, his eyes taking in my dark veil again I imagined him trying to picture my hideous form.

"Did you get your potions?" he asked.

"They aren't potions," I corrected, surprised he made an effort to speak to me. "They're medicines, for the queen and me."

"Where is your medicine?" He pointed to my hand that only held my coin purse. I didn't have to answer, because Gaven and Pru arrived just then. She scurried up to me with my purchases, and Xander waved her over. Reluctantly, she came forward, and he proceeded to search through my belongings, though for what, I wasn't sure.

"Poisons?" He looked up at Gaven, not even addressing me.

"Yes," I answered truthfully, and three sets of eyes stared at me in shock.

"Are you so unstable that you would admit to purchasing

poison to murder me within my presence?" Prince Xander questioned.

"No, because I would never lie to you." His face had gone stone cold, his eyes darkened, and I rushed forward to lift a dried herb and explain. "This is balinko. The leaves are dried and can be brewed into a tea for migraines, but the seeds, if ingested, are poisonous. As are most medicinal herbs. I use part of the monkshood root to cure blackouts, and yes, it is another name for wolfsbane, but I had nothing to do with harming your mother."

"You say these purchases are for you. Are you injured?"

"Yes."

"Show me," he ordered. Holding up my hand, I showed him my bandaged palm and wrist. His eyes widened and he sucked in his breath.

"Come here," he ground out between clenched teeth. His nimble fingers quickly unwound the bandage to look at the cut along my palm, the one I received from healing his mother. He ran his finger along my palm, and I shivered at his gentle touch.

"I've seen you heal the cut on my mother. Yet, you are unable to heal yourself?"

"That is correct. Magic is a very fickle thing."

Xander didn't release my wrist but slowly turned it over to reveal a smaller cut from when he cut away our wedding bindings. "And this one. Did I do this?"

"Yes," I answered, blushing, not wishing to sugarcoat what his recklessness did. I could have healed it easily, but I wanted to let it be a lesson to myself.

"I'll be more careful," he said. Prince Xander looked at me, his eyes red, his chin unshaven. Effects of staying up too late hunting the beast, most likely. But his pained look made my stomach drop and my breath catch. I couldn't let him affect me like this.

"So will I." I yanked my hand from his and headed inside, Pru on my heels carrying my packages.

"Your Highness, I have received disturbing news." A page bowed before the Prince and I slowed to hear his announcement.

"What is it?"

"The servant girl Herez has run away. A note was found saying she was too terrified to stay at the palace and would go home to her family in the country."

My heart ached for poor Herez, and Pru's head dropped in sadness.

"I see." Xander sighed.

"There's more. Other servants are gone as well. We do not know if it is because they ran away or because the b-beast got them."

"Gaven, will you do me a favor?" Xander asked.

"Anything, my prince." Gaven stepped forward.

"Please succeed where I have failed and find this mysterious beast. For I no longer believe we're hunting a normal creature but something of myth and legend, and that is your specialty."

Gaven nodded. "I will leave at once, Your Highness, and will not return until I have news."

CHAPTER ELEVEN

I focused on making a tea to help Queen Anya regain her strength. Humming softly, I placed the finished herbal remedy in a silk satchel and smiled, hoping it would help. Knowing it was better that Pru deliver them, I waited to hear if she took them. When Pru told me she did, I then worked on brewing more of my own medicine, an herbal remedy that kept the dreams at bay and the darkness away. Taking a sip, I was careful to hide my packets of wolfsbane tea in my small satchel. No one would understand why I needed it, and if they found out I had it, I would be shunned on the spot or accused of being the one to try and murder the queen.

When my tasks were done, I stared at the chair that still sat in front of the door that separated the prince's rooms from mine. I had yet to hear him enter the room, and I doubted he even slept there.

Moving the chair, I pressed my ear to the door and was greeted by silence. I lifted my hand over the lock.

"*Locherra.*"

I heard a clinking as the door unlocked and swung inward. Stepping into the darkened room, I realized my mistake. This was never the prince's room, or at least it hadn't been in a long time. All of the furniture was covered with sheets, the drapes were closed, and silver cobwebs hung from the chandelier.

A large portrait hung above the fireplace mantel. It was a fine depiction, painted by an expert's hand. Xander looked around five years old, his young face void of emotion, his eyes haunting as he stood next to his mother, the queen. I frowned. It wasn't Queen Anya in the portrait, but another woman, the king's first wife. King Gerald rested his hand on the young Xander's shoulder, and even through the painting, I could feel the heavy burden of royalty resting upon the young boy.

"Have you ever smiled, my prince?" I pondered aloud, knowing if the threat of war had been hovering over this family for years, there would have been little to smile about.

Moving about the room that seemed to be a mausoleum rather than a bedroom, I couldn't help but stop to admire the chessboard and pieces laid out on the table midgame. The black set was fey beasts, and the white set was majestic elves. But the beast queen was missing.

Looking below the table, I searched to see if it had rolled away, but didn't find anything. Checking under the bed, all I discovered were cobwebs and dust balls.

"What are you doing?" Xander stood in the doorway, his face grim. "Who gave you permission to enter here? It's off-limits."

"No one. I came here looking for you," I said, stepping away from the bed and noticing dust now covered my black veil and dress.

"What is the point of placing guards outside your door if you continually leave your rooms without them?"

"There is none," I snapped. "And why should I be kept in my rooms?"

"For protection."

"I don't need protection."

"From you," Xander said, his eyes narrowed and his lip curled up. "Leave!" he growled at me. Storming into the room, he grabbed my upper arm, but I shrugged him off.

"No. I need to speak with you."

"There's nothing you could say that I would want to hear." He paced back and forth, glaring at me.

"I don't trust the emissary from Florin. He is—"

Xander was shaking, his rage great, his hands clenched into fists. "None of this concerns you."

"How can you say that when the threat of war concerns all?"

"This is a matter between my father and me. No one else. We will find a way to solve this problem without you. Or should I say *despite* you."

"I can help," I tried to reason with him.

"No thank you! Don't think I don't know what a bargain with a daughter of Eville entails. My father made one years ago with your mother, and look what happened. I'm married to you."

"I am not my mother," I said, realizing the truth. As much as I strived to be like her, to make her proud, to turn my heart cold, I couldn't. I did care.

"You are *just* like your mother." Xander walked around me, keeping his distance as he looked at the dark veils that hid me. "Swoop in at a time of despair, make promises and then leave, reaping the rewards of our country."

"Why do you hate me?" I asked.

"I despise everything about you. Just looking upon you makes me sick to my stomach for what your family did to mine."

His words mirrored those of my mother, and they burned into my gut. I knew now why she became so coldhearted. I couldn't stay in this marriage or this backward, antiquated country. I couldn't stay here despite my mother's orders.

I dug my hands into the folds of my dress and glared up at him. "I know you never wanted me. You made that obvious from the very first moment you spoke to me. You treated me with disdain, had your servants ignore me, did everything in your power to belittle and embarrass me, and I have done nothing to you."

"I—"

"Let me finish," I yelled, and Xander looked up at me, shock at my tone evident in his eyes. "I was forced to marry you too. Do you think I wanted to be married to a coldhearted prince who I've never seen? I have no more desire to be married to you than you do to me."

That idea seemed to startle him. It looked like he had thought this was what I'd wanted all along. "But I'm a prince. Everyone wants to mar—"

My laughter burst forth uncontrollably at his confused expression. "Hardly. Not everyone wants to marry into the baggage your kingdom is carrying, and you are not the most congenial of suitors. But I am not unreasonable, nor am I my mother. I'm willing to make a deal with you—or should I say *despite* you." I smiled at my own rephrasing of his threat.

"More deals," he said in exasperation, waving his hands at me.

"No, listen. What do you want right now more than anything?" I asked.

Xander's chin dropped as he thought. "I want whatever beast that's plaguing our lands gone, and I want power to protect my kingdom from Florin."

"Deal," I agreed confidently. "And when I have succeeded at both, I will leave quietly into the night. After a few months, you can say I'm dead, have our marriage annulled, and be free to marry Yasmin."

"What if you show up on my doorstep years down the road?"

"I won't. There is nothing here that I want. Neither crown, nor land, not even you, Prince Xander." As I spoke the words, I could feel the power behind them. Fate was listening in, and I worried at what I had just spoken into existence.

"And what if you fail?" he asked. "What happens to me?"

"Nothing, for we are already doomed to war. I can't think of anything worse than war."

"Death?"

"No, there are worse things than death."

Xander paced back and forth in front of the cold fireplace. "You sure you're not going to ask for my firstborn or anything, like your mother?"

"I swear."

He nodded before unsheathing the gilded dagger from the belt on his hip. It was the same one he'd threatened me with the day of our wedding. Using the edge, he sliced his palm.

I was surprised. He himself was asking for our deal to be sealed in blood.

"You understand what you're doing?" I asked.

"I know all about blood oaths." Xander frowned. He handed me the knife, and I took off my bandage. My poor hand was looking quite pitiful, and I was sure one of the cuts would scar. I very carefully made another small cut in my palm and let the blood pool. Noticing we were without paper, I picked up the beast king from the chessboard and smeared my blood on the black stone before handing it to Xander. He mirrored my actions, and I took the piece back, speaking loudly and clearly.

"A bond made of blood cannot be broken. I will do every-thing within my power to aid your kingdom in its time of need, and when I am done, I will absolve our marriage agreement peacefully. I will leave the palace, never to return."

"No firstborn children," Xander reminded me cruelly.

"Nor will I take his firstborn child." At the word "child," I looked behind Xander and up to the portrait above the mantel. My heart ached for the stoic young prince. "I will free the prince to marry his true love."

Wind picked up my last words of promise and whisked them into the air. I felt the stone grow warm in my hand. My fingers opened, revealing the golden light that poured over our contract before fading into a dull chess piece.

When it was over, I smiled, handing it to Xander. I thought I had done a good deed, but from the absolute look of horror on his face, I realized I'd made a mistake.

"What have you done?" he said softly in bewilderment. "What have you done? You tricked me!" he roared and flung the chess piece across the room. It rolled across the tile and into the fire grate.

"I did no such thing!" I was confused; I had done everything he had asked, even tried to bless his future marriage.

"You used the blood oath to curse me. As a prince and future king, I don't have the luxury of marrying for love—obvious by our current arrangement."

"But Yasmin... I thought you loved her."

"I don't." His voice had gone cold, his lip curled. "As the rumors say, I am incapable of love."

My breath caught in my chest as I realized that, if his admission was correct, and once our marriage was annulled, I may have cursed him. "I can make this right!" I took a step forward, but he held out his hand to stop me.

"Don't! Leave, witch, before you curse my existence further." Prince Xander stormed out of the room, slamming the door behind him.

I kneeled by the fireplace and fished out the black chess piece, tucking it into my pocket while looking up at the royal portrait.

"You may not want my help, but the sooner I can provide it, the sooner I can leave."

CHAPTER TWELVE

O n the second morning after Herez's departure, news came and the palace was aflutter with servants running around packing, preparing for a hunting party. Gaven had found the beast's trail when no one else could, and it was on the run, east into the mountains, toward Florin. I secretly hoped he would kill it.

The prince was a possessed man who wouldn't rest until the beast was caught. He was gathering a small army, larger than any hunting party, with enough wagons and supplies that he could very well be gone for weeks. And according to a missive that I received from King Gerald himself with his own royal seal, I was to accompany them.

This is it! I squealed in delight. The king had acknowledged me. I could help and prove to them, and to myself, that I wasn't a threat or evil as everyone believed I was.

Once I heard the news, I ordered my trunks packed for the trip. I wasn't going to miss out on my chance to save myself from my sham of a marriage.

Throwing open what I thought was an empty trunk, I wasn't at all surprised to see Gobbersnot had claimed it for himself and had already moved his favorite dresses and accessories inside, along with what looked like a few bottles of wine.

My few dresses were packed along with my books, possessions, and medicines in the smaller of the two trunks.

"I think that's it." I dusted off my hands and directed Pru to have someone bring them to the wagons. It was time.

I hid my apprehension behind the dark shroud of my waist-length veil as I marched out of my room, down the hall, and out the doors of the palace and went to address the king and queen for our departure.

The trumpets pealed, announcing my arrival. When I stepped outside, a hush fell over the crowd, and a smile played on my unseen lips. I turned and gave both of them a curtsey, proud that it was flawless.

"How are you feeling, Queen Anya?" I asked.

"Much better, thanks to your tea. I'm getting stronger every day." She smiled sweetly at me. Her eyes held a hint of softness about them, and she reached out to touch my arm. She couldn't see my ecstatic response to her touch, or the tear that slid down my cheek.

The king wouldn't make eye contact with me when he spoke. "Thank you for agreeing to go on the hunt. I'm sure your help will be immeasurable. Our whole country thanks you for your sacrifice."

I frowned. "It's not really a sacrifice. I'm your daughter now, and I will do what I can to keep your kingdom safe." And I meant it. Despite my mother's wishes for revenge, I wanted to do the opposite and help them.

"Yes, yes, very good," King Gerald mumbled and looked toward Gaven, who was overseeing a group of hunters. Gaven was dashing in his furred cloak, his crossbow strapped to his back. He gave the king a salute.

I searched among the party that was going on the hunt and was surprised to see the Florin emissaries were accompanying us, especially after Earlsgaarde's warning to me about wanting payment for their queen's death. Was it because we were heading into the mountains close to the pass between Florin and Baist? I assumed so—if Prince Xander came anywhere near them with this large of an army, it would seem like a threat, but if the emissaries accompanied us on the hunt, there would be no deceitfulness.

Pru looked frustrated, as there seemed to be some confusion on where I was to be seated for the trip. Since this was a hunting party, most everyone was on horses, and there were two small enclosed carriages along with multiple supply wagons that would stick to the main roads. The hunters would be following the beast's trail and would be riding with minimal supplies, only reconnecting with the larger group when needed. There was a chance I wouldn't even see them most of the trip.

Pru had gone to take my small trunk to the first royal carriage, but Gaven shook his head. She looked up at me, and even from the distance, I knew something was wrong. I instantly recognized the passengers in the first carriage— Yasmin and her closest ladies-in-waiting. The second carriage was for me.

Why is she here? Why is she coming with us? He was publicly slighting me, telling the world that he placed more value on her than his own wife.

If my mother were here, she would have displayed her anger in a tangible way, and even though the cards were stacked against me, I knew I could play this game just as well. My veiled head held high, I grabbed my dress and made my way down the steps alone. I passed Gaven astride his horse as he moved ever so slightly to place himself between me and the prince's horse, his face one of distrust.

I slowed my steps as I passed Wulfbringer and reached out to brush my gloved hand along his muzzle, but Gaven pulled the horse's head away and out of my reach. Hurt all because of misguided perception, I weaved an illusion of an adder that appeared near the horse's hooves, spooking him and almost unseating the guard.

As I walked away, I heard him whisper to Xander, "You're right, there is something dark and unsettling about her. Don't worry, Your Highness. I will protect you from the witch clothed in darkness."

How little they understood. If only they knew my real secret.

To get to my carriage, I had to pass Yasmin and her servants. There was no hiding how she wore her own jeweled tiara to spite me. She sent me a knowing smile as she tapped her tapered nails against the side of the white carriage.

She didn't cower from me, but instead looked like a cat that had gotten into the milk. Gone were her tears, replaced by a confident and brazen young woman.

Once again letting my own temper get the better of me, I began to recite a poem in the old language of the dark fey. Their tongue had been forgotten by most, and I knew it sounded threatening as I passed by the noblewoman.

Yasmin's skin paled and she fainted in her seat. Her ladies rushed forward to attend and fan her, while I stopped in front of my enclosed carriage.

A guard opened the door, and I stepped inside and was warmly greeted by lush blue velvet benches and blue-and-gold pillows. Sitting down, I spread my skirt out around my legs just as Pru stepped in behind and sat across from me. Her plain linen servant attire was replaced by a dark blue dress with long sleeves and cuffs, signifying her rise in status. Her hair had been expertly braided and coifed, and she looked quite fetching.

The young woman had grown on me, and her fear, though

still near the surface, had subsided. She seemed to relax more in my presence, which was good, because I would need a confidant.

Her face had a wonderful glow of excitement as she sat across from me. "You look nice," I said, wishing I had come up with a warmer greeting, but I was still seething from what had transpired outside.

"Can you believe it? When I told the steward you requested me as your attendant, it was a promotion. Now I get new clothes and get to travel with you out of the palace. I've never been out of the palace, and now I get to see the world."

The door slammed on us then, cutting off any more congratulations I had. The carriage jolted forward, and I was unprepared for the movement, crashing against the back wall before toppling sideways. Regaining my seat, I took a deep breath and looked around. The curtains had been drawn, and it was instantly stuffy. I reached over to pull them open, but they were stuck. Every one of them had been tacked shut so they could not be pulled aside and tied back.

Pru's face fell with mine.

"I'm sorry your view is not very promising," I whispered as my hand fell limply in my lap.

She tried to smile, but I knew it was a struggle. "No worries." I could hear her disappointment. "But I still get to travel. It's a great adventure."

Knowing we would probably not be disturbed for a great while, I pulled the veil from my head and laid it along the velvet bench.

"Until a few years ago," I confided, "I'd rarely been out of my town of Nihill. Well, once in a while we would travel to visit our friends in the north."

"Nihill? Doesn't that mean—"

"Nothing," I answered. "A name very apropos for the

town." Leaning my head back against the sideboard, I closed my eyes and continued to speak. "A town so small, so filled with misfits on the border of Sion and Candor yet no country claims it. Filled with thieves and wastrels and vagrants, it has become a home for the lost and desolate. My adoptive mother was from the northern kingdom of Kiln. Her mother died in childbirth, leaving her to be raised by an ever-doting father.

"My mother is beautiful and was engaged to the prince of Sion. Her father was a well-known and wealthy shipping merchant, and when his largest trading ship was lost at sea, he lost his wealth, including her dowry. The prince refused to marry Lorelai, since she was a pauper now and devastated. Her father begged attendance at the yearly gathering of the seven realms and asked if anyone would honor the broken betrothal in the southern prince's stead. They all laughed, for what worth could a pauper bring to a kingdom? There was no coin to fill their coffers, no army to join in defense, no family lineage to strengthen. She had no value other than her beauty.

"'What of love?' her father asked the current king's father, who at that time was merely Prince Gerald of Baist. 'Her beauty is so compelling that surely someone would fall in love, if they take but one look,' Lord Eville pleaded.

"'Beauty means little, for one does not marry for love,' Prince Gerald had responded.

"All of the princes laughed in his face, threw food at him, and ordered him to be gone. When he clutched his chest and fell before them, they thought it was an act to amuse them. They didn't even realize the severity of the moment until Lorelai came running to him from the shadows—she had been there the whole time, watching and listening. She tried to save her father, but he died in her arms while they argued amongst themselves.

"But her father, Lord Eville, was right. When the seven

princes saw the beauty of Lorelai as she rushed to her father's aid, they each were stricken with an insane desire to possess her for their own as queen. Seven proposals came to her as she lay coddling her father's dead body. But the offers fell on deaf ears, and vengeance was born in her heart.

"'You are not worthy of my love, or my body,' my mother hissed. 'No one is, for while you argue and make a mockery of the very man who made you rich, you let the only man I have ever loved die.'

"Her anger only made her more beautiful to them, but Lady Eville could not be persuaded, and she swore vengeance on all seven princes and their kingdoms accordingly. Years later, here I am." I shrugged. "Fulfilling my mother's vengeance and forcing the king's son into a loveless marriage."

Pru had been caught up in the tale. Leaning forward, her eyes glistened with unshed tears. "What curse has she placed on the other princes' kingdoms?"

"I do not know, for that is not my story to tell," I answered.

"And what happened to Lorelai—I mean, Lady Eville after her encounter with the princes? Was she punished?"

"No."

"No?"

"She retreated as a pauper to Nihill, where she took up residence in an old abandoned watchtower on the edge of town and made a living selling charms and potions."

"How tragic." She sighed dreamily and clutched her own heart.

I nudged her foot with my own and gave her a look of admonishment. "This wasn't a story. This was my mother's history."

"Oh, sorry," she mumbled, and I felt slightly appeased, though not much.

A few hours later, we stopped for a break along the trail.

My hand was throbbing from the various cuts, so when the carriage was secure, I hurried toward the river's edge and took off my bandage, letting the wounds soak in the cool water while Pru gathered wood for a fire to boil water for tea. My black veil kept getting in my way, so I lifted it off my face while I was tending to my hand, wishing for the millionth time that I could heal my own wounds.

Heavy footfalls came up behind me, and I caught a scent of cedar and leather. *Prince Xander.* I reached for my veil and covered my face before I turned to him. He stood in front of me, the sun having given his skin a warm glow, though his eyes were still red and tired.

"Why did you come?" he asked.

I blinked in surprise. "I wanted to keep my end of the bargain to help you, and because your father asked me to."

"So you can leave?" He folded his arms over his chest.

"So I can leave," I confirmed.

"Nothing else? No other reason at all? You're not secretly in league with the emissary from Florin, are you?"

I snorted in response. "No, I am definitely not in league with Earlsgaarde."

Prince Xander's brows rose at my unladylike snort. He studied me silently before finally nodding and moving on.

With Pru's help, I rebandaged my hand, then prepared my special tea and sipped it.

Farther down the riverbank, I could see Prince Xander scowling, sitting on a log with his head in his hands. I prepared a feverfew blend and headed back over to him with a peace offering. Standing next to him in silence, I waited for him to acknowledge me so I could approach, but he didn't move.

Clearing my throat did nothing to stir him. "My lord," I finally said, and he turned his head and looked up at me.

"Yes?"

"For your head." I held out the cup, my fingers trembling. He didn't move to take it, and I felt his rejection in my chest. "Do you fear I would poison you?"

"Would you?" he asked, turning to give me his full attention.

"Not when I value my life," I said. "If I wanted to poison you, I would wait at least a year or more, not a week after our wedding. That would be suspicious," I teased.

Xander's brows furrowed and he cocked his head. I realized that, wearing the veil, he couldn't see my facial expression and was therefore left to read the tone of my voice.

Once again, feeling unfairly judged, I raised my veil with my left hand. He gasped at the movement, grasping my wrist to stop me. Wincing, as he'd grabbed my injured arm, I dropped the cup and spilled its contents onto the sand.

"What were you doing?" he hissed. "I told you to always wear the veil. What if I see you and become enchanted or put under a spell? My father swears that's what happened when he saw your mother."

My lips trembled as I tried to hold back the tears from the pain. Cupping my hand to my chest, I snapped, "I was only going to raise my veil enough to take a sip and prove to you that I wouldn't poison you, but I fear it wouldn't matter, Prince, because your heart is already poisoned."

Leaving the cup in the sand, I spun and headed back the way I'd come, passing my fire and kettle on the hill and entering the carriage. In the darkness, I let the pain overtake me and the tears fall as Pru doused the fire and cleaned up our lunch.

CHAPTER THIRTEEN

An hour later, we were on the road again, then stopped before sunset to prepare camp for the night. We found a trunk on a wagon with all of our supplies for setting up our tent, and thankfully, with a little help from my magic, I was able to get it up without help from the men.

Lanterns were out and hung on shepherd's crooks outside each tent, casting a warm glow on the ground. Not one used to sitting idly by, I tried to make myself useful. Picking up a sack of potatoes, I carried them over to the kitchen area near a boiling pot and set them by a crate that was being used to prepare food. Finding an unattended knife, I began to easily peel the potatoes next to another woman.

"N-No. You don't touch the food," Boz, the head cook, said, taking the knife from my hands. His eyes scanned my dark veil, and I could easily read his suspicion. An older servant came and whispered in his ear, and he blanched. "We're fine. We don't need you. Go!"

"But I can help. I don't mind," I said, but was promptly ignored. Even the servants wouldn't let me help set up the bedrolls or fetch water from the stream. I was a pariah.

Our tent was set up away from the others, and I asked Pru to come inside with me.

126

"What do you need, miss?"

"Switch clothes with me," I demanded, looking at her new dress. It still gave her more freedom than my own.

"What?"

"You heard me. I'm tired of being useless. If we switch clothes and you sit out in the open where people can see you, then no one will suspect me if I wander. I haven't the energy or talent for long glamour."

"I don't know. What if I get caught?"

"Everyone is terrified of me and won't speak to me. Who will know the difference when you're fully covered? You do want a break, don't you?"

"But, miss, you're much taller than me."

"I don't think anyone will notice." I waved my hands at her, dismissing the claim before removing my veil. "Come, help me with my buttons."

Half a mark later, Pru was wearing my black dress and veil, and I was in her attendant dress. Back in sensible fabric instead of layers of fabric and lace, I felt at rights with the world. My raven hair was already braided and wrapped around the base of my neck in a serviceable bun, and only a few strands had come loose when I took off my veil. I did have a bandage around my palm and wrist still, but I didn't think anyone would notice.

The one disadvantage was her skirt showed my ankles, but again, I was counting on no one paying attention to a servant.

This time when I approached the cook, he saw me and immediately demanded that I peel the sack of potatoes I had brought over earlier. Keeping my smile hidden, I picked up the knife and deftly cut the skin off in little spirals. When done, I began cutting them into cubes, then moved on to the carrots and added them to the boiling pot.

"You work fast," Boz said. "Faster than most. Here, take the tray and attend the prince." He handed me a silver tray with a pitcher of ale, a goblet, and bread on it, and nodded to Xander's tent.

"I-I don't think—" I stammered, unable to find an excuse quick enough. I just wanted to feel useful and have moments of not wearing my veil. I had no intention of walking up to the prince and getting caught or scolded after only a few minutes of freedom.

"You don't think. You're an attendant. It's not your job. Go!" he demanded, pointing to the tent.

My cheeks warmed as I carried the tray to the red-and-blue tent and waited outside to be announced. Two guards stood on either side of the flap entrance, and I paused and listened while the tray grew heavy in my hands. From inside the tent, voices carried, and I could catch bits and pieces of their discussion.

"What do you know of the Talon Pass?" I recognized Gaven's deep timbre. "According to the trackers, that's where it's heading. It may hibernate there during the winter months."

"It's almost impossible to navigate once inside, and it's home to many perilous creatures, like trolls, pucas, and goblins," Prince Xander said. "And the mountains are the only border between our country and Florin. Luckily, Yasmin's family has been protecting the border for years. But there's something not right about all of this."

"Like what?" Gaven asked.

"Hard to say, but why attack at the palace and then run away? Why run so far, and straight toward our enemy? It's almost like we're being led."

The first guard opened the flap, and I ducked under it and carried the tray inside.

Both men stopped their discussion as I entered.

Unlike the other smaller tents, the prince's was set up like the royal suite. A woven rug covered the ground, a table and two chairs placed to the side, along with three large trunks and an end table. My eyes drifted to the elegantly carved bed frame that fit together with slats and a mattress, covered with a soft fur.

Keeping my eyes down, I moved to the table and set the tray down, turning to rush out. *Please don't draw attention to me. Please don't call me out.*

"What are *you* doing here?" Prince Xander said in surprise, following my retreat with narrowed, suspicious eyes.

I froze. *Oh no.* I was caught.

He stepped around me and blocked my exit.

"You did order me to serve your wife," I quickly reminded him.

"Well?" he stated. "Are you going to tell me your name finally?"

I glanced toward Gaven, but he was refusing to look at me. I could see him swallowing repeatedly when I refused to answer. Finally, he spoke up. "Rose."

Xander stilled, his hand touching my dark black hair, his voice husky. "Are you going to pour me a drink or not, Rose?"

Keeping my head lowered, I stepped forward and proceeded to pour him a drink, my hands shaking so bad that I filled the goblet to the brim. Handing him the cup, I didn't realize until too late that I'd used my bandaged hand. Thankfully the prince took the drink and barely gave my hand a glance.

"You forgot something," he said.

"What?" I squeaked.

He held the cup out, and my heart beat wildly. *What could I have forgotten?*

Gaven widened his eyes at me and pantomimed taking a sip. *Of course, the prince never drinks or eats without someone tasting for poisons.* I rushed forward, taking the goblet back for a quick drink. I almost choked as the warm liquid rushed down my throat, and a few drops trickled out the corner of my mouth. I waited thirty seconds to prove I wasn't poisoned before placing the cup back on the table, curtseying, and backing out of the tent.

"Tell the cook I want you to bring me my dinner as well."

"I don't think that—" I began, but when Xander spun on his heel and gave me a cold glare, the words froze in my throat. "Yes, Your Highness." My retreat was followed by their laughter.

"What are you planning on doing with her after dinner?" Gaven asked.

I stopped at the entrance and turned to look at him quizzically. Xander's lip curled up into a suggestive smile, and the heat of his gaze left no question as to his intention. "I would like to get to know her better."

His reply made my heart race, though I wasn't sure if I should be thrilled or fearful.

This was such a bad idea.

As soon as I stepped out, I took off running for my own tent and demanded Pru relieve me. We switched dresses, and I was once again covered in a veil and back in my somber clothes when dinner was served.

I couldn't help but compare my tent to Prince Xander's.

Whereas his was enormous and filled with a luxury bed, table, and chairs, ours consisted of Gobbersnot's trunk, my smaller one, and two bedrolls over a dirt floor. I also had my imperial rose cuttings that I was mad to bring with us for the trip, but I wasn't yet done with my experiments.

Feeling bitter at the difference in treatment, I took one cutting and placed it in the ground, then took a pin out of my hair and pricked my finger, letting a drop of blood touch the thorns. This time I used magic and whispered, coaxing them to grow.

Then I touched the ground, whispering an enchantment. The grass grew long, and I spun my fingers in the air to weave the blades together into a grass rug. Thick vines sprang up, and, mimicking what I had seen in Xander's tent, I weaved them into two single beds off the ground. The roses wrapped themselves up around the tent poles and across the top before dropping down. Each opened bud glowed softly, creating a real flower chandelier.

A toadstool sprouted from the ground, and I perched upon it, a second appearing for Prudence. At the first hint of the magic transforming the ground beneath her feet, she let out a gasp of surprise, but held in her enthusiasm as she watched what I was doing. The large mushroom toadstool truly fascinated her, and she squealed in delight when she touched the flower chandelier.

"It's like a dream," she whispered in awe, then ran to sit on her bed, lifting the blanket to look underneath. "Will it really hold me?"

I nodded, exhausted and famished from the exertion of power it took me to create our haven. By the time Prudence brought me our tray of dinner, my head was also pounding.

We had just finished our meal of roasted venison and vegetable soup when a commotion drew us out of our tent. Two guards, Tipper and Fagen, were arguing outside.

"What's going on?" Pru asked.

"We're looking for your servant," Tipper said. "The prince has demanded we find her."

My heart dropped as I watched the disorder I had caused by refusing to attend the prince. Did he really care that much about a strange girl?

Gaven approached our tent with another guard and stopped before me. "We have been ordered to search your tent," he said stiffly.

"No," I answered coolly. "You will not find any servant girl in my tent." It was the truth, as Pru and I were both outside.

"Doesn't matter. I have my orders," Gaven replied without emotion.

My anger was rising. "I would prefer you not." I did not want him traipsing through my enchanted tent. I had made it homey for Prudence and me, and the thought of either of them in our private area really set me off.

Gaven motioned to Tipper, who went in. Immediately I heard the guard cry out in fright. "What in the blazes? Witchcraft and black magic."

Through the opening of my tent, I watched in horror as the guard took his sword and hacked at my floor, bed, tent, and trunks. Destroying everything I had built and created with magic.

"Gobber!" I cried out, but the trunk shattered, and the silky dresses spilled out. Gobbersnot was not in his trunk.

My hands shook in anger, and I had to close my eyes and focus on not cursing him to kingdom come. *Rosalie, do not turn him into a frog or a bat.* When my tent was thoroughly destroyed, he came out and shook his head at Gaven.

"I take it you did not find my servant." My voice was low and cruel.

"No."

"And that was reason to destroy my belongings?" I asked.

"That was Tipper keeping your evil at bay," Gaven said without any remorse.

"I am not evil, or should I say, I'm not as evil as my sisters. But you're making me wish I were."

"Where is she? Your servant?"

"Prudence?" I said, pointing to my one and only maiden.

"No, not her. Rose."

"Gone." I lightly touched my veil, pressing it to my face and reminding myself to pitch my voice lower so he wouldn't hear the similarities in our tones.

"If you have done something to harm her, by the heavens, I will—"

"Stop. She is alive. I promise you."

"When she returns, send her to the prince," Gaven said shortly.

"I will most certainly not."

But he had already moved on and forgotten me as they moved to search my carriage.

Stepping into my tent, I held back my cry of frustration. Tipper had hacked through the walls, the vine beds, the flower chandelier and even my trunk. The lid was demolished, and I knelt down to pick through the scattered pieces of dresses. All of my dresses were ruined, slashed to shreds, along with my few precious possessions, including my sewing kit and book. The dresses could be replaced, but I was furious about my book.

I stormed across the grounds toward the prince's tent. Two guards blocked my way, but with a flick of my wrist, I sent them spiraling into the air. They landed with a thud as I burst through the tent, letting my anger rage.

Prince Xander was sitting on his chair in front of his empty table, waiting for dinner.

"How dare you send your dogs to destroy my tent and my belongings," I roared.

His face blanched and his mouth dropped open in shock. He must not have known what had transpired. "I gave no such order to destroy—"

"You send the camp into an uproar searching for a servant —one you gave to me, mind you—and when I refuse to give her back to you, you have your guards destroy my property." I was so angry my hands were shaking. "How dare you treat me so! I am not a fugitive, slave nor servant, but your wife."

The guards came into the tent, but Xander held his hand up and motioned for them to go back outside. Then he launched to his feet, storming to meet me in the middle of the room, his face contorted into a cruel smile. "In name only, or did you forget? The title means nothing, you mean nothing, and it will not grant you power or any favors."

"So I've been told. It seems you care more for pretty servant girls than you do your honor," I snapped. "How does it look to your people and country that on this hunting trip, you not only bring along your ex fiancée but continually seek the company of other women?"

"That is none of your concern," he growled, and gripped my shoulder tightly.

I did not like the way he touched me. With a flick of my wrist, a powerful burst of air flung him across the room to land in a heap on his bed.

"Oomph!" he cried out.

"And as for granting me power," I continued, "I don't need any, for I have my own."

Opening my hands wide, I closed my eyes and muttered, "*Fiegro.*"

The candles turned into a blazing inferno, illuminating the tent. Xander sat up in the bed, his arms covering his eyes.

"If you want the girl so much, you will have to get through me," I threatened. In a final tantrum, I snapped my fingers and made the bed fall apart. He landed on the floor, the frame collapsing around him. If I couldn't have a bed, then neither could he.

In a flurry of black veil and skirts, I left the tent, passing the guards. With my departure, the candles extinguished, leaving the prince in darkness. My grin spread ear to ear as I headed back to my tent, but not before walking by a group of nobles that had gathered. My show of power, flinging the guards and illuminating his tent, had earned me quite a crowd of onlookers.

As I passed, I heard the more discriminatory terms thrown my way.

"Witch."

"Darkling."

"Evil incarnate."

With every insult, my heart ached, and I began to understand why my mother embraced her pain and cursed the seven kingdoms. If it were the other way around, I may have done the exact same thing in her shoes.

A cough had me turning toward a deep red tent, and I saw Earlsgaarde outside studying me. Looking back toward the prince's tent, he gave me a knowing grin that made me shudder. I had briefly forgotten he was traveling with us. It seemed he was for the most part running between the trackers and our camp relaying messages. He coughed again and might have tried to beckon me over to gossip, but I had no desire to trade small talk.

I headed to my carriage and sighed. It would have to do for our beds tonight. Each of us could take a bench seat.

Pru made herself useful, bringing in what she salvaged out of the blankets and pillows. Her pillow was ripped, and loose feathers kept floating around the carriage. My blanket was too short and wouldn't cover my body, but curled on my side on the bench, it would do for a night.

We had just settled in when I heard the door open and shut, followed by loud chewing. I looked over the bench in horror to see that Gobbersnot had indeed found something worth eating—a deer's foot, probably stolen under the cook's nose. Being very careful, I wrestled the leg from Gobber and tossed it outside of the carriage. I didn't get the door closed fast enough, however, and following a growl, he was out after the bone like a dog. I heard the cries and screams from Yasmin and a few of the ladies as the goblin grabbed the bone and took off running, scrambling up on top of my carriage to perch there as he sucked the marrow out of the bone.

"I told you she's creepy," Yasmin said to one of her ladies. I stood at the top step, watching them point to my goblin. "I mean, who in the world has one of those as a pet?"

Gobbersnot made me proud when he tossed the bone directly at Yasmin's head, causing her to scream and run away.

"Good goblin," I cooed as he swung back into the carriage. He curled up in my lap and proceeded to fall asleep.

A candle mark later, I was disturbed by a heavy knock.

"Yes," I said without opening the door, my voice cold.

"I'm here to apologize on behalf of my heavy-handed guard," Xander whispered through the door.

I sat up and leaned near the window, keeping my voice low as to not wake Pru. "Are you going to replace my things?" I asked.

He sighed. "I will personally see to it that your things are replaced."

"Also, I want you to stay away from my servant."

"Wait a minute, I demand—" he started.

My eyes narrowed as I imagined boring a hole through the door into his skull. "I would rethink your answer. Otherwise, you might find the next time you kiss someone, you'll end up a frog."

"Are you threatening me?" he asked incredulously.

"No," I said innocently. "I'm just discussing possible outcomes made from your scandalous life choices. You said you would never love me, and I can come to the agreement that it will be mutual, but I will demand you be faithful until our marriage is annulled. Or you may end up a rodent, frog, or some other creature."

"Fine," he growled.

"Fine."

I could imagine us glaring at each other before his footsteps faded away, and I sat back.

Prudence had sat up, her hands covering her mouth in awe. "I have never before heard someone speak to the prince in such a way."

"Well, get used to it, because I don't plan on stopping."

A heaviness came over my heart, and I leaned back against the bench and sighed.

Oh, Mother, what would you have me do? You've made the prince miserable, but in doing so, I'm also miserable.

CHAPTER FOURTEEN

We spent most of the following day cleaning up the mess from Tipper and waiting to hear from the trackers. Earlsgaarde had left in the middle of the night, as had Gaven and Xander. It was only the servants left, and of course Yasmin and her ladies. Listening to their ugly barbs toward me was enough to drive me batty.

Luckily, not all of my clothes were damaged. I did have the dress I was wearing, a red dress, burgundy cloak and the prince's pin. Fearing I may lose it, I pinned it to the front of the cloak and folded it up, placing it in a smaller trunk Prudence found for me.

By midday, Xander had returned, and he rode straight to me across the camp. I was sweating from working on cleaning up and was dreading my decision to wear all black in the sun.

Xander looked uncomfortable. "I came to tell you that our trackers have lost the beast's trail in the mountains, so we'll be taking the wagons and carriages the long way around and staying the night in Celia while they continue their search and will probably resume tomorrow."

"Thank you," I whispered, "for telling me in person instead of sending someone."

"Couldn't." He shrugged. "After last night's tantrum, there

wasn't a single page who was willing to deliver a message to you." I could tell from the tick in his jaw and how hard he was pressing his lips together that he was trying not to laugh at me.

"Tantrum?" I scoffed.

His lip turned up at me, and then the full smile burst forth. "Yes, I would call that a tantrum if I ever saw one. It's very female of you." Those eyebrows rose so high that I was about to chuck a piece of the trunk at him when Yasmin came sauntering over and began to complain loudly of the heat and having to stay outside.

"I've been so bored waiting for you," she whined.

Xander looked over at my mostly cleaned-up campsite and then turned to her. "I'm sure you could have found some way to help or stay busy."

She yawned, tapping her mouth with a gloved hand. "No, that's for servants." Yasmin cast me a side eye and then pulled Xander after her.

The wood piece I was holding snapped in my hand and I tossed it into the ground, wishing it were her neck.

Thankfully, we were quickly loaded and back on the road. By dusk, we were almost to the mountains and the small village they protected.

The carriage picked up pace, and a trumpet fanfare announced our arrival into Celia. Feeling sorry for Pru, I weaved a spell on the curtains, thinning them so she could see.

I didn't care to look at first—what was the point of looking out of a fishbowl if I'd never experience it—but I listened. Listened to the voices of the villagers cheering for Xander, hearing them scream and point at Yasmin, at first thinking she was his new wife, followed by the confusion as a second royal carriage pulled up behind them and people pondered the closed curtains.

Finally, I looked out at them.

Even though they couldn't see me, I couldn't help but hold up my hand and wave softly to my people. A tear of gratefulness passed down my cheek as I beheld them, young and old. They were my people, my subjects, and I was their intercessor on behalf of the king and queen, until such a time as I finished my bargain and left.

The carriages pulled to a stop, and Prince Xander dismounted Nova. He was led onto a stage, where he greeted the people and thanked them for the gifts they had brought and placed on the stage for him and his bride. He explained on my behalf that I had taken ill and preferred to rest, but I thanked them as well.

More lies. Anger pulled inward into my soul. How much could one person take? I feared the rest of the procession would taper out much like today, and I couldn't dare handle more. I would suffocate.

The leader of the town, a hefty man with a short red mustache and bald head named Steffler, was also the innkeeper. Our group had taken up all the rooms at the Three-Headed Dragon. Apparently the inn used to be called the Dragon and was destroyed shortly after it was built. Steffler felt it was bad luck to rename it the same, so he moved on to the Two-Headed Dragon, but sadly that one was destroyed as well, so we now were in the Three-Headed Dragon.

Knowing the current track record of the prince ignoring me, I figured we wouldn't be placed in the same room, and I was right. Prudence and I were given a room at the Three-Headed Dragon, and so was Yasmin. The prince decided he would sleep with his men in the stables out back. For something had got the men spooked. Whispers and rumors, that were for once not about me, but of a legend in regards to a great troll.

Once my small trunk with Gobbersnot was brought inside

and the guards put in attendance outside my door, I knew I needed to get out.

Opening the trunk, I pulled the only non-destroyed dress from around Gobbersnot's sleeping form. It was a deep dark red, perfect for slinking through the night and hiding amongst the shadows. Throwing off the veil, I motioned for Prudence to help me out of the black mourning dress and into the red one. It bared my shoulders and was a little low cut, but for the most part it was modest. Pulling out my braids, I let my hair flow down my back and slipped into short boots; slippers would not do for what I had planned. Finally, I donned black gloves to cover my bandaged hand, then a deep burgundy cloak.

I rushed to the small window, threw open the shutters and looked out into the cold night air. The window opened to the back of the inn and was awfully close to the next inn's roof. The jump would be child's play for someone of my height.

"What are you doing?" Pru asked.

"I'm going out." I smiled and tilted my head to listen to the music coming from the streets below. "There's another celebration, and I won't miss out on tonight."

"Wait, miss." She looked at the door, nibbling her lip in worry. "What if someone comes to check on you?"

An incredulous look crossed my face, and I raised my eyebrow at her. "Has anyone other than you ever come to my rooms to check on me?" Her worry dissipated, and I smiled. "Would you like to come with me?" I asked.

She shook her head rapidly, eyes wide. "What if the beast is out there?"

"I would protect you," I insisted, trying to squash her fears.

Prudence sat on the bed, her hands wringing her skirt with worry. "Don't go."

Sighing, I went to my bed, tossed my black dress under the

covers, letting the skirt hang out, then plumped up the pillows and my cloak into a good imitation of my body.

"There," I said smugly. "At least I'm still here, so you can go and get food and see the sights. Just make sure to bring back food for two, so no one gets suspicious."

Her smile widened, and she seemed relieved at the idea. I hid behind the door as she left. The guard interrogated her, asking where she was going. Her quick reply of downstairs for food pacified him. Through the crack in the door, I could see him lean in and glance at the bed before pulling back out into the hall and motioning her onward.

Once the door was closed firmly, I counted to one hundred before moving to the window. The distance to the next roof wasn't an issue, rather it was my long legs and pulling them through the small window that caused me discomfort, but once perched on the windowsill, making the jump to the roof was a breeze. Landing on all fours, I waited to regain my balance and then headed to the tree growing near the side of the roof. In less than a minute, I was down on the ground and wiping bark dust from my hands, looking up at the tree in victory. I didn't need Eden's glamour ability or Maeve's flight to go on adventures.

Sneaking down the alley, I followed the sounds of laughter and came upon two people hiding in the eve of a building kissing. The woman's pastel dress was like a beacon and impossible to hide, and her signature laugh made me cringe. She tried to move away, but the man pulled her back into the shadows and they continued to kiss, their hands wandering where none should stray. It didn't take a genius to guess the identity of her partner; after all, Xander preferred to kiss girls in the shadows.

Feeling extremely vindictive, I whispered a curse upon the two and had to hold back a cackle when I felt the air thicken as it materialized and floated over the two lovebirds.

"*Vesputin.*"

Yasmin sighed and pulled away, and I ducked behind empty barrels to watch as she adjusted her hair and lipstick before heading into the inn. Xander didn't follow her, the sound of his steps diminishing into the night.

The moon was full, and its light cast down upon me as I walked, making my skin slightly itch. Rubbing the back of my neck, I stretched my arms until the feeling passed. The town square had been hastily decorated with ribbon and brightly colored banners for the arrival of the crown prince and his new wife. A ragtag band of musicians was playing upbeat folk songs, and vendors continued to hawk their wares now that a new affluent group of buyers and soldiers had come to town. Little did they know we weren't here for a celebration but were hunting a threat to their community. If they knew, would they be celebrating so recklessly? I had to remind myself that the beast stuck to the woods, hunted alone and not near populated areas. The town was safe—I hoped.

A flash of red uniform caught my attention as I zeroed in on Lord Earlsgaarde leaning against a building, drinking and watching the villagers with a face akin to disgust. His eyes caught mine from across the square, and he lifted his tankard in a solemn salute. The side of his mouth curled into an intentional smile, one that alleged he knew my secret.

I shuddered at his salute and turned, ignoring him and moving through the crowd, putting as much distance as I could between us. I was surprised when I came to the edge of the square and saw troops stationed at the main road into town, and even more so that Xander himself was standing guard. Was there a threat we didn't know about? And more to the point, if he was here, then whom did I curse in the alley?

A lone deep rumble reverberated through the night, and I stilled in fear, turning to look beyond the troops and up the mountain. The rumble was followed by a second and then a third. The wooden tailor sign swung from its hinge and a mud puddle spiraled out with each quake, signaling a very large threat.

My breath caught in my throat and my skin tingled in warning as I scanned the treetops. The moon reflected off his grayish bald head, and I caught glimpses of a long bulbous nose the size of a pumpkin protruding from his face.

A troll.

He stepped out onto the road, dragging a downed evergreen behind him like a club.

The troll continued to march toward the town, not waylaid in the least by the first launch of arrows that came his way from Xander's troops. They bounced off his skin, none finding purchase.

Xander signaled another volley, but all they did was irritate the troll. He lifted the evergreen tree by the top and swung the trunk and roots down on a laden wagon, letting out a roar. The music stopped, and the townspeople looked up in terror before scattering like cockroaches.

Why was the troll here? What had caused him to leave his cave and attack a village with no provocation? Did something drive him here?

My mind filled with questions that had no answers as Xander took his sword out and directed a two-sided attack. They were trying to keep him from entering the town and drive him back into the woods.

With a mighty swipe of his tree, the troll cleared a path through the left bank of troops and began to march straight into the town as if drawn there like a moth to flame.

A child ran in front of the troll and froze, her legs quaking as she stared up at the great monster. His club was heading straight for her head.

With lightning speed, Xander grabbed the girl around the

waist, rolling with her out of the way as the tree embedded deep into the earth, but not without the branches scraping across the prince's back.

Joining the fight, I whispered to the earth, causing the club to sink deep into the ground. The troll struggled to free his weapon from its grasp, roaring in frustration.

Xander made sure the girl was all right and with her mom before he turned to attack the troll with the rest of his troops. He ducked as a mighty fist swung above his head, then spun, using his sword to slice in an upward angle across the troll's heel.

The troll let out a painful cry but did not fall, for the cut didn't sever a tendon, nor stop him from advancing toward the inn. Feeling vindicated and a bit amused, I continued to watch as the troll picked up carts and smashed them, overturned vendor tables, and spent a good amount of time destroying the now-empty stage and each and every single instrument.

The portly owner of the Three-Headed Dragon stood outside his inn, his hands on his hips as he wagged a finger at the troll. "Naw, you don't. Not again, ya hear? I've had enough of your destroying my inns."

The troll roared loudly as people began to pour out of the inn and into the streets, and I finally understood how the inns were previously destroyed. I glanced up at the inn and feared for Pru, who I had yet to see leave the premises.

"No!" Pulling the cloak low over my face, I ran forward, my hands trembling as I called power to me. Clapping them together, I called forth a bolt of lightning from the sky, which struck the ground in front of the troll, startling him. Knowing a cave troll's biggest fear was fire, I sent another lightning bolt to a cart filled with hay, setting it aflame.

"Keep going!" Xander yelled as his troops rushed forward. They grabbed the cart and pushed it toward the troll, who tried to dodge but fell backward into a house, crushing a corner of the roof down to the foundation.

Xander was at my side in an instant. "Can you drive him out of town?" he asked.

I nodded without looking or making eye contact, pulling my hood lower.

The wind blowing my cloak, I continued my mission, my head held low as I directed lightning like a composer, each melodious strike carefully calculated to drive the frightened troll back to the edge of town. He groaned at me, sounding disappointed at not being able to destroy the inn for a third time.

Pressure was building in my head, and I could feel the headache coming on, which meant if I wasn't careful, I could lose control. My hands burned from harnessing so much power, and an iron taste filled my mouth, as I had accidentally bit my cheek.

"You can do it!" Xander encouraged me as I paced back and forth like a herding dog getting a stray bull into the pen. The forest wouldn't do; he needed to go farther.

"We need to get him back to his cave!" I yelled to Xander.

Nodding that he understood my concern, he signaled his men to bring torches while he raced to the stables. They spread out, and with a few more timed lightning blasts to neighboring bushes, setting them on fire, the troll turned and ran into the woods.

"Don't lose him!" Xander yelled, riding up on Nova. Without stopping, he reached down and pulled me up into the saddle in front of him. My hood fell back, revealing the color of my hair, but I quickly pulled it down low and leaned forward, holding on to the saddle horn for dear life. Xander gripped me around the waist and pulled me back against his chest so he could see over my shoulder as he galloped into the dark woods.

Scared to be so close to him, but also terrified that we would stumble and fall to our deaths in the dark, I reached out and called forth a mage light, tossing it into the air to light his path.

"There!" I said, pointing to the destroyed path the troll had taken.

"I see it," Xander replied just as Nova leapt over a fallen tree.

I gasped, believing I was falling to my death, but once again, his hand held me close, keeping me safe.

The troll turned to attack us, but I sent another lightning bolt at the troll's bottom, scorching him. He howled in pain and ran on to seek the shelter of his cave. I thought we had lost him, but I heard the rumbling and scraping of rock as he pulled a giant bolder away from his hidden cavern and retreated deep inside.

Xander slowed Nova and helped me down, and I rushed over to the opening, sending the mage light deep into the tunnel. I couldn't see him. We had beaten Xander's troops to the cave, but I watched in horror as the prince unsheathed his sword and was about to go after the troll alone.

"Stop!" I commanded.

"If we don't kill him, he'll be back to terrorize the villagers again."

"Just because you don't understand something doesn't mean you should kill it," I hissed angrily.

"It's a troll. What's there to understand? They kill humans, and this one has been terrorizing Celia for years. It's my job to protect my people." Xander gripped his sword and pointed deep into the cave.

"If you go in there, you will die," I said coldly. "Troll caves are deep and filled with traps. You will not make it out again."

"What would you have me do?"

"Nothing," I said simply.

"Nothing?" he scoffed.

"That is a gentle Torperren."

"A what?"

"A troll that spends most of its life sleeping and only hunts goats and farm animals once every twenty years or so. If my guess is correct, every time the town has a noisy celebration, it disturbs the Torperren's sleep, and he comes in and destroys the inn."

"You're kidding me." Xander laughed.

I shook my head. "The best thing to do would be to spell him back to sleep and soundproof his cave."

"You can do that?"

Hiding my grin, I moved forward and cupped my hands, whispering a lullaby into them. With a flick of my wrists, I released my bespelled song into the air and watched as the glowing trail flew into the cave, searching for the troll. It wasn't as powerful as Meri's songs, but I knew it would do the trick.

We waited a few minutes, and sure enough, we heard the echoing rumble of a snore coming from deep within.

Xander moved to the giant rock and began to push it. Ever so slowly, he rocked it back and forth until it closed over the cave.

I found a sharp rock and began to dig sigils deep into the stone around the cave. Each one glowed faintly before fading away. Xander kneeled near me to watch, and I glanced away, keeping my hood between us, my heart racing in fear. This country hated magic, despised what I stood for, yet I had seen the wards around the palace. Now that he had seen me use my magic again, did he loathe me even more? Would I be punished?

"That's amazing," he whispered in awe as he watched me etch another symbol, which then faded and disappeared.

I stilled in surprise, keeping my head averted. That was not the reaction I was expecting from the prince.

"I want you to know I was wrong about the troll." He sighed. "I tend to judge too quickly, and that is a fault of mine I will try to overcome." My lips pinched in irritation, and I wanted to snap at him that he'd judged me unfairly too, but he interrupted my internal rant. "I was also wrong about you." He patted the rock and stood up, moving away from me to look down the hill and into the woods, where we could see the torch and lanterns of the rest of his troops.

I was left speechless, uncertain at his admission. I stood, my trembling hands reaching for my hood as I began to pull it back to reveal I was Rose, the servant girl he seemed so infatuated with, but I was scared of being rejected again. But I hesitated too long, and Gaven rushed from the darkness, his crossbow at the ready, eyes scanning the woods. I pulled my hood back up and moved out of sight.

"Prince Xander, where's the troll?" Gaven asked.

"Gone. It seems we have the troll problem under control for now. In twenty years, we'll have to fill the forest with an offering of goats, but I think the town and inn will be safe for a while. One beast down, only one more to go." He laughed and slapped Gaven on the back. His eyes twinkled with mirth, and I understood that I was catching a small glimpse of the future king, one who took joy in helping and protecting his people from harm. I was proud of who he could become, but it almost wasn't such a happy ending. It could have ended in his reckless death, because he judged everyone by his or her appearance.

As more of his troops gathered around the cave and he continued to explain what we had done, I slipped back into the shadows. This was his moment, and I feared the feelings that were bubbling up within me. He looked around for me, his once joyous face turned to one of concern, but I had already disappeared into the darkness. My absence was quickly forgotten, as his guard Fagen hefted his fist into the air and yelled in triumph, "Long live Prince Xander!"

"Long live Prince Xander!" Tipper followed.

Casting a smaller mage light was difficult, as my hands trembled from the exertion, but I began to make my way through the woods and back to the inn. Happily humming as I did so, I clasped my cloak and then froze as I felt the cool touch of the rose pin Prince Xander had given me that I had attached for safekeeping. No, not me—Rose.

Did he see it?

I was so caught up in my thoughts that I missed the dark shadows that separated from the trees.

"You're coming with us, witch," a gruff voice demanded from behind me as a knife was pressed against my exposed throat.

Blinking in surprise, I glanced up at the kidnapper who dared accost me. His clothes were fine, black to blend into the shadows, and a mask covered his nose and mouth.

"No," I said coolly. I was not in the mood to be trifled with, nor waylaid at this hour. I had lost sight of Xander, and now I was irritated.

"You will obey or die." A second man stepped from the shadows and came up to face me. Dressed similarly as the first, his hat brim hid his features, all but for a small mole on his neck.

Ever since the knife had touched my skin, I hadn't moved, barely breathed. Anger rolled through my body, and I felt a growl low in my throat, a challenge.

"Remove the knife at once," I snapped.

"Or what?" The first man pressed the blade closer to my throat. "You'll scream?"

"No," I threatened. "You will."

A fine powder was flung into my face, and I tried to fight the effects of the sleeping drug. A haze came over my mind, and I could feel myself slipping, losing consciousness.

A deep throaty growl surrounded us, and then their screams rent the night air.

CHAPTER FIFTEEN

Come morning, I found myself back in my locked room in the inn, with no memories of crawling back through the window or how I had escaped the men in the woods. Prudence was lying on a mat near the door fast asleep, her hand over her eyes. Her chest was moving, and a slight snore could be heard.

I was still wearing my red dress from the night before. My head pounding, I struggled to walk to the table without falling over; the floor seemed to move like waves beneath my feet as I grabbed the wall for support. Making my way to the table with a washbasin and pitcher of water, I wet my hands and splashed my face.

Looking down, I gasped—the water was tinged with red.

My hands shook as I brought them up to my face. There were specks of dried blood all over them. Whose blood? Mine? Panicking, I checked my neck in the mirror, but there was only a small scratch across my throat from the thief's knife, no other significant cut.

Then I saw the dark patch of red on my skirt. The fold of my red dress had hidden it, but there was no mistaking the blood.

Fear raced through me as I clawed my dress, trying to rid myself of the bloody shroud.

"What's the matter?" Pru asked as she awoke and rushed to my aid.

"Get this off me," I cried out. Her fingers made swift work of the laces where mine had fumbled, and then the dress was off.

It landed in a pile on the floor as I crawled into my bed, pulling my knees to my chest and rocking back and forth as I tried to piece together what had happened.

A loud snore came from the trunk, and I knew if Gobbersnot was comfortable enough to sleep and not worry, then I could be as well. But I didn't.

"When did I come in last night?" I asked anxiously, my eyes wandering around the room, searching for clues.

"I don't know. I fell asleep a few hours after the troll attack and didn't hear you return."

"And what time was that?"

"A little after the tenth mark?"

Closing my eyes, I tried to push down my fears. It was okay —my curse had just reared its ugly head, and I had another episode of memory loss. But I would need to double or triple my dose of wolfsbane to keep it at bay so it wouldn't happen again. Maybe I was weakened from using so much magic away from the ley lines that it left me vulnerable to the episodes.

"Miss, are you okay?" Her words comforted me. She seemed to actually care about my well-being.

"I will be, I hope." My voice lost its hard edge, one born of defense, and my tone changed around her. I was warming up, becoming a softer person.

Pru went downstairs and came back with hot water, and I dropped my special tea bag in, letting it steep longer than usual. I would need to make a more concentrated dose, but this would do for now. When it was ready, I took a sip.

I wasn't sure anything had happened, aside from the blood.

It didn't mean anything. My head was throbbing, and I rubbed my temples, blaming it on using too much power yesterday.

A loud knock came at the door.

I hadn't dressed yet because I didn't want to disturb Gobbersnot, so I grabbed the quilt, wrapping it around my body and rushing to stand behind the door as Pru opened it.

"Are you and the... the *princess* all right?" I recognized Gaven's voice and didn't miss as he struggled over the word "princess."

"Yes, why wouldn't we be?" Pru asked.

"Because two men were found dead in the woods early this morning."

My heart froze, and I couldn't help but imagine the crumpled red dress that was tossed in the middle of the floor as a blood pool. From my spot I could clearly see the red stain, but I prayed he didn't notice or suspect.

"That's horrible," Prudence exclaimed, not needing to act. "Those poor souls."

"I wouldn't call them poor souls. It looks like they were bandits and tangled with the wrong mark, except...."

"Except what?" she pressed.

"I inspected the bodies, and I'm not so sure a man killed them."

"A woman? You think a woman could have killed them?"

"No, not a—" Gaven paused and scanned the room. Then he took a step back and looked between the open crack of the door, and our eyes met.

Mine opened in surprise; his narrowed. I was still in a manner of undress, so I did what any woman would do who'd been caught half naked—I slammed the door closed in his face.

A knock followed, and I pressed myself against the door to hold it closed. "You cannot enter. I am not in a suitable state of dress," I called out.

"Understood," he said from the other side. "But you didn't happen to hear or see anything in the middle of the night, did you? Your window overlooks the woods."

"No," I answered hastily.

My wardrobe door swung open, and I heard the loud snoring from inside. *Could it have been Gobbersnot?*

"Very well." Nothing further came forth, so I assumed he left.

"What would you like me to do with the dress?" Pru asked.

"Burn it." I was saddened because now I was only left with my black somber dress.

Pru went over to the fireplace and tossed in the rolled-up dress and bloody cloak. The embers that had died down in the night picked up again at the new source of fuel.

It wasn't until the dress was engulfed in flames that I remembered the token, the pin Xander had given me.

"No!" I rushed to the fireplace and grabbed the dress with my bare hand, pulling it out and trying to smother the flames. When it was doused, I searched the dress and the burnt ashes for a glint of the pin. Soot and smoke poured out from the fabric ball, and I coughed as I searched.

"Rosalie." Pru came and grabbed the poker from the stand. "Let me." She searched the ashes and didn't turn up anything. "What was it?"

"Nothing of importance," I lied, knowing it was a gift willingly given to me by my husband. At the rate we talked and saw each other, I wasn't sure if I would ever receive another. "It's gone now."

"That's not true." She pointed to my red and blistering hand. "You don't burn yourself over nothing."

The throbbing only began once I noticed the burn. Once given my full attention, it proceeded to dominate my thoughts. My wrist was already blistering, and I had a hungry-looking goblin poking me in the side, fully awake and licking his lips at the smell of burnt flesh.

"Did you murder those men in the woods and then bring me back here?" He shook his head. His feet danced in excitement as he moved his mouth closer to my injured hand. "No, Gobbersnot." I had no intention of giving him a piece of my flesh.

He pouted, then swung the dress around and sashayed back to my trunk, giving me a rude hand gesture before crawling back into his bed.

CHAPTER SIXTEEN

B ack on the road, Prudence and I slept fitfully in the carriage, but thankfully my dreams were quiet and not plagued with the thoughts of a murder or death. I awoke with a crick in my neck and barely remembered packing up and leaving Celia, my brain in such a fog of worry and exhaustion. I fell into despair, biting my thumbnail as I tried to calculate what of my meager store of potions and tea was left. It wasn't good. Tipper had destroyed most everything I had, and I was down to my last few tea bags.

The beast's trail went cold, so I heard talk from the men of stopping at a noble's house on the western side of the pass. It meant little to me. Tracking the beast was no longer a main priority—hiding my inner darkness was. I couldn't shake the fear that I was the one who killed those men and then blacked out. I must have used my magic to get back to my room. There was no other explanation. I chewed on my lip in worry as the scenery changed and the carriage slowed.

We pulled up to a magnificent three-story manor with immaculate landscaping and what appeared to be woods for miles beyond. It was at the base of a mountain pass, with guard towers scattered along the tree line.

"Whose house is this?" I asked Pru when we arrived. She held the door open, and I stepped out of the carriage.

An elderly man in his sixties wearing a dark coat came down the stairs.

"Papa!" Yasmin cried out and ran into her father's arms. The girl began to cry extensively, and I couldn't help but feel responsible.

"What is this, my poppet?" Yassa declared. "What happened to your face?"

My head snapped up and a sly grin rose to my lips as I tried to smother my glee. I had almost forgotten the curse I had placed upon Yasmin and her midnight lover. A curse that wouldn't appear until the light of day touched their skin.

"It's all her fault." Yasmin pointed her perfectly polished nail my way. Instead of cowering, I walked straight up to the both of them and took in the red pox that now covered her face and hands. She kept trying to scratch it with her gloved hand.

"A soothing lotion and staying out of dark alleys will definitely cure what ails you," I quipped.

"Papa," Yasmin whined, scratching the back of her neck.

"Enough, Yasmin," Yassa admonished before turning to Xander.

"Thank you for going ahead and hosting us while we deal with the problem at hand," the prince said cordially.

"You're here now, and so is he." Yassa turned and nodded toward Earlsgaarde, who was giving instructions to two of his men; the rest were nowhere to be seen. I wondered if they were sent out ahead to Florin now that we were so close.

"What is this?" Yassa continued softly, but not quietly enough that I couldn't hear him. "I thought that at least by the time you had arrived, this matter would have been settled."

"It will be in due time. I will personally take care of it," Prince Xander replied stiffly. "But there is a matter I need to take care of in town, so I expect that you will act as host in my stead and make sure everyone gets settled while I'm gone. Including the emissary from Florin."

As he spoke, the emissary in question was across the yard speaking with Gaven, both of them deep in discussion. Then they turned to look at me, and Gaven's eyes narrowed suspiciously, his hand tightening on his crossbow. I wanted to rip off my veil and shout, "It's me, Rose!" But there was something about his expression, the way he leaned in too eagerly and listened to Earlsgaarde. I shuddered.

"Of course, Your Highness." Yassa bowed and touched his hand to his heart. "Then we can begin the hunt."

Prince Xander stumbled and caught himself, rubbing his red eyes. "I make no promises that we will find anything. The trail has suddenly gone cold."

Yassa leaned forward, placing his hand on Xander's arm. "You look unwell. Are you sure it is not *her* doing?"

"I would bet my life on it," Yasmin said while rubbing her arm. "You should be rid of her."

How dare they continue to belittle me, and within earshot no less? Do they have no manners? They call me evil, but at least I'm civil. They are truly beasts.

Knowing they weren't worth my time, I stepped back toward my carriage. *Breathe. Focus. Do not curse them.*

Even though the manor was large, my room was on the small size. A slight I believed meant to wound me, as the prince's bride, but it was still larger than my room in our tower.

I was silent and contemplative as I sat in the wooden chair in my room overlooking the front of the house. We opened the trunk and I was dismayed to see Gobbersnot was gone; he must have snuck out when we were unloading. I had a feeling he was probably raiding Yasmin's closets and jewelry boxes for pretty things. I was too exhausted to care, and frustrated because I had no clothes to change into—and I would not stoop so low as to beg for clothes from Yasmin or Yassa.

After a few hours, I had neither seen nor heard from Prince Xander, so I thought he must have forgotten our deal. I would see to my things myself. I knew farther down the mountain path there was a village. If I hurried now, I could make it before dark and have some dresses sent up to the house.

Excited about my plan and my own excursion, I left without telling Pru or anyone. I wasn't used to having to tell people where I was going, and at Yasmin's house there were so few guards available, I didn't have anyone watching my door.

Heading to the stables, I was dismayed to see the carriage horses had been unhitched and most of the stable hands and servants were gone. An old man took pity on me and brought me out a roan to borrow.

"Where are you going?" Xander asked as he rode back into the yard with Gaven and his guards. This was the first time I had seen Gaven up close in a while, and his face, neck, and arms were covered with a creamy pink-tinged paste. My cheeks burned in embarrassment as I realized who the other target of my curse had been.

"I'm going to town to replace my things," I said stiffly, looking away from Gaven and directing my answer to Xander.

"Are you sure you can ride? The last time you were on a horse, you were practically sliding off it," Xander teased, referring to our ride in the woods.

I clenched my skirt and stared up at the horse, who had all of a sudden grown five times higher than I remembered. Ride? I wasn't sure, since this horse was livelier than Jasper. Then I looked over at Xander and knew it was a challenge. He was trying to prove to me how unworthy I was, give me tasks that would embarrass me.

Challenge accepted.

Gritting my teeth, I bunched my skirt up in my hand, placed my left foot in the stirrup and, gripping the pommel, pulled myself into the saddle. The horse, unlike our old one from home, stood perfectly still. Readjusting my skirts and veil, as it had caught on a buckle and almost tore from my head, I reached for the reins and looked over at Prince Xander and Gaven, whose faces were a mix of laughter and disbelief.

What's wrong? I glanced down and realized I wasn't sitting sidesaddle, as was proper for a lady. Rather than get down and readjust, I just clicked my tongue, pressing my heels gently against the roan's flanks. It wasn't that I couldn't ride a horse, it was that my horsemanship skills were seriously lacking. I had dug my heel in a little too hard, and the horse took off at a canter that jarred my teeth.

Prince Xander, Gaven, and three other guards followed as we headed into the valley and back into town. Unsure of exactly where I was going, I dropped back to the middle, content to follow behind the prince. There was no laughter or jokes, the procession somber and mellow and heavy with tension. I kept quiet even when we rode up to Dandy Leona's, a beautiful dressmaker shop with a dandelion flower in the window.

My dismount was anything but graceful, my muscles betraying me. I stumbled when my feet touched the ground and fell backward, but was steadied by a strong arm. Following the hand, I realized it was Xander who had reached out to catch me.

"Thank you," I mumbled and then quickly pulled away from his grasp. Lifting my skirts, I headed inside the shop, surprised when they didn't follow me but waited outside. My heart dropped, and I felt a lonely pang.

"Greetings, mademoiselle. I am Miss Sou." A young woman came out from the back room and froze in place when she encountered my dark and veiled form.

"Greetings," I said, glancing outside to see the prince and Gaven deep in a serious discussion, looking at a map and pointing back up the way they came, then to the east. Frustrated and relieved, I lifted my veil. The woman sighed, probably at not finding a horrible monster. "I am in need of a few items."

"We will be more than able to help you." Her smile brightened, and I knew it was going to be a great afternoon. "Are you looking for more mourning clothes?"

I was done wearing black, hiding and being ostracized. "No, this is a celebration."

Heavy footsteps sounded on the doorstep, and I pulled the veil back over my face. It was Prince Xander. "There's been talk of a sighting of a beast at the edge of town. Send the purchases to Yassa Nueva's house." He didn't look at me as he tossed a sack of coins to Miss Sou. He also didn't say if he would be back to escort me.

She frowned at his sudden departure and gave me a curious look. "Why do you hide from such a handsome man?"

"Because he doesn't wish to look upon me."

"That's not right."

"It is his order."

"Then we will have to give him something else to look at." She wiggled her shoulders and gave me a sly wink. I couldn't help but laugh.

The next hour consisted of Sou fitting me and, with the help of her seamstresses, quickly taking in a few of her ready-made dresses. When we were done, I had two gowns, plus a lovely day dress of cornflower blue and a riding dress.

I was so in love with the cornflower blue, I had to wear it right then. It felt so freeing to be in a lighter dress, not layered down with heavy skirts. She'd even fashioned a soft gauzy veil to a fascinator and clipped it into my hair to cover my face.

"It's lovely," Miss Sou gushed. "The dress accentuates your small hips and draws attention to your elegant long neck. And the veil is short enough that it barely brushes your chin. Your other one hid everything that was womanly about you. You'll have to forgive me, but when you first walked in here, I thought you were an evil spirit come to whisk me away."

"You don't know how close you were to being right."

"Make sure you get back before dark. It's not safe after dark," Miss Sou warned.

Stepping out of the shop in not only my new dress but new shoes, I felt lighter and had a little bounce in my step. Feeling free, I wandered the streets without a chaperone, guard, or lady-in-waiting. Now that I was no longer the walking epitome of death in black, I actually gained a few appraising looks from passersby. Miss Sou was right; my other dress did little to accentuate my assets. But living in the tower, we weren't trying to find a husband—we were studying, training, and learning. Knowledge was power, and power was always our goal.

Strolling through the marketplace, I picked up a few books from a vendor, a sweet roll, and candy. We never had the money to blow on candy, and it wasn't something readily available in our town of scalawags and misfits, so I was thrilled to tuck the small bag of hard candy into my skirt pocket.

A chill was coming on, and I noticed the sun had sunk lower toward the horizon. It was time to head back. Quickly I rushed back to the dress shop to see it had closed for the evening. The horse was still there, though I didn't see any evidence of Prince Xander or Gaven.

Pursing my lips, I debated what I should do. Yes, it was silly of me to have wandered off without my guards, but they weren't really there to protect me, more to make sure I didn't commit harm to the public. They had also abandoned me and left me on my own.

Sighing, I retraced my steps to the town square and noticed most of the market had begun closing as well, and the streets were emptying as the villagers went home to prepare dinner. There was no sign of any of our party.

It was only a mile or so. I could find my way back—I hoped.

My elated feeling gone, I mounted the horse and began the long journey back to the manor. It seemed like a fairly easy jaunt, if I remembered right. There were only two turns, or were there three?

A loud rustle in the forest startled a flock of birds, and they flew right up in my face. Startled, I yanked on the reins too hard, causing the horse to rear. I lost my seat, falling to the ground. My vision spun as the wind was knocked from me, and my magnificent steed raced off into the woods without me.

Grumbling, I pulled myself up and dusted off my new skirt. I would have to travel the rest of the way on foot. My new shoes pinched my toes painfully, but I picked up my pace, trying to hurry. The sun had almost set, and I shivered knowing I would be making the rest of the trek in the dark.

In the daylight, the woods didn't seem as threatening, but as night fell, I couldn't help but worry. The darkness surrounded me, and I felt a chill in my bones. I created a mage light to brighten my path as I walked back in the direction I thought led to the manor.

The thundering sound of hooves came up behind me, and I moved off the road into the tree line to let the rider pass. The horse thundered by, kicking up dust in the road. Recognizing the rider as Prince Xander, I stepped out of the woods just as he passed.

He reined in Nova, who didn't enjoy the sudden change in speed, then turned around and cantered back to me. He did not look pleased, his brows furrowed, his mouth pinched together in anger. "What are you doing?"

"Taking an evening stroll, obviously," I said sarcastically.

"Why are you alone? Why didn't you wait for my return? Don't you understand it's not safe to be out after dark?"

"I'm not scared of the dark, and I had no reason to believe you would return for me."

"You're my charge. I have a right mind to leave you here and let the beast take care of you."

"That's fine with me. I might prefer the beast's company over yours any day!"

He looked away with a deep scowl. Internally, I counted to ten before I tried to speak civilly. "Did you find anything at the edge of town?"

He shook his head. "My men stayed behind to try and pick up its trail, while I came to take you back."

Xander dismounted, took the reins and stood in front of me. I was incredibly conscious of how close we were, and how just the tiniest hint of wind could blow my veil away; then I would be at his mercy for disobeying a direct order. Standing this close, I saw his eyes drop to my waist and felt his slow perusal up my body, lingering on my exposed neck.

He reached out and brushed his hand under my chin, my breath catching in my throat. My heart thudded loudly, pounding in my ears. He was going to look upon me, and I became anxious at the thought. Would he curse my name even more when he learned the truth? My stomach dropped.

"I wonder...," he breathed, lifting my veil.

"No!" I panicked and turned away. A hard thud hit my chest, pain exploding outward from the sight, and I gasped. It hurt to breathe. When I looked down, I saw an arrow protruding from my shoulder.

"Get down!" Xander yelled, pulling me behind his horse and into the woods.

The pain wouldn't stop, and all I wanted to do was pull it out. I clutched the shaft and was about to yank when his firm command told me to cease. Instead, with strong hands, he broke off the shaft, leaving the arrowhead in my shoulder. Then he tossed me onto the horse and jumped on after me, and we rode like a fury into the woods and away to safety.

With each step the horse took, the silver arrowhead burned and dug into my shoulder. White-hot flashes appeared in my vision, and I started to black out.

"Stay with me, Rose," Xander called out urgently. "Don't go to sleep."

Too late.

CHAPTER SEVENTEEN

A throbbing ache came from my shoulder. "Where am I?" I mumbled, trying to blink and focus on my surroundings. I was in an unfamiliar room, resting on a large stuffed mattress with a flowered quilt tucked around my lap. Across the room were a wood-burning stove, kettle, table, and two chairs. Next to the washbasin was a shelf with a few table servings, cups, plates, and a glass jar that held the silverware. Three shuttered windows took up a large portion of the walls, and an old rag rug covered the floor. Dried herbs hung from the rafters, keeping a pleasant aroma in the cottage when I expected it to smell musty. As cute and organized as the cottage was, it was obvious it had been abandoned, for there were no personal effects in the room.

Xander sat on the bed next to me, pressing a cloth to my shoulder.

"You'll be fine. The arrow didn't damage any major muscles," he said.

The pain had subsided to a dull ache. While I was passed out, he had removed the arrowhead, cleaned it with hot water, and bandaged the wound. My new dress was destroyed, the shoulder torn and the sleeve gone, but I was still modestly covered. He had used strips of my skirt as bandages.

I sighed wearily as another beautiful dress was unnecessarily destroyed. Looking up at Xander, I realized how crystal clear he was and I inhaled deeply, reaching for the veil—that was gone.

"It got in the way," Xander answered, his face emotionless and hard to read.

"No, it didn't," I argued. "It was only a few inches long.

"Okay, well, maybe I was tired of you lying to me."

"Lying to you?"

"I knew the day you served me in my tent who you were." Xander lifted my bandaged wrist. "What are the odds that two different women would have the same injury in the same place? Not to mention I recognized my mother's pin on your cloak."

"And yet you demanded I come back to serve you dinner. Are you mad? Weren't you worried I was going to poison you? I seem to recall that conversation as well."

His lip twitched. Was it a hint of a smile? "Are you going to poison me?"

"Depends," I said.

"On what?" He stilled.

"How irritating you continue to be."

"Woman, if you rate whether a person should be poisoned based on how irritating they are, I fear there will be no men left in the kingdom." He barked out a laugh.

I snorted, and his eyes widened in disbelief. Maybe real ladies didn't snort? Well, I wasn't a lady. "Then maybe I would be doing your kingdom a favor. Women tend to not be so rash in their ways or thinking."

"Women can be just as irritating." His eyes narrowed, and he pointed to me. "As for serving dinner, I wanted to see which version of *you* would show up. And how obedient you were. Turns out not very."

"Get used to it," I snapped, then leaned back onto the

pillow and waited for the harsh words to follow. How he was angry that I had fooled him, lied to him about who I was, and also disobeyed his order to not be seen by him, a few times.

My reddened cheeks gave him the affirmation he needed.

He sighed dramatically and leaned closer to me. "Why did you come to the wedding celebration that night when I forbade you to?"

"I hadn't eaten all day and was famished. It seems your staff are not very hospitable."

"Ah, that's right. You did say you were just there for the food."

I nodded.

"You looked beautiful that first night. I didn't know who you were. I was trapped in the despair of my own doing, and I spotted you hiding in the shadows across the room. Your face glowed with delight and innocence. I was drawn to you and snuck closer just so I could watch your reactions, for here was a woman who didn't seem to be burdened with darkness. Light spilled forth from you. I was a moth, and you were the flame. Had I only known then who you were."

It was difficult to swallow at his admission. Waiting for the hammer to drop. Nothing but silence. When the tirade didn't begin, I searched his eyes and he searched mine. I felt naked without the veil, my true identity revealed. We were truly seeing each other for the first time. Did he have no feelings on the matter? Then I realized how angry he was, because he was silent.

"I'm sorry," I said coldly, looking away to stare at the wood floor. "For deceiving you."

It was his turn to sigh. He leaned back so he was parallel to me on the bed, his arms stretched above his head to cradle his neck. "I was a fool to ever give you that order. It's a good thing I hadn't seen you before we were married, because my father was right—I would have let your beauty surely dazzle me." He reached for my chin and brought my eyes up to look into his. He searched my gaze, and I wished I could understand what he was thinking and feeling. Instead I saw a tortured soul.

The heat of his hand on my face made my heart flutter, my breathing ragged, and I realized we were utterly alone. His eyes dropped to my lips, and then his grip tightened and he pushed me roughly away from him.

"You *are* a witch," he said angrily. "You bespell me every time I see you, for I have this asinine desire to kiss you... again."

"That was never my intention. I tried to obey you, but I can't live behind a mask for the rest of my life."

"Why not? I do. It's what protects me from those I hate." His handsome face turned cruel, and I moved away from him, putting my back to the wall. He laughed. "Oh, now you run away?"

"Did you try to kill me?" I asked suspiciously.

"What?" He was obviously shocked by my accusation.

I swallowed and looked away, trying to keep my tears at bay, hiding my insecurity behind bitterness. "I overheard your discussion with your father in the library. He told you to take care of the *inconvenience.* You took me into town with your guards and left me, and then someone tried to murder me in the woods. It sounds to me like an elaborate assassination plan if I ever heard one."

"No, I do not know who shot you." Xander swallowed and glanced away, but I could read it on his face.

"You lie," I accused angrily.

His eyes flashed as he gripped my shoulder. "I'm not."

"Why did you bring me here?" I asked. "Instead of heading back to the house."

"Because it was dark and closer than the manor."

"Which means if you kill me, no one will find my body," I surmised.

"Why are you so obsessed with the idea that I'm going to kill you?"

"Aren't you?" I was pushing his buttons, trying to rile him up. It was easier to deal with him when he was angry. The other side, his softer side, where he gave me warm looks and his hands grazed my skin, drove me crazy. That was the side of Xander I feared the most.

"If I wanted to kill you, you would be dead already," he said simply. "Plus, why bother when we swore a blood oath that as soon as you save my kingdom, you leave. If I kill you, you can't help. And after all, you saved my mother when you could have let her die. You helped save a village from a troll. I'm inclined to believe you will try and save my kingdom." Xander crossed the room and sat on the bed next to me. His leg pressed into my thigh, and his nearness made my cheeks burn.

"I... I think we should leave." The pain from my shoulder was driving me batty, making my thoughts not very coherent. I would probably regret everything I was about to say if we continued talking.

Feeling brave, I slid to the edge of the bed, stood up, and tried to walk to the door, but the floor betrayed me again by moving. I wasn't going to make it, felt myself falling.

"You aren't going anywhere," Xander growled as he caught me and carried me back to the bed. The scent of cedar and leather tickled my nose, his pleasant aroma drawing me to him. Ever so gently, I was laid back on the bed, and the barest of fingers brushed my hair across my forehead. "It's already dark. I've stabled my horse for the night. We will be safe until morning."

Safe. Safe from whom, exactly? There was only one bed, and Xander had already stretched out next to me on top of the quilt, his arms bracing behind his neck and his eyes closed as if to sleep.

"I don't think you should sleep here."

"Hush, woman. There's plenty of room for the both of us."

"That's not what I mean."

Xander turned on his side, bringing us even closer together. His amber eyes slowly roamed over my cheeks and then stopped on my lips. I couldn't breathe. He had sucked all of the air out of the room with his hungry look.

"Oh, I see." He smiled. "You want to finish what we started the night of our wedding? I could most definitely oblige."

"No!" I said adamantly. The pain of our sham of a marriage hurt more than the arrow. "If you touch me, I will curse you." Turning, I buried my head into my pillow and closed my eyes, praying he kept his distance.

Xander's fingers trailed along my cheek, brushing back my hair behind my ear. "Like you did to Yasmin and Gaven?" He chuckled.

I sucked in my breath at being caught so easily.

He leaned in, his breath tickling along my neck, his voice husky. "For you, I would take that chance."

It took every single ounce of my willpower to not respond to his touch, not turn and raise my lips to his and kiss him truly. But I dared not, knowing he would throw me away as soon as I saved his kingdom. The kiss would be fleeting, for it was not love. He'd said it himself, he could not love.

Do not fall into temptation, Rosalie. You are stronger than this.

In an uncomfortable silence, we lay next to each other. I was extremely aware of every breath he took, each sigh and every time he shifted on the bed. Neither of us was going to sleep soon, and I almost wished he would kiss me again. Not out of drunken lust or because he was bespelled by my beauty but because he *wanted* to kiss me—for me.

Anything that would happen now wouldn't be real, because he didn't love me. But did I love him? I had to ask myself the question, and it only created more uncertainty. I had feelings for him when I wore the guise of a servant, but when I was his wife, he was absolutely despicable toward me, thus making me despise him. Now the charade was gone, and there was only me—the real me. The daughter of Eville. Only time would tell if the prince could love my inner darkness.

My legs were restless, and I was about to turn over and give in, throw my arms around Xander and kiss him, truly kiss him, and see if he ran away or returned the gesture. I wanted to feel his lips on mine and know what love's first kiss was all about.

Just when I had gathered my courage to face my husband, I felt the bed dip as he moved.

My body froze, my breath caught in my lungs, and my eyelids squeezed shut as I feigned sleep. But Xander didn't move closer. Instead, he got out of bed. Immediately a chill came over me as I felt his absence. His footsteps moved away, and I heard the door of the cabin open and close.

Prince Xander had left, taking his chances out in the cold of night rather than with the cold woman in his bed.

I sighed, momentarily relieved and at the same time depressed that he ran away from me.

CHAPTER EIGHTEEN

I was running through the woods, the moonlight easily lighting my way as I searched for my prey that kept trying to elude me. His pitiful cries led me right to him. It was a young man, not more than twenty, his hair a russet brown that was cropped short, his boots splattered with mud. His scent wafted in front of me and I changed course, wondering briefly if his skin would taste as sweet in my mouth, if his blood would be infused with fear. I hoped it would.

In a few long strides, he was within my grasp. The crossbow fell empty into the mud, having spent his arrows wastefully on my shadow. I raised my clawed hand to strike and quickly ended his whimpers.

I was going to be sick.

Rolling over and tumbling from the bed, I rushed for the basin and emptied my stomach. Shaking, tears falling down my face, I crumpled to the ground and began to cry hysterically. The dreams had returned in full force. I even preferred my blackouts to these vivid nightmares.

Pressing my back to the wall, my knees pulled up to my

chest, I stared into the dark room and tried to calm myself. His scent—the victim's scent.... I could still smell it in my nostrils, and my mouth was filled with a bitter iron taste. His blood.

Crawling back to my knees, I was sick a second time before crumpling to the floor and crying, praying for the vivid dreams to go away. I couldn't bring myself to look down at my feet; I didn't want to see the mud that would be splattered across my legs. I knew it was there. It was always there.

Eventually I did fall asleep, because I awoke to Xander touching my arm.

"Rosalie," he whispered, but I didn't answer. "It's time to go. We're safe now." He took off his cloak and wrapped it around my shoulders, properly covering my ruined dress. His kindness was melting my cold heart. Finally I looked up at him with my red and exhausted eyes.

"Are you okay?" he asked.

"No, I'm not," I answered truthfully, but didn't elaborate even when he pressed. Instead, I tried to turn the blame onto him. "You left me," I said stiffly, pulling the cloak closer around my neck, covering myself and standing up to face him. My eyes were drawn to his lips before glancing up into his own sleep-deprived eyes.

His breath caught and he looked away, avoiding eye contact. "I had to leave. You wouldn't be safe."

"You said we were safe here," I reminded him.

"Yes, from the outside, but you weren't safe from me." He looked down at the ground. "I had to leave for fear I would do something I would later regret."

His words were a sharpened dagger into my already fragile heart. *Regret?* He was already regretting being close to me. My throat constricted, and swallowing became difficult.

"I see." Stepping around him, I headed for the door. Pulling it open, I was blinded by sunlight pouring through the treetops.

The tiny cottage was nestled among a grove of trees. Two thrushes sang proudly, and I paused to listen to the melody of the birds, the whisper of the wind, and the call of the rushing creek a stone's throw away.

It was beautiful. This cottage had at one time been someone's home, and I was hesitant to leave.

Xander brought Nova around. "You ready?"

Nodding, I reached up for the saddle horn, put my foot in the stirrup and tried to mount on my own, but I slipped. My shoulder screamed in agony, and white flashes danced across my vision as I came crashing down into Xander's arm.

He caught me, pressing me close to his chest, and I heard the worry in his voice when I couldn't immediately open my eyes to his call.

"Rosalie," he called. My eyes fluttered open, and I realized how tight he was holding me.

"I'm fine. Just give me a minute," I said, pulling away from him, which only seemed to anger him.

"You fainted."

"I slipped. It won't happen again."

"No, it won't," he growled. Then his hands grasped my waist and I was up, feet in the air as his strong hands lifted me onto the saddle. Seconds later, he was up behind me, lifting me a second time so I was now sitting sideways across his lap.

Distressed, I tried to slide off, but he ordered, "Don't. Move."

I didn't. I couldn't, because Nova had started moving, and I feared I would fall and be trampled under her hooves. Xander shifted me again and wrapped his hands around me, pressing me close. My head lay in the crook of his arm, his vest against my cheek.

This close, I couldn't help but study the threads of his long sleeve. Along the cuff was a dark red stain.

He didn't speak, and now that I was close to him, I didn't feel scared. I was safe. After a terrifying night, I found myself at peace enough to fall into a light sleep. Just as I was nodding off, I swore I felt the lightest feathery kiss across my brow.

"We're back," Xander whispered when we were within sight of the manor.

Opening my eyes, I noticed the hard clench of his jaw, the tenseness he carried in his muscles. His left hand was wrapped around my waist to keep me from slipping, and even his arm felt like iron. Why would coming back make him so apprehensive?

Our arrival back at the manor was completely different compared to yesterday's. Guards lined the entrance, crossbows resting against their hips. Their faces were grim and mirrored the worried look of Yassa himself, who stood next to a wagon. We rode up, and I could see there was a body lying in the back, wrapped in muslin.

My mouth went dry. I could tell from the tall stature that it was a man. My heart pounded fast, and I couldn't help but wonder if he had russet brown hair like my dream.

"Oh, you're safe, Your Highness," Yassa cried out, stepping down from the front steps and wringing his hands. "We thought the beast had gotten you too." He pointed at the wrapped corpse.

"I am fine," Prince Xander said firmly as he dismounted.

An urgency filled me, and I struggled to get off the horse. Xander was loath in letting me go, but finally he sighed and carefully held on to me until my feet were firmly planted on the ground. Veil forgotten, my heart was in my throat as I moved toward the body. My hairpins had fallen out, and my eyes were red-rimmed and dry from lack of sleep; I assumed I would look closer to a ghost than a princess. Stopping inches from the wagon bed, I glanced over and saw a tanned hand sticking out from the canvas, fingers covered in dirt and mud.

My approach had caused the conversation to halt, as Yassa and Prince Xander watched my movements with renewed interest. Their opinion didn't matter—only he did. I reached for the edge of the canvas and lifted, my hand trembling as I saw his dark brown hair and what was left of his face.

I knew what I was about to do was taboo and against everything the kingdom of Baist stood for. Only those with my gift, or curse, could call this power.

I slipped my hand down his cold arm and touched his fingers. His fear consumed me, and I gasped in pain. I could almost see his attacker as his death vision touched me. The last few seconds of his life flashed before me. His terror was my own: black fur, teeth, blood, and then death.

I dropped the cloth and clutched my frightened heart, trying to calm my shaking hands and regain my breath. Tears streamed down my face as I struggled under the weight of his death all over again.

"It was the beast," I confirmed, turning to look at Xander accusingly. He had come here to stop the killings and had failed. I had to grasp the wagon to keep myself from sliding to the ground.

"Witch!" Yassa called out. "She touched the dead. You saw her. She is unclean and must leave our pure lands." He pointed at me, the jowls under his chin shaking in rage.

"Watch your words," Prince Xander warned. "Know who you are speaking to."

"Apologies, my prince," Yassa said, only apologizing to Xander and not me.

"Don't fear, Yassa. We will get a party together and search for the beast. We won't stop until it's found."

"Thank you." Yassa bobbed his head and turned, signaling for the coroner to take the wagon to town.

Xander ignored me as he addressed Gaven. "When? Where?"

"Early this morning. He was tracking the beast when he was killed. Found a half mile from the manor."

"Footprints?"

"Only the young man's," Gaven answered.

Xander sighed and turned. Realizing I was within earshot, he cleared his throat and motioned for me to go inside the house. I disliked being dismissed with a nod and clenched my jaw in anger before meeting Gaven's scrutiny.

He looked confused, glancing to the horse we had both rode in on, to the prince and back to me. He was about to say something, call out to me perhaps, but Prince Xander spoke up. "What?"

Gaven croaked out in disbelief as he regained his footing and looked up at me in awe. "It's you," he whispered. "You're her." I knew what was coming next. As if I had dreamed this nightmare over and over. "You're the witch."

"Not here, Gaven," Xander corrected.

"But that's—"

"I know who it is. It's my wife," Xander snapped before turning and rushing toward me. He gripped my right elbow painfully as he dragged me up the steps after him into the main house.

I hissed between my teeth as he torqued my shoulder. I could feel fresh blood begin to pool from the wound he had recently bandaged.

"Stop!" I demanded once we crossed the threshold. When he didn't let up, I felt dizzy as the wound stretched.

He was breathing heavily, his eyes wild.

"Xander," I cried. "Please!"

My use of his first name snapped him out of whatever spell he was under. He saw the fresh red blood leaking through the bandage and dropped my arm in horror, eyes wide and mouth agape as he backed away from me.

"I didn't mean to hurt you. I forgot you're injured," he gasped out. "I knew if I didn't get you out of there, Gaven's careless words might cause me to hurt him, but instead you bore the brunt of my anger."

Breathing slowly, I waited for the room to stop spinning before I spoke. "Don't touch me!"

Xander stood in front of me, his face pale. He shook his head roughly, as if he couldn't believe he had so carelessly grabbed my injured arm. He was about to say something when I heard a clearing of the throat come from the stairs above.

Yasmin sauntered down the steps, her head held high, hair curled and impeccable.

"My prince," she purred, her gaze locking on Xander, her hips dipping with each step, drawing his gaze. The woman knew how to appeal to a man's senses, and she was using all of her power and charm. When she reached the bottom step, she curtsied, and I couldn't help but notice how low cut her dress was. My lips pinched in distaste. The rash on her face was completely hidden beneath layers of powder, and she looked barely fazed by the curse that would wear off in the next few hours.

But the show hadn't even started yet. Her eyelashes fluttered and her bottom lip quivered. "D-Did you hear? The beast is here." She reached to clutch his jacket, pulling herself into his arms right in front of me. "You'll protect me, Prince Xander? You'll not let the beast get me?"

The force with which she threw herself into his arms made Xander stumble back, and he had to grasp her to keep from falling. She buried her head into his chest, and I was sickened by the display. I wasn't even sure if she knew who I was, or cared.

A growl of discontent started in the pit of my stomach.

"My lady!" Pru called, rushing down the steps. "I've been so worried." She halted abruptly when she saw my ruined dress. "What happened?"

"Your mistress needs tending to," Xander ordered, his arms still wrapped around Yasmin, who looked to be completely at home. "See to her needs... or else."

I was confused by his sudden change of heart in regards to my welfare. Was it because he felt guilty for how he treated me? It must have been. It wasn't because he cared.

Keeping my back stiff, I let Pru lead me to my room and didn't dare look back. But I still heard Yasmin's contented sigh, and my stomach rolled in displeasure.

CHAPTER NINETEEN

P ru continued to fuss over me, her words alighting on the air like a butterfly filling the void. "I can't believe someone shot you with an arrow. Who would do something like that?"

But her words and worry fell on deaf ears. My wound and heart were numb as I replayed the scene over and over again in my head. My cruel words to Xander. Yasmin's successful attempts at wooing him. And in the middle of it, my own confusion about what I was feeling toward him. I could feel the jealousy seeping into my heart and poisoning my soul.

A gentle touch of Pru's hand as she brought out a needle and thread and moved to stitch the wound interrupted my thoughts. Shaking my head, I glanced down to inspect that it was thoroughly cleansed before pointing a finger to my shoulder and whispering, "*Numera*."

Numbing the area around the wound was dangerous, because if my finger had slipped, I could have numbed my heart. Though that may have been preferable.

"Okay, I'm ready." I gripped the armrests of the chair as she stitched. My charm worked; I didn't feel the slide of the needle through my skin or the slight tug as she stitched.

Gobbersnot kicked open the trunk, and I saw the tip of

his nose first as it wiggled and smelled blood. Then he crawled out wearing a petticoat that wasn't mine, he lips smeared with red. At first I was worried it was blood until I saw the waxy texture. It was red lipstick—also not mine. I smiled as I imagined Yasmin using the same lipstick as my goblin.

Gobbersnot pawed at my knee and looked up at me with big pouty eyes. I knew that without a doubt that, if I didn't watch him, he would be licking my wound in my sleep. I handed my bandage to him, and he gave me a kiss on my elbow, leaving a smear of lipstick, before muttering in goblin and crawling back into my trunk.

A sound captured my attention, and my eyes went to the front yard. Gaven was trying to ease his own rash by rubbing his back on the corner support beam of the stable while organizing and directing the hunting parties out toward the woods. I prayed he would find the beast and the merciless killings would end.

Xander led Nova into the yard while laughing at Gaven's itchy predicament.

Yasmin ran out of the house and slowed, waving to Xander before he rose to climb on Nova's saddle.

Prince Xander rode forward, bringing his horse up beside Gaven's, and leaned forward. She reached up, placing a scarf around his neck. A token of affection? My breathing had picked up, and my fingers scraped along the arm.

I watched the prince's face for a reaction, but he was emotionless, already pulling away and turning toward the woods, his mind most likely focused on the coming hunt.

They rode off, heading deep into the forest, and I waited as the woods swallowed them whole. Glancing down, I saw the dark wood slivers under my nails, the deep gouges they had left in the armrests. Spreading my fingers, I carefully tried to cover up what my anger had done. How was I so strong? Was my jealousy really that powerful?

Pru stepped back. "I'm done."

I nodded, acknowledging her. There was nothing left to say. I was an empty shell.

"That will be all," I said, feeling the ice queen's return.

"Would you like me to bring you food?"

I shook my head. "I would like to be left alone."

Pru cleaned up her work, picking up the rags and bowl, and left the room, closing the door behind her. I went to the side table and picked up a small gilded hand mirror, then reached for the needle. With a slight prick on my fingertip, the deep red drop welled, and I stared at my lifeblood. We all were taught how to call each other using reflections and blood. I whispered an enchantment and let the drop fall onto the glass. Instead of spattering across the surface, it passed through like a water droplet, causing the mirror's reflection to wave and spiral outward.

"Sister," I said, hoping one of them would be near a mirror and hear my call.

Nothing.

I spoke a little louder. "Sister!"

The reflection moved as someone picked up a mirror and bright green eyes met mine.

"Rosalie!" Meri exclaimed excitedly, her voice ringing out, my name on her lips as lyrical as a song. "It's you!"

Oh, how I missed Meri's musical lilt, her childlike enthusiasm, and her mischievous banter.

"Mother came home but hasn't told us anything about your husband," she pouted. "No matter how much we begged. Just last night we were debating whether to summon you through the mirror but were afraid it would make your husband's heart stop in fright." A nervous giggle followed. "Is he cute? Has he kissed you yet?"

Of course, she would be more worried with looks than anything else. She was as passionate and fiery as her hair, which was as red as the setting sun. But Meri's excitement meant she could barely hold her mirror straight, and I kept getting an up-close view of her pert nose and red lips.

"Meri, Mother has need of you in her workshop," another sister called out.

"But it's Rosalie," Meri told her, then turned the mirror toward her and passed it off.

"Aura," I said, trying to get her attention as her chin came into view.

The shaking stopped as my sister Aura brought the mirror up and looked at me. "Rosalie, how are you doing?" Her smile fell from her lips and her brows furrowed as she read my melancholy expression through the mirror. Aura was adept at reading emotions when she wanted to, and sometimes minds if the person wasn't good at closing off their thoughts. "Oh." Her voice dropped. "That bad, huh?"

I swallowed. "It's nothing more than as it should be. No more or no less. I'm married."

"But—"

"There's nothing more to be said on the matter. I'm here. Married to a—"

"Prince!" Aura interrupted and grinned playfully, as if this were a game she easily won.

Darn it! She easily went through my wall. I retreated further into a mental thorn bush to keep her from picking at my thoughts. I wished anyone else other than Aura had picked up the mirror.

"If you're going to keep reading my thoughts and expressions, then why should I even bother calling you?"

"Sorry, Rosalie. I couldn't help it. My enthusiasm was just too powerful for me to hold back."

"You must learn restraint," I admonished, sounding more like my adopted mother. "One day you'll read the wrong person and learn more than you ever want to know."

She smiled wickedly at me, and I knew she had been privy to many dark secrets already. Except for our mother. Aura had been unable to crack our mother's thoughts or feelings. Anytime she tried, Aura was stricken with a horrible headache. Whenever she became extremely tiresome on us, Maeve would dare her to try and read Mother Eville. Aura was never one to back down from a challenge, and would then spend the next few hours in bed with a pillow over her head, whining about the pain.

"Okay, then stop with the ice queen act and spill," Aura demanded. A shadow passed over her shoulder and the mirror tilted, Eden's golden blonde head popping into view.

"Who is it?" she asked.

"Nobody." Aura tucked the mirror under her chin, and my view was blocked by the print linen pattern of her green dress.

"It's me," I called out loudly, hoping my second-oldest sister would hear me.

"Rosalie?" Eden pulled the mirror from Aura's hand, and I heard a screech of disappointment.

"Give it back," Aura pouted.

"Hush!" Eden demanded, then held the mirror so both of them could speak with me. "Tell us, where are you?"

I blinked, trying to hold back my tears. Aura's face melted as she read my emotions. "I'm in the kingdom of Baist."

"What?" Eden said. "That backward, magic-banned kingdom? Do you even have running water? Water taxis, moving picture boxes? What are you doing there? Where's your new husband?"

"I'm married... to the crown prince."

The mirror fell out of Eden's hands and landed facedown on Aura's quilt coverlet. It was dizzying to watch through the mirror as the room spun.

Aura was the one to come away with the mirror. "It's okay if he doesn't love you, Rosalie, because we do."

"What do you mean, he doesn't love her?" Eden asked.

"Oh, well, she married their prince, but he doesn't love her. He loves someone else, and Rosalie is really depressed about it. And then there's this monster that's murdering people, and someone tried to kill her."

"Rosalie!" Eden gasped. "Is it true?"

My anger smoldered and I wished I could smite my mindreading sister through the mirror. I didn't mean to relay so much, but the magic came from my blood, so when Aura held the mirror, she had a closer connection to my mind, which allowed her to pry deeper than if we were in the same room.

My mouth pressed tightly together, I glared at Aura, who quit talking when she saw my expression. She handed the mirror back to Eden and quickly escaped, her shadow moving out the door and down the steps to, I would assume, spread the news to the others.

It was Eden I needed. She was the one who understood me the most. When my nightmares were too much, she was the one who crawled into my bed and held me until they subsided. She would take an acorn or a thorn and transform it into a wolf, then place it by my bedside, telling me it was my protector and would chase away the dreams. Though it was never the wolf who kept me safe but my family. Now my fears and uncertainties about myself and my bloodline came flooding back to haunt me.

"Who tried to kill you?" she asked.

"I don't know."

Eden's face turned red with anger. "How dare they touch a hair on your head? Do they not know how powerful we are? That we are the daughters of Eville? To harm one of us is to ensure the wrath of us all."

"I'm not sure if it was me they were aiming at," I said, then explained the adder that appeared in the maze to harm Ameline, how Prince Xander's mother had mysteriously been poisoned, and how I was accosted by two kidnappers and woke up with no memories of how I got back in my room, covered in blood.

"Do you think...?" I hesitated. "Maybe my dreams, my blackouts... I'm...?"

"No, never, Rosalie," Eden replied. "You would never harm someone unless they were trying to harm you or your family." Her blue eyes sparkled with unshed tears. "You are not a killer. But I do have one thing to say, dear sister. Your magic is strong, and you've got a good head on your shoulders. Use both to your advantage."

Hearing it from Eden calmed my fears. It was good to speak to her and hear how my other sisters were doing in my absence. Mother hadn't told them anything about my departure, and it made me unhappy that she could drop me off with little fanfare and then not speak of me. Raised and then discarded to fit her means.

We talked until my body grew weary. I fell asleep on the bed holding the mirror, letting Eden's voice speak reassuringly to me as I dreamed.

CHAPTER TWENTY

A whinny of a horse awoke me from my slumber, the mirror slipping from my fingers to drop on the floor. Picking it up, I felt its cool surface and knew my sister must have closed the spell. Going to the window, I saw the party was back. I watched as Gaven took Xander's horse and led her to the stable, while Xander stretched and looked about the yard thoughtfully. Their hunt hadn't been unsuccessful. He glanced up to my window, and I stepped back into the shadows. Had he seen me? Did he even know which room was mine?

I was drawn to him: his strong muscular shoulders, his brooding eyes, and his angular chin. He was a fine specimen of a man. A smile befell my lips.

He is mine, and mine alone.

The dark thought came suddenly, and I turned and clutched my chest. *What was that? Where did that thought come from?* Startled by my sudden obsessiveness over him, I quenched those feelings and calmed my heart. He wasn't mine. He'd declared it many times.

My door opened, and one of Prince Xander's attendants was standing there next to a grinning Pru.

"Yes?" I asked at Pru's beaming face. Her lips were pinched together as if she were holding onto a secret.

"Prince Xander has requested you attend him for dinner," the man said.

"If he thinks I'm going to serve him, he has another thing coming."

"Miss." Pru had gone to the wardrobe and pulled out one of my new dresses. "Not serve him dinner. He wishes you to be at his side."

"Why now?" I asked suspiciously.

"Why not? You are his wife," she answered.

"No," I said shrewdly to his attendant. "You can tell him I refuse. I will not be hidden or paraded about for his every whim."

"My lady, I won't tell him that. I can't." The attendant's face paled.

"Fine!" I snapped and moved toward my hand mirror. Lifting it, I repeated my demands to the reflection and then handed it to the man. "Give this to His Highness and you won't have to say a thing."

He held on to the mirror with trembling hands and disappeared out the door.

"An enchanted mirror," Pru exclaimed in awe.

"Not exactly. It still holds a bit of my blood, so it will work to relay messages for a short amount of time."

"That's amazing," she exclaimed, looking at me with doe eyes. How far she had come, from fearing me to idolizing me. "What do you think will be the prince's response?

"Oh, he won't like it, for sure, but I've played his game long enough. Now it's time for the rules to change. And he doesn't want to face me when I'm angry."

We didn't have to wait long before Xander was pounding on my door.

I didn't make Pru open the door but did so myself, having

used the time to fix my hair and change into a new deep burgundy, velvet, long-sleeved dress.

I gasped dramatically. "Why, Prince Xander, what brings you to my door?"

Xander held up my hand mirror and shook it. "What witchcraft is this?"

He couldn't see my smirk. "It's not witchcraft. It is actually a quite useful form of communication. Other kingdoms have been using mirrors to speak and send messages for years. Baist is, how can I say, a little behind the times. How could you have not known?"

He stared at the mirror as if it were a snake that would bite him. "Really? Even Sion?"

"Most of the kingdoms. Even my small town of Nihill has one enchanted mirror.

Xander's face was pale as he chewed on his lip in worry, and I slowly began to understand his fears. I hadn't seen much of the country of Baist, but I had noticed a lack of charm stalls and hedge witches. A magic mirror like this wouldn't cause such a ruckus unless he had never seen one before.

He stared at the mirror and swallowed thickly. I held out my hand for it to be returned to me, but instead he clasped his hands behind his back, the mirror out of sight.

"Back to the matter at hand. I had asked you to attend dinner with me."

"And I gave you my answer."

"I am not ordering you," he said softly. "I am asking you."

"Why?" My own voice was barely above a whisper as I tried to hold back my hope.

"Because I'm willing to concede that maybe you were right. That maybe I judged you too quickly. I'm here offering an olive branch."

"You sound like we're at war with each other."

"I thought we were. There was so much stigma, hatred, and fear coming from my parents, from the stories, that I had believed I was being betrothed to my enemy, but I'm willing to start anew. Just have a meal with me."

I accepted because he was being polite. "All right. Give me a few moments."

He nodded and left.

Once the door was closed, Pru rushed to a jewelry box and threw it open, crying out in dismay when I didn't have an array of precious jewels or combs. "How can this be? You are to have dinner with the prince and will be compared to Yasmin. She's already been preparing for an hour for dinner. We have but a few minutes, and you have no jewelry."

"I don't need jewelry," I said firmly. Moving to the mirror, I began to take out all of my pins and combs, letting my dark hair fall to the middle of my back, and touched up my lips with a dark rouge.

Yasmin would overdo her wardrobe with ruffles, necklaces, rings, pearls, and scents. I knew the only way to outdo her was to not even try. Let my beauty be the only decoration I needed.

When I was done, I turned to Pru and she inhaled. "Yes, I see what you're doing."

When dinner was announced, I made my way down the stairs and to the dining room. The long table was set for twenty, and I could see Yasmin and her maidens dressed in their finest huddled together in a large group.

Hiding in a pack didn't make you stand out; instead, you became lost in the masses. A true gem stood alone. Once I reached the bottom step, I faltered, unsure where to go or where to sit at the table.

At a soft touch on my elbow, I turned in surprise to see Gaven. His hair was wet and styled, his clothes fresh.

"So, you were already married." His expression filled with

distrust. "I now understand why you rejected me in the garden. But be fair warned, witch. The kingdom of Baist does not take kindly to your kind. Magic is and always will be unwelcome here, and the prince and this kingdom are under my protection," he threatened with a smile.

I actually liked this side of him better.

"Good. And just so you know, if you fail him, I will kill you, and no one will ever find the body." I laughed and the tension in the air left. We were no longer friends because of our different views but were now equals with similar goals.

My laughter drew attention from Yasmin, whose brows were furrowed so deep in confusion that she gave herself a unibrow. She whispered to one of her girls, who looked at me and shrugged.

I sighed. It didn't seem like Yasmin knew what to do with me. I wasn't dressed as royalty, so she had probably assumed I was a lady-in-waiting earlier. But now that I was here, she wasn't sure how to place me in person, because she didn't know who I was.

I knew when Xander stepped into the room, because Yasmin's eyes flicked over my shoulder and her face pulled back into a toothy smile. Her flower girls—for that was what I deemed to call them, each one dressed in a complimentary pastel color—curtseyed as well. My deep red dress was a stark contrast to their almost frail and sickly shades.

Xander nodded in greeting. Then Yassa stepped forth and clapped his hands, and everyone moved to the table to sit. Xander moved to the seat at the head of the table, and I was most appalled when Yasmin stepped forward and moved to his left. That may have been where she sat when he visited her on previous occasions, or even at other meals, but it left me with a sour feeling in the pit of my stomach, and I froze.

Xander glanced over to me and waited. It didn't seem like

he was going to address the issue of where I should sit. He had already dictated that our marriage was not like others—I couldn't ride in the same carriage as him but behind him, didn't sleep in the same bedroom but had my own suite. How was I supposed to assume that seating arrangements for dinner would be any different?

He didn't sit, just stood at the head of the table and waited, which caused the whole room to awkwardly stand as well, since no one sat until the highest-ranking monarch sat.

Xander sighed and seemed a bit perturbed at my inability to decide or move. He glanced quickly at the chair to his left and gave me a slight nod, encouraging me to take it from Yasmin. He was making a statement publicly and using me to do it.

I clicked my tongue in my mouth in irritation as I fought back my temper that was about to run forth. His eyebrow rose in challenge, and I knew he was testing me.

This time it was I who cleared my throat and stood next to Yasmin.

"Excuse me," I said coldly.

"Yes?" She spun around. Her hair smelled of lavender.

"You're at my seat."

"No, I'm no—" Her words died on her lips when she looked me up and down. "Who are you?"

"I'm his wife," I said snidely.

"But I thought you wore a veil and never came out of your rooms... ever. I thought—"

"Wrong," I finished. Using my magic, I pulled the chair back, causing her to stumble. Stepping in front, I waited and watched Xander's face as he pinched his lips together. Finally, he sat, and I sighed as I took my seat next to him.

When he picked up his fork to eat, I couldn't help but see the silver utensil shaking in his hands. He was laughing.

"Glad you find this so amusing," I said, a bit perturbed.

Yasmin moved the guests around until she was next to her father, and when she plopped herself down on the chair, she gave me a heated glance. In fact, most of the room couldn't pull their eyes away from me. Some of Yasmin's flowers didn't even try to hide their disdain or voices, and their comments reached my ears.

Slowly, I turned to direct my gaze at each of the girls, staring at them as I flicked a finger under the table, directing a breeze their way. My magic added just the right touch of theatrics. A sudden chill accompanied my direct gaze, and I smiled as one by one, the heads turned away and they shivered.

This was a trick I had learned early on from Mother. "Most of the population is blind to our magic. They can't see what we do, but you can make them instinctively fear you," she would say. She taught us how to command the breeze and that it could be swayed and moved to send a chill across your enemies, a wave of fear accompanying it. This was a tool I had used many times to keep unwanted attention from men away, one I had watched my mother use when we burst into the palace, and one I recycled now.

I briefly glanced back to Xander. His fork had stopped midair, a piece of pork dangling off it. "What did you just do?" he whispered so only I could hear. He wasn't in the direct line of my spell, but he somehow felt the effects. Interesting. Maybe he wasn't as blind to magic as I had thought.

"I put them in their place." Slicing the meat, I took a bite and chewed. Focusing on my own plate and on the prince, it was easy to ignore the table of onlookers.

"Maybe I should learn this trick," he said.

"I don't think you have the strength."

"Careful, you're insulting the prince, and therefore the king and the crown. You should fear for your life because of that insult," he teased.

"Do I look like I scare easily?" I challenged. "If you haven't learned yet, it is you who should fear me." I took another bite and smiled.

His eyes darkened. "Very little frightens me."

"Could have fooled me with the way you treated me when I arrived." I reached for my glass and took a sip, savoring the cider as it rolled across my tongue.

"Let's see if we can eat a meal together without killing each other." Xander crooked an eyebrow at me.

The smile, though small, was there. I couldn't hold it in. "Don't count on it."

"Then I will be sure to keep my weapon close." He rested his hand on the ornamental dagger at his waist. "Don't be distracted by its pretty outside. It's more than a decoration."

"Same goes for me," I teased, and he smiled warmly back.

The meal, though magnificent, wasn't to the same standards as the palace. Dinner was strained, and I found myself quietly observing Yassa and Yasmin, who kept sending each other nervous glances at my sudden arrival at the dinner table.

I was here to help catch the beast. Once I had done that, I could go and live my own life away from my sisters. Away from the town of Nihill and away from the prince.

Suddenly, the thought of having control of my own life and destiny seemed exhilarating. I could go anywhere, do anything. Maybe create a new life and start over where no one had heard of the daughters of Eville. I could become a hedge witch, maybe work in a small town healing people and brewing potions.

The daydream became real and started to overtake my thoughts until Earlsgaarde cleared his throat. Touching his napkin to his mouth, he stood to address the table.

"Thank you so much for your hospitality, and for hosting us on the behalf of the king of Florin. I know that through this hunt and finding this beast, justice will be served!" He raised his glass in a toast, and everyone did the same. I caught the way he glanced not to Xander but to his glass and watched the tic of his mustache.

Feeling a moment of panic, I reached for Xander's glass, and our hands collided as he lifted it to drink. I grabbed his glass and switched it with mine, knowing I had already drunk out of it. He gave me a curious look, but I silently pleaded with him to trust me. He took my cup, and we raised them in salute and drank.

I brought the glass to my lips and sniffed, careful to not take a sip or let the liquid touch my lips. Then I saw it, the slight crystalized powder on the inside of the rim. Someone had not poisoned the wine, but the cup.

My eyes flashed angrily toward Earlsgaarde, but he wasn't looking at me, intent on his discussion with Gaven. Their discussion must have ended badly, because Gaven got up and left the table, heading out of the room.

"What's wrong?" Xander whispered to me.

My hands were shaking in anger as I put the glass back on the table.

"Someone poisoned your cup." I placed my hands back in my lap and tried to settle my face. It wouldn't do to let the would-be poisoner know his plan wouldn't work. Or maybe it was a she? Poison was a woman's trade, after all.

Yasmin's mouth was ugly as she continued to frown in my direction. As much as I wanted to hate her, I believed she would have poisoned me over Xander.

His knuckles were white as he gripped his fork and slowly put it down on the table. He clearly wasn't going to chance eating either. "Are you sure?"

"Yes, positive."

He wiped his mouth with the napkin and whispered, "Thank you for saving my life."

He scanned the table, most likely trying to assess who had it out for him.

"Earlsgaarde," Prince Xander called out. "Please tell us why catching the beast is so important after all this time? Why now?"

Earlsgaarde stood to address the group. "Because the beast lives in your lands. It needs to be dealt with, as you can see by the unfortunate murder last night. And if you won't hunt it down, then we have no choice but to bring our troops over and do it ourselves."

"You speak of war!" Xander stood up, pounding his fist on the table.

"I speak of justice. What happened to our dear queen when she came into your kingdom? No one seems to know. Your father has been very vague on the matter of her disappearance. After this many years, we can only assume they're dead. But how and by whose hand? Maybe this strange beast murdered them? Maybe it was a plot to harm our kingdom? But nonetheless, if you can't solve a royal disappearance or find this strange beast, how could you possibly find yourself fit to rule?"

"We don't know what happened to the queen of Florin and her child, and I'm very sorry for our failure." Because I was so close to Xander, I heard the hitch in his voice and caught the lie. Hopefully, I was the only one. "But I can tell you we will not fail a second time. We will find answers. We will find this beast." Xander stood up, taking his knife and plunging it into the table. "I won't stop until it is dead."

Scattered handclapping came from around the dining table until it built into a roar of applause. Earlsgaarde slowly sat back down. His face unreadable behind his stony mask.

Xander was riled up and continued his rant. "And I want to know where it goes in the daylight. How is it continually hiding from us, only to strike our men when we least expect it? Where's its den?"

"You won't find a den," I cut in, "because you're hunting a shapeshifter."

The room stilled, my own heart thudding loudly in my chest at the words that even I was terrified to announce. Because of my dreams. I was connected to its thoughts, and even though they were gruesome, they weren't animalistic. There was a human element to the thoughts, and the fact that I couldn't get over the feeling that we were being baited.

Yassa hissed through his teeth at the word. Yasmin gave a cry and fainted. Only Xander turned to give me a curious look.

"They are just tales," Yassa said, pounding his fist into the table. "There are no such things as shapeshifters."

I fingered the sleeve of my dress and looked directly at Yassa, the old man squirming under my gaze.

"Oh no, they are very real, and that is probably why the creature has eluded you for so long. The beast is probably one of us, here in this room. Some are shifters by birth, whereas others become a were-animal after being bitten by another and thus shift because of a blood curse." At that, Xander's body stilled. I could feel the heat of his gaze boring into the back of my neck.

"How do you kill a shapeshifter?" Yassa asked.

My hands were wringing my napkin in my lap, and I could feel all eyes on me.

"Silver will stop the transformation," I whispered, meeting Xander's gaze. His eyes were begging me, pleading with me to stop, but I couldn't. "And then he reverts back to his normal form, and you can kill him. But you don't have to kill him. There are other ways to subdue—"

No one listened. The room had turned to chaos as Yassa, Earlsgaarde, and his men stood up and began to speak out at once.

"Quick, gather the silver candlesticks."

"Heat the fire."

"We'll find the beast tonight!"

Yasmin, who had woken up with the help of her ladies, had once again fallen into a faint when she learned of the new hunt they had planned. Dinner was ruined, and I knew I could no longer eat. The one who had remained silent through all of this was none other than Xander.

His face was cold, his eyes dark as he stood up and glared at me.

"Look what you've done!" he snapped. In a fit of anger, he shoved his plate away from him, and it clattered along the floor. "More blood will be spilled because of your careless words!"

"I'm sorry," I said, and I truly was. "But whoever is murdering these innocent people must be brought to justice."

"I came here to do just that. But you don't understand what it is we're hunting. You don't know what happened on the road eighteen years ago. You weren't there."

"And you were?"

"Yes!" he snapped. "You are right. It was a shapeshifter. A werewolf to be exact."

I gasped. "I'm sorry. I didn't know. I thought no one knew what happened that night."

He glanced down in shame. His voice lowered to a whisper, "There are only a handful of people who know the truth."

"Then why don't you tell Earlsgaarde. Explain to them about the werewolf and stop this."

"I can't. Because no one would understand. The lie is far better than the truth. It is a secret that will go with me to the grave."

"I'm sorry. I was only trying to help."

"You've done enough."

"No, really—"

"That is an order! Leave here! I should never have brought you down. It was folly on my part," he yelled. Gripping my wrist, he pulled me away from the table and spun me out into the hall toward the stairs. The momentum wasn't much, but I was unprepared for the servant who crossed my path. I collided with them full-on and fell onto the stone steps, bruising my rib cage.

I gasped at the pain, wincing as I pulled myself up from the stairs. Xander was gone.

CHAPTER TWENTY-ONE

My skin burned and stretched, and my bones ached as I shifted. My eyes tuned to the darkness as I caught the scent of the hounds. Hungry. I was hungry. A burning in my stomach drove me. The moon's light was enough to guide me as I sniffed the path. Not just horses. Men. Lots of men.

I feared no man.

I shook my head as their familiar scent now disgusted me, then howled, alerting their hounds to my presence. I scratched the trunks of a nearby tree, left footprints in the mud leading into the mountains—a trail that would keep them confused for hours while I hunted closer to home.

My long legs carried me back to the house, and I looked upon the manor. Lights were on in many of the rooms, and I smelled the horses in the stables. They caught my scent, and I could smell their fear. Their meat was not as pleasing to my tongue, but blood was blood, meat was meat, and I was hungry.

Laughter made me recoil, and I hunched down in the woods and watched as a couple came out of the house and made their way to the stables.

Yessss! Meeeat!

Saliva dripped from my lips as I remembered my master's orders and growled.

I bolted upright in my bed and rushed to the window, scouring for the beast. I had touched his thoughts while I dreamed, and I recognized the stables and house he had come to.

It was this one.

Donning a robe over my chemise, I threw open the door to my room, rushing past the guards outside.

"Halt!" one of them commanded, but I dared not stop. Who knew if I was too late to save the couple? He might've already been attacking them.

My breath came in ragged gasps as I raced down the steps, briefly realizing that I had left my shoes back in my room. As soon as I made it outside, the rocks cut into my bare feet, and I regretted my hasty decision. Picking up speed, I bolted toward the stables, searching the darkness beyond for the beast.

"C'mon," I murmured. "Please don't let me be too late." I barreled into the stables and saw a dark form looming in the stall in front of me. A lantern swung softly on a peg, and I acted without thinking.

"*Fiergo!*"

The lantern's fire blazed brighter. With a flick of my wrist, I sent the fiery furnace directly at the shadow, preparing to light it up in a blaze of magic fire.

"Holy hell!" Xander cried out as the lantern hit him, and I gasped, realizing my mistake.

"*Difinite!*" I shouted the extinguishing charm before I burned the crown prince alive.

He patted his burning cloak and spun around to confront me. "What in the blazes are you doing? You just tried to murder me!"

"Not true. I thought you were the beast!" I said.

"I am not the beast!" he roared, and I saw a small form shaking behind him. Yasmin stepped out a moment later.

If they were the two in my vision coming out of the house, then that meant the beast was still here, and I was wrong about Xander being the shapeshifter. Spinning on my heel, I ran out of the stables, scanning the woods. Closing my eyes, I reached out with my senses, my power. Focusing all of my will, I waited in challenge with my hands spread wide, ready to call forth the very earth to crush the beast, praying I could do it.

I knew when Xander had come out of the stables and stood behind me, his scent as familiar to me now as any of my sisters. I held up my hand to silence him as I paced back and forth, searching for the dark presence but finding none.

"You are not welcome here!" I said threateningly, making sure the wind carried my voice into the woods and to the beast if it was listening.

"You can't tell me where to go," Xander seethed, and I gritted my teeth angrily. He thought I was speaking to him.

Stupid man. Did he not understand the supernatural battle that was going on around him?

"Leave!" I commanded, thrusting every ounce of compulsion I had toward the woods, hoping the beast was still there. To try and draw it out into battle right now could also endanger Xander. I would leave this battle for another day.

The hair on my arms rose as I tried to reach deep into the ground, searching for magic and power to aid me in case of attack. Sweat beaded across my brow. Xander was oblivious. He reached for me, and my power unintentionally blasted him backward to land in a pile of straw.

I released the power and rushed to him. I was the stupid one. There wasn't anything out there, just my own delusions. In trying to protect them all, I had injured the prince.

As Xander pulled himself out of the pile of straw, Yasmin

was next to him, cooing as she pulled each piece out of his hair and jacket.

Bile rose in my stomach as I pictured them in the stables together, rolling around in the hay. How far would it have gone had I not arrived? Neither of them even knew I'd saved them.

Xander pushed Yasmin's hand away as he rushed at me, gripping my arm painfully.

"You struck me!" he roared, the veins in his forehead protruding. I tried to pull away, but he wasn't allowing it. "You tried to light me on fire."

"I *thought*"—I yanked away from him—"you were in trouble."

He cocked his head and went silent before his laugh filled the air. "Trouble." He turned and pointed to a smirking Yasmin. "From her? Now that is amusing. I do tend to get into trouble with the ladies, but rest assured, I do not need saving from them." He laughed again, and the little bit of understanding we may have had was gone. A wide chasm opened between us in its place.

"Not from her—from the beast." How could I possibly explain my vision of the beast, my connection to it, without implicating myself?

Xander's laughter stopped, and his expression turned to one of wariness as he looked toward the forest. "It was here?"

Did he believe me? Maybe the chasm wasn't as large as I thought.

"Yes, I think so."

"How do you know?"

"I just do."

"Then you know nothing," he snapped.

Now he really was wearing my patience thin. Spinning on my heels, I stepped closer to him, looking into his eyes. Even barefoot, he was only a few inches taller than me. "No, Your

Highness." I sneered. "But rest assured, he would have attacked you if I had not shown up."

"Why *did* you show up?" he countered. "Were you jealous? Following me?"

I snorted. "No."

"Then how did you know the beast would come tonight, to this location, if you're not in league with the beast?" Xander's voice had dropped to a deadly whisper.

"Xander," Yasmin spoke up. She was shivering in the cold and looking terrified at being out in the dark.

"Go into the house, *darling*," he said, his eyes never leaving mine. His endearment was not lost on me.

"But—" she countered.

"Go! Let me deal with the witch," Xander growled.

With each cruel word, I felt the slice of his tongue across my skin and the burning pain it left behind. Again, I was no stranger to these derogatory remarks, but they hurt more now than from a stranger.

Steel yourself, Rosalie.

When Yasmin was inside and we were truly alone, I became uncomfortable standing barefoot and without a proper shawl or coat. Only now did the chilly night air attack me, the cuts on my feet stinging as the adrenaline wore off. My stitches burned from running, and I was now doing everything in my power to mask the pain I was in. I would never give him the satisfaction of seeing me weak or powerless.

"You are a fool," I snapped. "You underestimate the beast. It's smarter than any animal. Its thoughts are—"

"If I didn't know better, I'd say you're connected to it with the way you talk."

"N-No, I can sense it. And when I dream, I...."

"You what?" he asked.

"N-Never mind," I said, glancing away, my lips pressed

firm, my arms crossed to ward off the chill and my shaking. I would not give my enemy any information about the beast.

"Why did you touch the dead man?" he asked.

Here it comes. More accusations. More fuel to the witch fire.

"It's one of my gifts."

"What is?" Silence. "As your future king, I demand that you answer my questions. You say you do not lie—then don't. I know we may not know much about magic, but you could teach me. Tell me the truth."

"Very well. I will tell you the truth, but in no way does this prove me in league with the beast or in a conspiracy against you or your kingdom. Do you understand?"

"Let me be the judge of whether you're forming a conspiracy against me."

"You'll be the judge or the executioner?" I queried.

"Rosalie." He said my name in exhaustion. My full name. It was almost my undoing. I sighed in contentment at hearing it cross his lips.

"If you want answers, then you need to be ready for a history lesson, my liege, and one I am not prepared to give you in the middle of the night, in this state of undress."

Xander glanced down upon my nightdress and bare feet. His eyes widened, and seeing me in this state seemed to undo him. He spurred into action, rushing forward to lift me into his arms. Instantly, I felt the heat of his chest against my side and almost melted into him.

Xander marched me into the stable and headed to the back stall, grabbing two folded horse blankets from a shelf. He placed me down on the ground, my feet crunching the straw as he wrapped a blanket around my shoulders, then spread out another one on top of the straw.

He gestured for me to sit, but I refused to move. How dare

he assume I could be so easily duped into putting myself into an unladylike situation? I was not Yasmin.

"Sit," he demanded.

"I will not."

Xander grabbed me around the shoulders and pushed me down into the straw. I yelped in surprise and prepared for his attack, but nothing happened. Once I had fallen on the ground, he stepped out of the stall and came back with another lantern and more blankets. Under the blanket was a long wooden handle.

"Why do you have to be so infuriating? I've never met someone who tries my patience as much as you." He pulled the stall door closed behind him, crouched low, and wrapped another blanket around my shoulders, revealing the wooden crossbow. Xander unshouldered a quiver full of silver arrows and set it against the door.

"Where did you get the arrows?" I asked.

"I had already brought them down here earlier in the day."

"Why?"

"To hunt the beast. I was coming to lie in wait in the stables when Yasmin caught me in the foyer and followed me out. She refused to leave me alone despite my warnings of danger."

"Why would you do something so foolish? Where are your guards?"

His eyes flared with fire. "Did you not see Gaven's men across the yard near the woodshed, Tipper and Fagen by the well, and Yassa's guards hidden along the property?"

"No." I shook my head.

"Then hopefully the beast wouldn't either."

"It's a trap," I realized too late.

"Yes. We tried to find the beast's trail during the day but found nothing, so we resorted to laying a trap. We were hoping we would catch the beast in the act, but obviously you ruined any plans of that. So now, as your punishment, you must sit here and keep me awake until dawn. What was going to be Yasmin's job has now been bequeathed to you." His eyes twinkled mischievously, and my breath caught. He couldn't possibly mean for me to be close to him.

His eyes lowered to my lips, and heat filled my cheeks.

I stood up to leave, but Xander grabbed my hand and pulled me back down. His strength caught me off balance, and I landed in his lap. Struggling, I tried to move away, but he gripped me tighter.

"Hush! I hear something," he ordered.

Fearing it was the beast, I stilled and waited. My heart beat loudly, my breath caught in my lungs, my ears straining to hear beyond the confines of the stall.

Nothing.

I looked into Prince Xander's amber eyes and saw the heat within them, the curl at the corner of his mouth, and knew he had fooled me.

"Now who's the foolish one?" he said. "You're freezing, I'm cold, and we have a long night ahead of us, so just sit still."

I wasn't angry—the opposite, in fact. I was relieved the beast hadn't returned.

He held me gently in his arms. Neither of us spoke, but we listened to the sounds around us in the semi-dark. His slow, even breathing, my heart thudding furiously. The soft rustle of straw as he shifted to settle me into his lap easier. The swish of the blanket being adjusted to wrap around both of us tighter. I pressed my hand ever so lightly against his chest, keeping a physical and mental barrier between us. He reclined against the wall, and I slid down against his chest, my head cradled in his shoulder.

"Now, isn't this better?" he asked.

My cheeks burned, but I was unable to comment out of

embarrassment at the closeness of our bodies. The crossbow was still within a hand space away. We were both warm and safe.

"So, you were saying?" he pressed.

He was completely comfortable, but I was as stiff as a log against his side, unused to physical touch of any kind, least of all from a man I found attractive. He couldn't possibly want me to remember what he had asked me, right?

"What?" I asked.

"You said you were going to tell me about your gift. The truth now. No lies."

Oh, Mother. You never told us how much we were to keep secret. I sighed. *Here goes.* "If I touch those who have recently departed, I can see their death."

"What?" Xander leaned forward to look at me.

"The final moments of their death. Not only that, but I dream of their death. Sometimes it comes as a vision, or a warning. Other times it's after they're already dead."

He didn't speak, and I knew he was processing the information. Judging me as if I were indeed gruesome or repulsive. I thought back to the day I'd learned about death visions and how my life would forever change.

I'd had an episode when I was no more than eight seasons— a blackout—and when I had come to, I was in my bed, covered in mud. It was Eden who had noticed my mud-covered feet and my ripped nightdress.

"Rose? Wake up, Rose." She opened the shutter, and light streamed into my room, revealing my disheveled state. "Did you go roll in the garden?"

Sitting up, I saw my fingernails were covered in dirt, and twigs were tangled in my hair.

When Mother learned of my nightly dream excursions, she

said, "It seems your gifting may be one beyond my knowledge. I must contact Lorn and schedule your day of testing."

I expected the day of testing to include quills, scrolls, and lots of spells. I didn't expect him to walk into my living room holding two woven baskets with lids.

"Put your hand in, but don't look," the elf said, holding out the right basket.

I closed my eyes as he helped guide my hand, keeping the lid closed. My fingers brushed the top of something soft, and I jumped as it moved and fluttered its wings.

"Oh my, Lorn!" I laughed as I settled my heart and let my fingers caress the top of a bird. Thinking it had something to do with guessing the type of bird, I rose to the challenge. "Too small for a chicken, too big for a sparrow, and it's not a pigeon," I said confidently. He pulled the basket away, and I grumbled. "Wait, I wasn't done guessing!"

I opened my eyes and saw he had put the basket on the floor. He then presented the second one. Expecting another bird or animal, I wasn't as nervous this time, knowing Lorn wouldn't have placed anything dangerous inside.

I was wrong.

Nothing moved within, and I searched, reaching farther into the basket until I was almost touching the bottom. Then my fingers brushed the feathers, and I seized up.

Escape! Escape! The feeling of being trapped overwhelmed me. I was outside in a pen. I looked up as Lorn, impossibly tall like a tree, loomed over me, his hands going around my neck, and then pain and darkness.

I screamed, pushing the basket away and falling to my rear. I cried, tears rushing down my face, grasping my own neck as I could feel Lorn's fingers tighten around it.

"Y-You tried to kill me," I cried out sobbing.

"No, Rosalie. I didn't!"

"Yes, you did. I saw you!" I pointed at him accusingly as I backed away from my fey tutor.

"You were mistaken. It was not you but the bird," Lorn said calmly, kneeling to pick up the dead dove that had fallen out of the basket when I knocked it from his hands. "You shared in the bird's death vision."

"What?"

"You, Rosalie, can touch the dead and see their final moments. Death calls to you, and you come—sometimes unwillingly."

"I don't understand." What he said did not make me trust him or come any closer to the dead bird. I was still reeling from the feelings of Lorn's hands around my neck; even now, I could still feel the pressure as he prepared to snap it.

"The night you woke up in the chicken coop, a fox had come in and killed the rooster."

I was going to be sick. Running out of the room, I made it to our sink and lost the contents of my stomach.

That was the day he taught me about a group called the Death Seekers. They were called upon to give answers in death, specifically the how—finding out if someone was poisoned by a jealous lover or merely died in their sleep. The gifting was extremely rare, and it paid well since only a few were in tune enough to see a person's death vision.

"I don't want this gift! Lorn, please take it away!" I begged.

"Nonsense. You have been chosen for a reason, and it is not good to deny your gifts."

"I can't do it."

"It is as I feared," Mother Eville said from the doorway. "She has the Death Seeker gift."

"Yes, and as she grows, so will her powers," Lorn replied.

"We can't have her chasing after the death of every live-stock or butchered animal in the middle of the night, can we?"

"No, but when she sleeps is when she is most vulnerable, and her magic will draw her to them."

"Then I will find a way to temper her gift," Mother said confidently.

"Lorelai, there is no way to—"

"Don't you tell me what I can and can't do." Her voice dropped to a growl, and she retreated to her potions closet. Days later, she emerged, hair a mess, eyes red and bloodshot from lack of sleep, holding a potion in the form of a dried tea that did indeed keep the blackouts and dreams away —until now.

"And now here I am years later, using my gift willingly," I finished. "Those men who were murdered in the woods... they tried to kidnap me."

"And you saw their murderer?"

"No, I blacked out and woke back in my room, covered in their blood."

"I'm sorry you had to experience their death like that," he said sincerely.

Xander didn't ask any more questions after that.

Leaning against his chest, I felt myself slowly begin to relax. He never made a move to touch me, and I could almost hear his mind processing, taking in the information I had relayed.

"What of your real parents, not Lady Eville?"

"I don't remember them. Mother never speaks of them other than to say I was bartered away, traded like goods, and she saved me. She said it doesn't do well to dwell on where you come from but to instead focus on where you're going."

He leaned down and rested his chin on my head. "You are an amazing woman to overcome so much."

"What?" My breath caught in my throat. I was surprised at his sudden praise.

"Don't get my wrong. You are also extremely stubborn and frequently cause me grief." I grinned in response. "But that only makes you more irresistible to me." My heartbeat picked up at his admission. "The kingdom will fall to war, but I don't care anymore as long as I have you." He groaned softly, pulling me closer to him. He nuzzled his face into my neck and breathed deeply, sending goose bumps up my flesh. I could feel his hand along my waist pulling me closer. "Why couldn't I have met you a year ago?"

"You still would have hated me. Nothing would have changed; you would have just disliked me sooner."

Xander sighed. "So much could have happened in a year. We may have actually learned to get along." His lips moved along my neck as he spoke, each word like a soft kiss.

"Maybe," I laughed. "Or at least tolerate each other's presence."

"Yes, eventually I would have chipped away at your icy exterior with my charm."

"You? Charm?" I laughed out loud. "I would at least have pretended indifference as you bungled your way through courting me."

"You love my charisma."

"You called me a witch and an old hag the first night we met and again a few minutes ago."

"Only because you are a trying woman, and you know how to wear my patience thin. For that I am sorry." He kissed my chin. "See, there's something about us that we can't deny. I was drawn to you ever since I first laid eyes on you, and I've been fighting that pull since day one. You were the one who ran from me."

"I thought you were a married man."

"I was—to you."

"But you didn't know that at the time," I said, aghast, my

hand pressed against his chest.

His mouth curled up into a devilish smile. "You can tell yourself whatever you want to believe." Xander smirked. "But even without seeing you, you've drawn me like a beacon on a watchtower. You're a light in the darkness, and I have forever been searching for you. Now, I'm done playing the gentleman. I'm going to kiss my wife."

His eyes glowed in the lamplight. My heart pounded as he leaned in close, his hand raising my chin so I was staring into warm amber pools filled with desire. His lips brushed across mine ever so softly before nudging them, asking for permission. Meeting his lips, I answered his longing with my own. I didn't know it, but ever since our wedding night, our first kiss, I had been slowly drowning, wanting more. Needing to be saved from the desire Xander had started.

"Douse the flame," I whispered huskily, breaking our kiss.

Xander groaned. "The lamp is all the way across the stall, hanging on the wall."

"Fine." I smiled. "I'll do it." With a snap of my fingers, I snuffed out the lamp. But in the dark, our fiery passion could not be so easily extinguished.

I sighed in happiness. A feeling that I had never truly understood before. Until now.

Shivering, I rolled over, pulling the wool blanket closer to my chin to stave off the cold. A prickling against my nose irritated me, and I opened my eyes to gaze at the offending piece of straw. Sitting up, I realized I was alone in the stall as darkness surrounded me.

Where is Xander?

A loud commotion came from the yard, and I heard voices

raised in anger. Tipper was there, gripping the uniform of one of the soldiers and lifting him into the air, his face inches from the other man's as he berated him mercilessly. It seemed the night was not over.

I rushed out into the yard.

"You were lax in your duty!" Tipper yelled.

"No, sir, I wasn't!" the young man said. He couldn't have been much older than eighteen seasons. "I swear the beast didn't come near the house."

"You were stationed on the far side. You were the one closest to the back door. If anyone saw the beast or heard someone cry out, it was you."

The beast must have come back in the night. Death always created a spectacle.

I scanned the crowd, looking for Xander, but couldn't find him among the group.

"I'm telling you, I didn't see anything," the soldier whined, the tips of his boots scraping the gravel as he struggled to find purchase.

Tossing the wool blanket to the side, I only then became aware of the dried rust color across my feet.

Blood.

I became light-headed and crumpled to the ground.

No! Did it happen again? Did I sleepwalk? Have I done something to Xander? Is it his blood? Did I kill him?

Maybe I was wrong about everything, and my own paranoia deceived me.

My mouth was dry as cotton, and a bitter taste filled it as my worst fears came to light—me covered in blood and Xander missing.

It was me.

I was the murderer.

I was the beast.

CHAPTER TWENTY-TWO

My tears soaked the wool blanket upon which I lay. My right hand curled into the straw-covered earth as I silently screamed in horror, sobbing, letting my heart cry out but refusing to make a sound other than soft gasps. I mustn't alert anyone of my troubles. My blackouts, the visions, the killings. Too many times I'd awoken covered in blood and shredded clothes to not put two and two together. My mother and Lorn were wrong. They had to be. It was why I was so closely connected to the killer, because we were one and the same.

The medicine no longer worked to keep my darkness at bay, and because I lacked the access to readily available magic here, it weakened me, making me succumb to the beast within. This kingdom really was cursed. Leaving was my only option, hopefully before I injured another person.

Washing my feet, hands, and face in the horse trough, I tried to hide and destroy all evidence of the blood. Grabbing a rucksack, I packed it with what little provisions Xander had brought to the stall, as well as extra blankets for my journey. It seemed the only way to keep my promise to the prince was to leave. Only then would he be safe. If I were a strong enough person, I would try and take my own life, but I was a coward, and I feared death.

I wrapped the blanket around my shoulders and headed deep into the woods, using a compulsion to keep everyone from looking my way. I turned back only once to the manor house and saw the compulsion hadn't worked on everyone, for Earlsgaarde was staring right at me with alert and perceptive eyes.

Had he known all along what I was?

He didn't raise an alarm at my sneaking away; in fact, he seemed quite calm. He even gave me a nod.

Turning my back on him, I picked up my pace, hoping to avoid the guards who had already began their search for the missing person.

It wasn't until I heard the search party call out the person's name for the third time that it truly registered how evil I was and what I had done.

"Pru!" Tipper's voice echoed in the woods. "Prudence!"

My knees buckled and my legs gave out as I fell to the ground shaking.

No. Not Pru! Had I killed the one and only person who I could call my friend?

Getting back to my feet, I fought the tears and continued to run through the woods in the darkness, away from the sounds of the hounds.

I stopped and listened. Through the boughs of the trees, I could see a faint torchlight and hear the crashing of horses through the dried leaves and the calls of the men searching for Pru. A fluttering object on a tree branch caught my attention, and I slowed enough to recognize the blue hair ribbon. It was Pru's.

But I dared not let the men find me before I found her. I needed to know for sure.

The bushes near me wiggled, and I heard the crisp crackling of leaves and Gobbersnot's cussing. His beady black eyes looked at me hungrily through the long blades of overgrown grass.

"Oh, thank the stars. Gobbersnot, can you distract the dogs and lead them away from here?"

He nodded but grumbled out, "Dugaday?" trying to bargain with me.

I rolled my eyes. "No, you cannot eat the dogs."

The goblin held his hands parallel about a foot apart and repeated, "Dugaday?"

"No, not even a small one."

Gobbersnot did not like that answer, and I feared I wasn't keeping up my end of the bargain. "Please, Gobbersnot! I promise I will get you blood when we're done."

He sneezed at me and disappeared back into the bushes. A few agonizing seconds later, I heard the dogs bay again and change direction, heading away from me.

Spinning on my heels, I scanned the ground looking for clues, hints of her whereabouts. If I could find her, then maybe, just maybe, I could right a wrong and still save her. Taking the ribbon, I tossed it into the air and commanded it to "Seek." The ribbon lifted from my hand and floated in circles above my head as it began its search.

But using a blue ribbon in the dark wasn't going to help me. I would need light. Creating a mage light, I cast it low to the ground to glow about my feet. The ribbon was already on the move, and I was following close behind.

The forest became darker the deeper I traveled, and the sounds of the search party faded away. Gobbersnot had done well, for we were heading in opposite directions. Normally, I would have been scared, but my fear for Pru spurred me on.

The ribbon danced and turned abruptly, and I knew I was getting close. A snapping noise from beyond stilled my movements as I listened, hunting with my ears for sounds of her cry or moans. Closing my hands, I raised the mage light and spun, searching the darkness, and saw a hint of a blue dress near the edge of a gully.

"Pru! Pru! I'm so sorry." I rushed to her, grabbed her shoulders, and turned her over. Her eyes fluttered weakly, and I breathed a sigh of relief. She was still alive, though her pulse was weak, and there was a nasty claw mark in her side that was bleeding profusely. Guilt assailed me, and I knew it must have been me. I didn't mean to hurt her. My hands glowed, and I closed my eyes, pressing them to her wound. I could feel her skin slowly knit back together.

"I never meant to hurt you, Pru. I promise I'll go away, somewhere far away, where my inner beast can no longer hurt you or anyone else. Do you hear me? Just promise me you'll wake up."

Pru's eyes fluttered open weakly, and she breathed out a sigh. "You came for me. I knew you would save me."

"No, I'm not good at saving people. I only hurt them. It's me. All my fault. All of those deaths. All because I truly am evil, a murderous beast."

"N-No, you're n-not a beast," she cooed softly. She reached up to cup my face weakly. I put my hand over hers and she smiled. "I saw you. When the beast took me, and I thought I was dying for sure. You appeared to me, like a ghost or a dream, but you didn't say anything. You were here and then vanished."

What she was saying was confirming that she was indeed close to death and had summoned me to her while I slept. I had been here, but I didn't remember.

"I thought for sure I was dead, but then he said...." Her eyes widened in fear.

"Who said?" I asked. "Who's he?"

Pru leaned forward, putting her forehead to mine. Wrapping her arm around my neck, she murmured, "Rrrrn."

"What?" I asked again, scared that maybe I had inadvertently hurt her.

Pru struggled to breathe out her warning again, but this time I heard her desperation. "R-Run, Rosalie." Her breathing was ragged as she looked behind me in terror. "It's a trap!"

Goose bumps traveled up my arms, and I sensed we were not alone.

"You cannot have her," I said firmly, sending the mage light high above my head to try and cast its rays onto the beast.

The cracking of branches echoed around me as the beast moved in the darkness. I spun, trying to find it again, to keep the threat in front of me, not behind. Knowing that may be the only warning I'd have if it attacked, my hands crackled as I harnessed my power, focusing it as I prepared to defend myself.

"It's not a beast," Pru whimpered fearfully.

"What is it, then?" I asked.

"It's Gaven," she whispered.

A slow clap came from the woods, and I turned as Gaven stepped out from behind the tree line. "But that's where you're wrong, little girl. For I am more than a beast. I am invincible." He fingered the fur he wore on his back, and I eyed it suspiciously.

"It's enchanted, isn't it," I said, nodding to the black fur.

"I told you I was the greatest hunter alive. I killed a legendary brackenbeast. I'd heard tales of their powers, so I skinned it with a silver knife while under a hunter's moon and took its fur as my prize."

"You killed a fey. Why would you do that?" I gasped in horror, realizing that by doing it under those conditions, he had embedded some of the fey's magic into the skin, making the wearer a shapeshifter.

"I was bored of hunting with arrows." Gaven grinned. "Now I hunt with teeth and claws, and it is exhilarating. And no one can stop me. Not even you."

"I will stop you. I guarantee it," I threatened.

"We could have been good together, you and me," he said, shaking his head. "But then you had to go and ruin it by being her—a daughter of Eville."

"It wouldn't have worked." I shook my head, still reeling from the shock of his betrayal. "You're a murderer."

"No, I will be hailed as a savior, for I have rid the kingdom of you."

"What?" I said in shock.

"When the envoy from Florin learned the prince's new wife was a daughter of Eville and heard the rumors of how much the prince and king hated the arrangement, he approached the king with a proposition. He wanted you, and King Gerald wanted peace and the witch's spawn gone. Earlsgaarde laid out a trap to get you away from the palace and closer to Florin."

"You became the beast and created a trail for us to follow."

"The kingdom has been plagued with tales of a harmless beast that roamed the woods for years. I just turned that fairy tale into reality."

"You killed Thomas. And that's why Herez screamed when she saw your cloak. You tried to kill her."

His eyes glittered with joy. "No, I did kill her. You didn't think Herez really ran home to her parents in the middle of the night. I couldn't let her live, in case she told others. I killed her and the others, all laying the trail to get you far away from the palace, past the wards and into Earlsgaarde's hands."

"The failed kidnapping." I nodded in realization. "And you were the one who shot me!"

Gaven nodded. "Xander is stupid. He doesn't see you for how evil you truly are and tried to protect you."

"No, you're the evil one. You are murdering in cold blood."

I was secretly relieved to discover it hadn't been me. I wasn't the beast. But Gaven's story still didn't explain who killed the kidnappers in the forest.

The whole time we were talking, I had walked, drawing him farther away from Pru, who had used my distraction to run away, hopefully for help. Now it was just the two of us.

When Gaven noticed his prisoner had escaped, he gnashed his teeth. "No worries. I'll hunt her down soon enough. After I kill you." He lifted the black fur over his head.

The air hummed with the current of magic as he changed and I gathered power to me, preparing to cut him down. I watched as the fur bonded to his skin, shifting and stretching. Two large horns grew from his head, and his mouth elongated, sharp, pointed teeth filling his muzzle. A brackenbeast—the legendary creature of Sion with the head of a lion, horns of a bull, and the strength of a bear.

Even though he loomed before me, a terrifying beast that had killed and hunted down people in cold blood, all I could think about was the man who had made me smile in the stables, danced with me in the ballroom, and had even tried to kiss me. These were basic human emotions my mother warned would make me weak, and I struggled with them.

My hesitation was a fateful error, as he lunged straight at me. Slipping on the wet leaves, falling backward, I released a bolt of lightning that missed Gaven. I slid down a small gully, my head smacking against a rock before I collided with a rotting log that rolled over my body, pinning my leg underneath. Pain filled my mind, and while I tried to push it away and escape, I was hopelessly trapped.

As the brackenbeast drew close, his hot, rank breath warm

against my neck, I looked up as its mouth opened in a snarl and saw its deadly teeth. I was paralyzed with fear, unable to think or conjure a spell in the midst of this great horror.

Of all the deaths I had seen in my lifetime, I had never seen mine—until now.

I closed my eyes and prayed over my soul, wondering briefly who would see my death vision.

A blur of fur brushed past my face, and then the bracken-beast was gone, knocked away from me by the sudden attack of a second beast—a great copper wolf the size of a horse.

The wolf placed himself in front of me, his hackles raised against the much larger brackenbeast.

The fight between two beasts of fey lore was both terrifying and awe inspiring. The brackenbeast was larger and more massive, but the wolf was quicker and more agile.

The wolf growled in challenge, his back tense as he paced, most likely looking for a weak spot to attack. The brackenbeast wasn't intimidated; lowering his head, he led with his horns and charged. I heard the cry of pain from the wolf and was spurred into action.

Focusing through the ringing in my head, I blasted the log off me, the repercussions reverberating through my head in a throbbing headache. My ankle was starting to swell already, but I limped to my feet and tried to focus on the two dark shapes fighting to the death before me.

One shot. I would have one shot if I were lucky before I passed out from using so much magic.

A yelp of pain drew my gaze. The brackenbeast had the wolf pinned down, the wolf's throat exposed as the beast pulled back his clawed hand. They were too close. I couldn't hit one without hitting the other.

"No!" I shouted in fear.

Gobbersnot rushed out of the grass, a silver knife glinting in his hands as he jumped onto the beast, stabbing it in the side over and over again.

The brackenbeast howled before grabbing the goblin with one hand, his claws digging into Gobbersnot's skull as he stood up and tossed the goblin farther down the gully and into the raging river. His body disappeared under the dark water.

"Nooo!"

Amid my grief, I realized Gobbersnot had given me my only opening. I wasn't going to waste it.

"*Enchanti fiergo!*" I screamed, and with a blast of fire that almost ripped my head in two, I engulfed the brackenbeast. I heard his cry of pain as his fur caught fire, and then the beast dashed into the river. But it was an enchanted fire and could not be so easily extinguished, unless Gaven shed the skin. I heard his strangled cry as he ripped the burning fur from him, but I could not see him, nor did I want to imagine the pain it must have caused. I chose fire for a reason; it had a purifying property, and removing a burning skin would be as painful as being skinned alive.

Gaven's cries of pain continued for a moment, and then they fell eerily silent.

The wolf lay on the ground before me, and I found myself wobbling over to him. The world faded in and out around me, and I knew I wouldn't be conscious long. Falling to my knees, I ran my fingers along the wolf's body and felt the warm pool of blood. His tongue was hanging out of his mouth, and he was panting fast. He was dying.

He whined.

"Shhh," I whispered to him. "Hold still, will you." His ears fell back under the weight of my command and another whine came forth. "It's okay," I murmured soothingly.

The wolf looked at me, his amber eyes pleading, then becoming fearful as they flickered to the sound of the hunters and their hounds. Laying my hands on where he was injured, I sent a trickle of magic outward, searching for the source of the bleeding. First, I needed to fix the internal injury, and then I could reknit the muscles and skin.

Got it. Sealing it with a whisper, I pulled my hand back and felt the first wave of nausea hit me. Gritting my teeth, I tried to stay awake. *No. I'm stronger than this.* I had to stay awake and help him. I would not let Gobbersnot's sacrifice be in vain.

Tears burned in the corners of my eyes as I pressed harder on the wound and focused more of my energy. It was going slowly, the wolf's body fighting my magic. But then it was done, the bleeding stopped and the wound healed. The fur beneath my hands shifted and disappeared, leaving baby-soft skin.

"It's okay. I know. You don't have to hide from me." The wolf let out a growl, and then he got up and shook his fur. I watched in fascination as the copper wolf transitioned easily into my copper-haired prince.

Xander. A werewolf. It didn't shock me once I'd figured out his curse, but seeing him as the wolf was another thing altogether. Part of me was frightened, but part of me was curious. His skin was warm to the touch, and I could see the slight trail of silvery scars that were years old.

"You're not scared of me?" Xander asked softly.

I shook my head. "You were the one who killed those kidnappers in the woods that night. You rescued me. Why didn't you tell me?"

Xander nodded. "I had done a terrible thing. I murdered two men to protect you. And yet, I still had doubts about who you were. You were still a daughter of Eville." His words, meant to be comforting, instead stabbed me in the heart, and I pulled away as doubt crept in.

"Is what Gaven said the truth? Did you know your father planned to be rid of me?" I asked angrily.

Xander swallowed and staggered to his feet, grimacing in pain and clutching his side. I knew he would be fine, but newly healed muscles were stiff and uncomfortable, and he would probably be scratching at them for a while.

"Rosalie—"

"Yes or no," I demanded.

"Yes," he said, "but let me—"

"No. Say no more to me. Ever."

Stumbling away in exhaustion, I headed deeper into the woods, away from the river and away from him. I fought the tears that blinded me as I crashed through the bushes, forging my own trail as I became lost, promising to cut my heart out and to never love again.

He had betrayed me.

A wave of light surrounded me, and I blinked painfully, the mage light causing my head to ring in pain. I smelled the stench of dark magic encircling me and heard a male voice whisper a spell I knew quite well.

"*Somnus.*"

A wave of nausea hit me, and I fell forward and passed out.

CHAPTER TWENTY-THREE

I awoke with my hands bound. At first I was confused by the large manacles clamped onto my wrists. Then I was livid.

"Mmmfff?" I cried out. My shackles were connected to a chain and anchored to a post in the ground. Standing up, I pulled at the chain from every angle, but I couldn't force the clasp to budge.

Tipper, in full armor, warily came close, reaching forward to tug the rag around my mouth down.

"Tipper, what's going on? Unchain me," I demanded.

His face was unreadable, his eyes dark. "You are being charged with the murder of Gaven Hostler."

"That's nonsense."

"My men found you in the woods, with the body, covered in blood. With this." He held up the burned skin of the brackenbeast. "You are the beast."

"No, I didn't kill him. I mean, yes, I did, but that's because he was the beast. Please, Tipper," I cried out. "You must believe me. Xander, where's Xander? He'll explain."

My plea for Prince Xander made Tipper look at me with utter disgust. "We haven't found him yet. He's gone. You probably murdered him as well."

Tipper shook his head and signaled for the guards. They

hauled me up by my forearms and dragged me to my feet, scuffing them across the ground as I tried to fight them. I reached deep inside for my power but was met with intense pain. I screamed as the bands around my skin began to heat up and burn me. When I released my power, the burning stopped. The pain was so excruciating that I struggled not to pass out.

Earlsgaarde walked over to me, his face covered in a smug smile. "It's no use. The bands are enchanted and will bind your powers. You will no longer be able to harm anyone."

"But I've never harmed anyone."

"Yet you are the daughter of Eville," Earlsgaarde said. "It is only a matter of time before you walk in your mother's footsteps and curse us all. When I heard you were the prince's new bride, I immediately knew what must be done. We must rescue Baist from your evil."

"Release me. I am the princess," I growled.

Earlsgaarde began jumping around, waving a scroll in the air. "Not according to this. The king of Baist agreed to surrender you to us." With a flick of his wrist, the scroll unrolled, and I could see the new peace treaty in a hastily written script. "I once asked you what you were willing to do for peace." Along the bottom of the scroll was none other the royal seal of Baist and King Gerald's signature.

My mouth went dry as I realized what had been done. I was betrayed, traded to protect their country from invasion. Even after I had saved Queen Anya and Princess Ameline, it wasn't enough. For the good of the crown, I was being sacrificed to save the many.

I scanned the growing crowd of onlookers and couldn't help but see the horrified look on Pru's face. I was relieved she was safe. She was crying and being held back my one of the guards. I smirked as she kicked him in the shin to release her, and she ran to me.

"Miss!" she cried out, but was stopped when another guard stepped in and grabbed her around the waist. Lifting her in the air, he physically removed her from the yard.

"It's okay, Pru!" I yelled out. "Be brave. Be strong."

She settled at my words, and the guard put her down. Pru buried her face in her hands, her shoulders shaking with her sobs.

Behind Pru stood a smug Yasmin, who in the last hour had changed into one of her more extravagant dresses. No longer was her face pale with worry, but instead it glowed with happiness. And why wouldn't it? She was getting what she wanted. I was imprisoned and would probably be executed in a foreign country, leaving Xander free to marry her. Baist would have peace, and Florin would be happy because they had what they wanted—me. Their own revenge on Baist. An eye for an eye; a dead princess for a dead queen.

This wasn't right. I needed to hear it from Xander himself. He couldn't have agreed to trade me away. But I couldn't find his amber eyes and dark head among the crowd. He was absent. My heart broke as I realized our love was nothing more than a distraction. His pretty words were lies, and he knew all along that Florin would eventually take me, so he wouldn't care if the blood oath failed or not.

Mud pelted me in the face, and I glared at the mob, unsure of whom it was who had dared throw something at me.

"Monster!" a random voice yelled.

"Murderer!" a second followed.

No one tried to help me. Most stood before me with looks of hatred, fear, and confusion.

Clenching my eyes and fists, I tried to fight back the tears that were burning in the corners of my eyes, a sensation that matched the one in my heart as I felt it shrivel and die. My mother was right. Love brought nothing but pain and suffering. Heartbreak could make one weak.

But she was also wrong about another thing.

Lifting my head, I quenched my tears and looked with hatred upon the crowd.

Vengeance would be mine, but I could be patient.

"So be it," I said, turning my back on the people of Baist. They never were my people, as much as I wanted it to be different. They would never accept me.

I was hauled past the stables and tossed into a cage on the back of a wagon. A guard linked my chains through a pole in the side, attaching an iron lock. The emissaries of Florin prepared to depart. Servants loaded their trunks, and I watched as Earlsgaarde directed more guards to surround my cell.

Tipper came to stand near the cage. He wouldn't meet my gaze, turning his back to speak to me. "Glad to finally be rid of you!" He waved to Earlsgaarde, then brought his fingers up to his mouth and let out a piercing whistle. The horses started moving, and I lost my balance and fell to my knees. Grasping the bars of my prison, I watched as I was taken away.

The crowd jeered at me and tossed garbage my way.

"Good riddance to the beast!"

"Now we will be safe!"

"Hooray!"

"I'm not the beast," I shouted back, but they couldn't hear me over the din of their cries.

A well-thrown rock made it through the bars and cut my cheek. A tomato followed, striking me in the chest, the red juices running down my shirt like blood. Then came dung.

They were the same as all the others.

Heartless souls.

And they would pay.

I remembered little of my trip into Florin, too wrapped up in my hatred. It burned, feeding me, keeping me warm on the cold trek through the mountains.

Twice a day we stopped, and they would let me out to relieve myself and give me a plate of food. Then back into my mobile prison I would go. Only once more did I try to use my powers to break the enchanted chains on my wrist, quickly deciding I liked being alive. For when I reached for power, the manacles would burn and then quickly drain away my energy, and my mind would be in a fog for hours afterward.

The terrain changed and became warmer. Flowers bloomed along the hillside and their aroma calmed me, reminding me of my family.

My family. What would my mother say when she found out how easily I was captured and subdued? Not at all becoming of the Eville name or legacy.

Earlsgaarde would frequently ride along next to me and gloat. He was the worst kind of man—cruel to animals, greedy among his men, and all in all a greasy little weasel. My fingers weaved a pattern in the air, unconsciously forming the spell to transform him into such an animal, but nothing would come with the manacles.

My wrists were burned and gave off a rancid smell. Without proper clean water or ointment, they would probably become infected, and there was a good chance I would either die from sepsis or they would have to be amputated.

Neither was a favorable option for me. I would have to escape or die trying.

Picking up a spoon, I ate what little food they had given me for dinner—a weak porridge, which tasted strangely sweet. It was better than the bland porridge I had been given for breakfast.

Just when I thought I was recovered enough to attempt an escape or break the enchantment on the manacles, the world started to tilt and the faces blurred. Dropping the spoon, I kicked the pewter plate away in disgust.

Drugged.

They had drugged me.

CHAPTER TWENTY-FOUR

T he wagon stopped, the door of my cage opened, and footsteps drew near. I tried to open my eyes, but I was too weak.

A shadow passed over me as someone kneeled by me to take stock of my wrists. A curse fell from their lips as they touched the burned areas. I moaned, the excruciating white pain blinding me.

"Is this her?" a deep but somewhat familiar voice asked.

"Yes, Your Majesty," Earlsgaarde's whiny voice answered. "This is the girl I told you about—Eville's adopted daughter."

I tried to open my eyes, to take in the new speaker, but all I saw was a dark blur. He gasped when our eyes met.

"It can't be," the strange man said. "I don't believe it."

"Believe it, Your Majesty. Test her and you will know I speak the truth."

"It's really her?" he asked. "She's alive after all this time?"

My head rolled and I muttered incomprehensibly. My wrist moved and pus leaked out from beneath the shackles, a rank smell along with it.

"By the stars, Earlsgaarde. What is that stench?"

"It's her wounds, my king. They are festering. She will die soon, so maybe we should move up the execution."

The king's voice was muffled as he spoke through his sleeve. "No, send for a healer immediately. Take her to the guest suite and make sure she's comfortable."

"As you wish, Your Majesty."

Time was nonexistent in my prison. The next time I opened my eyes, there were two more blurred shapes standing over me. Based on the shapes of their brown, dirty boots, it was one male and one female.

"This is going to hurt." The man carefully began to clean around my shackles with a damp cloth. He lifted the manacles, but my burned skin came with it. I screamed in agony as white blindness came over me again, and then I mercifully passed out.

Warmth. I was warm. After shivering for hours, I finally felt warmth, or maybe I had died. A rough wool blanket was tucked over my shoulders, and I opened my eyes to find that I was no longer in the cell but in a clean bed. My wrists were bandaged carefully in white linen under the heavy manacles, and the smell of disinfectant hit my nose.

I didn't recognize the bedroom but cared little because the pain had stopped.

The bed dipped as someone sat on the mattress near my hip, but I didn't look, just stared off at the stone wall.

"Oh, Rosalie." His soft voice speaking my name broke my heart. "Rose. What have you done to yourself?"

"You did this to me. You abandoned me."

"No, that wasn't me." Xander's voice changed, became deeper in resonance. His blurred shape grew fuller until the person sitting next to me was a stranger.

His face was full, covered by a well-groomed black beard. His red robes were trimmed in fur, his buttons gold. Wealth adorned his brow in a gold circlet. I looked upon kind yet sad brown eyes.

235

"Who are you?" I asked, my throat sore from disuse.

"I'm King Basil of Florin."

Hearing his name instantly made me want to lash out at him. I raised my hand, but he carefully clasped it between his large ones to keep me from hurting him or myself.

"My executioner," I gasped.

"Your savior," the king corrected before yelling out, "Earlsgaarde, bring forth the imperial rose."

Earlsgaarde entered carrying a dying rosebud on a plate, and I trembled when I looked upon it. He lifted the tray and offered it to me, but I refused to touch it.

"Touch the flower," King Basil commanded, and I froze, already knowing what would happen.

Earlsgaarde put the tray down next to the bed, grabbed my wrist, and pricked my hand with a needle.

I barely flinched when the prick caused a red drop of blood to form.

Earlsgaarde placed the rose in my hand. As soon as the thorns touched my blood, the sickly rose began to bloom, its petals unfolding, the color becoming brighter.

"You see, Your Majesty." Earlsgaarde grinned. "The imperial rose does not lie. She is of royal blood and your heir to the throne."

The king sighed. "So it's true. You *are* my daughter."

I stilled and gazed upon the stranger. We couldn't be related. It wasn't possible. Yet we had the same black hair and light eyes.

"I don't believe you," I whispered.

"That's fine. I hardly believe it myself. Sleep now. We have much to discuss when you are well."

It wasn't true. It didn't make sense. I couldn't be a princess, because Mother had said my parents didn't want me. It couldn't be true.

King Basil left me alone, and I slept a full two days before waking up feeling refreshed. My wrists still bore the manacles, and although the long chain was gone, they were still enchanted. The binding magic was strong, created by a powerful sorcerer. The magic residue seemed familiar, but I wasn't sure where I had felt it before.

I had the freedom to leave my room. The two servants who had taken me from the cage were an elderly married couple, who were now in charge of my care.

"Oh, Rose," Magda twittered as she came into my room carrying a tray of scones. "I've got your favorite."

"My favorite?" Rubbing the sleep out of my eyes, I looked at the tray she'd placed across my lap. The cutest blueberry and lemon scone cut into squares sat on a flowered porcelain plate next to a dish of clotted cream. The hint of lemon tickled my nose, and my mouth began to water. Picking up the square scone, I ignored the knife and dipped it right into the cream, then took a bite. My taste buds exploded as the pleasure receptors in my brain began firing. I did indeed love these scones.

"How did you know?" I asked.

"Because I made them for you every morning when you were a child."

It seemed pointless to point out that I thought she was mistaken, so I continued to devour every single scone, even the crumbs. When I was satisfied, I stepped out of the bed, proud that I only slightly wobbled as I walked over to the wardrobe. Opening the door, I was greeted with a vast array of silk dresses to befit a queen. Pulling one from the hook, I held it up to my neck and was surprised it fell to the floor, the perfect length.

"They were your mother's," Magda answered before I even asked. "I had them pulled out of storage, cleaned, and pressed for you."

Unlike the dark colors I normally favored, this one was pale yellow and reminded me of Yasmin. I brushed my fingers across the pearl buttons, and my emotions battled within me. Truth and lies. Dream and real. I wasn't sure how to process the new information. Taking a deep breath, I told myself to keep my emotions in check. This could all be an elaborate scheme. After all, they had tried to kill me only a week before.

Magda helped me into the dress. The thick manacles made getting my arm through the long sleeves difficult, and little slits had to be cut to accommodate them, but once on, the cuffs of the dress completely hid them. She gave me a complementary navy cloak lined in fur, and I ran my fingers along the soft, luxurious pelt.

My days in the prison aside, my time with my enemy had been far more pleasant than that with my husband's family.

Don't compare, I chastised myself.

Magda moved to the double doors and opened them, beckoning me to follow. I stopped before crossing the threshold into the hall and looked at either side for an armed guard. There weren't any.

My teeth ground together, and I had to focus on putting one foot in front of the other as I made my way down the hall. We passed the throne room, and I couldn't help but glance up at the two golden chairs under the large banner of an imperial rose.

"Why hello, Miss Rosalie." Peder, Magda's husband, crossed our path carrying a large bouquet of flowers. "I was just bringing these to your room to help spruce it up. No one's lived in it for years, so it smells a bit stuffy. Just going to bring the outside in a bit, you see." He grinned, wrinkles lining his face and around his merry eyes.

"That would be lovely, Peder."

"Yes, miss." He beamed, and I wanted to reach out and hug

him. There was something about the elderly couple that seemed comforting.

Magda gave Peder a quick kiss on the cheek before heading into a drawing room. A crackling fire blazed under a large stone mantelpiece, and above the mantel was the stuffed head of a great wolf. It was one of the largest wolves I had ever seen, except for Xander's shifted form. I paused and wondered if it indeed was a werewolf.

Seeing the majestic creature turned into a stuffed trophy made me a little uncomfortable, but not as much as seeing the two men who rose from their chairs to greet me. One I remembered from the other day, my so-called father. The king of Florin. The other young man, about eighteen winters, was a stranger.

"Ah, Rosalie! Come, come. You must meet your younger brother, Aspen."

Brother? Aspen didn't seem inclined to accept me as quickly as his father did. His hair a dirty blond, his nose and jawline were similar enough, but that was where the resemblance ended. He looked nothing like me.

"I don't think that's true, Father. I still think this is some cruel trick they're playing on us. My sister is dead. Mother is dead. Nothing can bring them back, but their deaths can be avenged."

Ah! There's the family resemblance. We both shared the same fiery spirit. I could see it in the stubborn clench of his jaw, the way his nose flared when he disagreed with someone. I had seen the same characteristics in the mirror.

"I'm sure you have questions for us." King Basil came and patted the chair across from him, nearest the fire. I followed directions, scooping the dress out from around my legs to fan out when I sat. He sighed and looked up at a royal portrait of our family, and I stiffened, recognizing me as a small child, sitting on my mother's lap.

I studied her familiar face, my breath catching in my throat. It couldn't be. The hair was the wrong color, but the somber eyes and frail form were the same. Right down to the familiar gold rose pin—the same one Xander said his mother had a fondness for. The hair on the back of my arm rose as I began to put two and two together.

"This can't possibly be my sister." Aspen snorted.

King Basil picked up a book he had tucked in the side of his chair and sent it flying. "Insolent pup! I have every right to strip you of the throne and pass it on to your elder sister."

"You wouldn't dare!" Aspen paled, and the glare he cast me was one of an enemy. "Just because you see a ghost doesn't mean the ghost can rule."

"I have no wish to rule, King Basil. If you remember, I am already married to the prince of Baist."

"Yes, yes, and that is a problem." He sighed and tapped his fingers along the upholstered armrest. "I have spent so many years searching for vengeance on my enemies, Lorelai Eville and Florin. And in my pursuit for justice, I have found the answer to my prayers."

"Forgive me, Your Majesty, but there is much I fear I do not understand."

King Basil's eyes turned glassy as he tried to recall the story. "It is because of one of the deals we made when you were a little babe. Your mother, Queen Hyacinth, became ill after you were born and was unable to conceive a second child, but we needed a son. She sought out Lady Eville and begged her to bequeath Hyacinth her greatest desire. Eville said we would have a son to inherit the crown, if we were willing to give you to her in exchange.

"Your mother refused, but I desperately needed someone

who could lead Florin into battle against Baist if at all possible. I knew no man would follow a woman into battle. It would be suicide. So I pressured your mother. After your brother was born, we knew you wouldn't be with us long."

"You bartered me away for a son," I said, aghast. I glanced over to Aspen, who had moved to stand by the window, refusing to look at me. His knuckles were white as he gripped the sill, his back painfully stiff.

"And we paid dearly for it," King Basil cried out. "I sent you and your mother to Baist for asylum, but you were attacked on the way by magical beasts that killed everyone—including you, we believed. It was Lady Eville's doing. Her revenge because your mother tried to run away with you."

My mind went reeling back into the past as I tried to remember the night I came to the tower. Nothing. I remembered very little and could only assume it was because of a spell Mother Eville had cast over my memories.

"So it was Lady Eville?"

"She did this to you, I swear," he said, holding his hand up.

I was grateful for the chair underneath me, because surely I would have fallen over. My whole life was a lie. I had a family, one that had traded me away for a male heir. Again I was made to feel less than worthy, powerless because of my birth and sex, but no longer. Mother Eville had taught me to be strong, powerful, and sure of myself—but she was the one who'd sent the beasts on the caravan that night.

"You don't know how long I have burned for revenge," King Basil growled. He stood up and knocked over a glass on the end table next to his chair. "I blamed Baist for what happened to your mother and you, but more than that, I blamed Lady Eville. Finding out one of her daughters was married to my enemy was all I needed to know. I would have my revenge twice over."

"And now?" I asked.

"I swear I didn't know you were my daughter. I never even suspected that Lady Eville had taken you that night, or that you were even still alive."

"You should have suspected," I snapped. "You made a bargain." I pointed to Aspen. "His life for mine. You can't seriously have expected a different outcome! Nor should you blame Baist. The whole idea of war is a fool's errand."

"Is it? Every good king wants their kingdom to grow. I wanted a son to rule and for you to marry into the country of Baist. Then if the prince should die, our kingdoms could become one. When you disappeared, I knew my only other option was to take the kingdom by force."

"War doesn't do anything but bring bloodshed and tears."

"War brings prosperity. It thins out the weak, leaving only the strong. It has been that way for generations."

Listening to his mad ravings was giving me a headache. Baist was a large kingdom. Florin was waterlocked; the only way they could expand was westward into the kingdom of Baist. It didn't matter what excuse they came up with, war would be on the horizon.

I shifted in my seat and brought my hands together, the bands clinked loudly.

"If I am your daughter, then will you release me?" I asked, keeping my voice neutral, hiding my anger deep so my emotions wouldn't betray me while studying the king for his reaction. It wasn't good.

He flinched and blinked one too many times before looking away. I could see his throat bob as he swallowed, and sweat glistened across his brow. He was afraid of me.

Rising to my feet, I carefully took a step toward him and kneeled on the rug before his chair. Keeping my eyes lowered, I raised my wrists to him. "Father, please, release me from these painful bonds."

Aspen had come to stand just behind the king, his hand resting on his sword hilt, preparing to cut me down if I harmed my own father. It saddened me that they could not trust me. Even if what they said was true, and I was their own blood, they still feared who I had become. It seemed I had exchanged one palatial prison for another.

"I fear I cannot, daughter. I do not know how deep Lady Eville's influence goes."

"I see," I said stiffly, rising to my feet and backing away. "Then what am I to do here? Live out my days wearing these?"

"Well, we just don't know how much Lady Eville has poisoned you against us."

"She never had to. You're doing a fine job of it yourself." My lips curled and I spun on my heel, leaving them.

"I never dismissed you, daughter," King Basil roared.

Stopping just short of the door, I could see Magda in the hallway waiting for me. Her love was evident, tears filling her eyes. That was what a parent's love should look like, yet after eighteen years apart, I didn't even get so much as a hug.

I sighed deeply. Gathering my courage, I looked back at my father and made my decision. This was not my family. It never would be.

"You're wrong. You dismissed me the day you traded me for an unborn son."

CHAPTER TWENTY-FIVE

I t wasn't until wandering a wing of the castle that I came to a hall that felt familiar. I knew where I was and picked up my pace, turning left at the cherub statue and then right by a bust of the first king of Florin. I slowed and stopped outside of a door, resting my hand on the handle.

"It's all right, Miss Rosalie," Magda spoke up. "You can go in."

"What will I find?" I asked.

"Answers."

Swallowing, I turned the handle and stepped through the door right back to my childhood. It was a nursery fit for a princess. White lace curtains, now yellowed with age, hung above the windows. The four-poster bed was stripped clean of bedding and pillows, and years of dust covered the table and bookshelves, but nothing else had changed.

It was my room.

Crossing the bare floor, I sat upon my old bed and lay on the mattress to stare up at the ceiling. How could I have forgotten this place? The bed, though old, was three times the size of my bed in the cramped tower. There were stacks of children's books on the floor and every available surface. Reaching for the closest one on the table near the headboard, I pulled it toward me and removed the bookmark. It was a tale about an evil fairy who kidnapped children and replaced them with changelings.

I swallowed. Even as a child I had wished to be taken away, or maybe that was every royal child. Thinking back, I couldn't remember their faces, but I remembered the feelings of insignificance, the indifference and the lack of affection, as my parents had saved it all for Aspen.

A tear slid down my cheek and I wiped it away, grateful I didn't grow up here, that for whatever the circumstances, I had grown up at Lady Eville's tower. I may never understand her reasoning for keeping my past from me, or why in the world she would bargain for the life of a firstborn child. She was not one to give explanations but would rather we come to our own conclusions, although she did carry an intense hatred for the seven kingdoms, and that bias did get passed down. But from what I had learned in a short time from the two kingdoms I had now been in, her hatred was justified.

Mother had saved me. I knew that now, and I hoped that if I were ever put in the same situation, I would have the strength to do the same. This should have changed my opinion of my adoptive mother, but instead I understood her better.

I sat up, my dress covered with a layer of dust that I patted off, sending clouds into the air. I sneezed and a female voice said, "Bless you." But I was alone. Magda had not followed me into the room, and the door was closed.

My heart began to beat in excitement as I called out, "Aura?"

"Over here!" she laughed, and I frantically began to search the room for a mirror. It was attached to the wall, and when I pulled the sheet from it, I could barely see her under the layer of dust. Using my dress, I wiped the glass and almost sobbed in relief to see her smiling back at me.

"Oh, I missed you!" I cried out.

"Yes, we've been trying to message you for days. Where have you been?"

"Really? Why did I not—come to think of it, there is a general lack of mirrors in the palace. This is the first room I've found one in."

Aura's brows furrowed when she saw the bonds on my wrist. "Who did that to you?" I didn't have to answer. "No—your father? Grrrr! That makes me so angry. It's a good thing I'm not there right now, or I would show that king of Floof what for. Oh, wait, you're a princess? Of course you are. Ah, and you have a brother."

"Careful, Aura," I tried to soothe her, knowing what could happen when she lost her temper. She could literally bring the whole tower down around her. "I'm fine for now. Just don't tell Mother!" I warned, scared of what she might do if she found out I was back at the kingdom of Florin. But more important, I wasn't sure if I could trust her.

Aura frowned, her eyes cast to the side guiltily. "Why do you want to keep it from her? Oh... I see."

I sighed in relief. In some ways I wanted to confront Mother, but at the same time, I wanted to be able to prove myself to her.

"Okay, I need to get going. I just wanted to see for myself that you were okay."

Tears flooded my eyes at the love I saw in my sister. *This is what family should be.* "Thank you, Aura."

"Oh, one other thing?"

"What?"

"Is your brother handsome?"

"Bye, Aura." I sighed and closed the call.

I replaced the sheet over the mirror and made my way out of the room. Closing the door behind me, I turned and, sure enough, Magda was still there waiting for me—silent as ever, her eyes twinkling with joy.

I headed back to my room, Magda walking close on my heels. I could feel her sympathy, and it only made me grit my teeth.

"There, there, child." Magda patted me on the shoulder. "All will be made right. I guarantee it."

CHAPTER TWENTY-SIX

L ife should have been better here at the palace with my family. Instead, I longed for the days of the kingdom of Baist. At least there I had my magic and glamour to let me move about the palace freely. I had come to enjoy my masquerade as Rose and walking amongst the servants while outsmarting the guards. Here, there were no guards, only Magda and Peder, who took turns following me everywhere, seeing to my needs.

After I had spoken to my sister, I immediately headed for the palace doors to leave. I would head out on my own, hitching rides if I had to, but I would not—*could* not stay here. But once my foot crossed the threshold, my bands began to burn around my skin.

"No!" I cried, stepping back into the entryway and running my fingers along the doorframe. Sure enough, someone had recently added wards across the entrance to keep me from leaving. I traced the divots where someone had enough knowledge to chisel out the symbols into the floor and frame. With the bands on, it kept me from reading the caster's signature, and I couldn't see the glowing power showing they were active. I could try scratching them out, but there would still be a residue, and I could die trying to leave.

Picking up my skirt, I raced to the nearest window and found the same marks etched in the stone on each and every one. A deep dark pit opened up around me, and I felt my world start to slowly close in.

This was worse than the kingdom of Baist. They were prepared for me.

That night I sat at the table alone, eating in silence, with only the clink of my manacles interrupting my dark thoughts. My righteous outburst had not gone unnoticed, and it seemed I was to be punished with solitude. Of course, there were servants, but instead of cowering in fear, they simply ignored me.

As much as my family avoided me, I found myself avoiding them as well. Baist was safe for now. Earlsgaarde had handed over the signed treaty to Tipper, and that should have been the end, but sadly it wasn't so. I had come down the stairs and heard Earlsgaarde and my father discussing in quiet tones in the dining room. Keeping out of sight, I watched through the crack in the door as they pored over a map.

"Your daughter saved the young princess child from my adder."

"Pity, but their queen should have immediately succumbed to the wolfsbane poison. Why didn't she? Why did she survive?"

"I do not know. I even tried to speed the process along by slowly bleeding her out, but her will is strong and I was constantly under watch." The body was Earlsgaarde, but the way he was speaking was wrong.

Then I made the connection. It was Allemar. Or Earlsgaarde was Allemar. The healer had never left the kingdom of Baist. He was trying to slowly take out the royal family. My stomach dropped as they continued with their scheming.

"I wish you would have gotten a drop of the queen's blood.

Then I could have settled the rumors once and for all," King Basil sighed. "My daughter, how is she faring?"

Earlsgaarde became frustrated. "She should have been raised here under my tutelage. She would have been an even greater weapon against Baist than her brother," he whispered. "Though I do fear she won't go along with our plans to take the throne by force. It seems she's grown close to the prince and their family."

"If she can't follow orders, then I have no use for her," King Basil grumbled. "She would be better off dead. In fact, after we take the kingdom of Baist, I want you to see to her demise. Make it look accidental."

"As you wish, Your Majesty," Earlsgaarde said softly. He rolled up the map and turned toward the door. I backed up but wasn't fast enough before the door opened, and I looked into the whiskered face of Earlsgaarde.

"So we meet again, Allemar," I sneered.

Earlsgaarde grinned evilly. "The truth has come out. Although, I'm surprised you didn't notice sooner." He reached under his tunic and pulled a wax string that was threaded around a small finger bone. A bone that probably had at one time belonged to the real emissary of Florin. With a tug he snapped the necklace off and tossed it to the side.

Allemar's body shifted, the white-mustached emissary disappearing. I expected to see the healer with his exotic skin and sharp features, but instead he became a tall man with slicked-back gray hair and a peppered goatee. His fingers were long and boney, his dark eyes hidden under hooded lids and his teeth curled up into a cruel grin.

"You were the one who tried to kill the royal family!"

"If it wasn't for you. I would have succeeded."

The door to the drawing room swung open and King Basil

stood there, not surprised in the least by the sorcerer standing in front of him. "What is going on, Allemar?"

"We have a snoop." Allemar flung me down on the floor in front of the king.

"You're a liar," I accused my father. "You were never going to leave the kingdom of Baist alone."

"Really, Rosalie. I'm very disappointed in you," the king sighed. "I had such high hopes that you would see we're your family. That you would understand your place here."

"My place," I sneered as I pulled myself up to a standing position, "is to stand in opposition right between you and Baist. If you want to get to them, you will have to go through me."

The man who stood before me transformed, his round face turned dark and ugly, his eyebrows narrowed. "No one stands between me and what I want."

"I know. Because you wanted a son and were willing to throw me away."

"It was the best decision I have ever made!" King Basil bellowed.

My voice had gone cold. "I agree. The day I was taken from you was the greatest day of my life. I will gladly sacrifice it if it means keeping you from getting your greedy hands on Baist."

King Basil swung his thick, meaty hand, connecting with my face and knocking me to the ground.

I reached for my power, but the bands burned into my wrists through the bandages, the pain agonizing as I tried to break through the enchantments binding me.

"Do you like them?" Allemar asked capriciously as he leaned over me. "I made them just for you. Let's see who's more powerful now."

He reached for my skull, and white-hot pokers blinded me as my eyes rolled back. Gasping, unable to take a full, deep breath, I could feel unconsciousness coming back.

"Take her from my sight," the king said. "Make sure she never crosses my path again."

"With pleasure." Allemar grinned.

CHAPTER TWENTY-SEVEN

I awoke in a dank, dark cell. From the little light that trickled in through the barred window no larger than a loaf of bread, I estimated that it had to be almost sundown. Sitting up, I pressed my back against the wall and looked out the window.

"Xander," I muttered, hoping he would come but knowing he wouldn't. He had found a way to get rid of me for good.

Tears of frustration burned my eyes, and my heart ached at the betrayal. I had known love for a few hours and now knew heartbreak. This feeling—it was horrible. My chest was empty, like someone had carved out my heart with a dull spoon and filled it with a burning stone.

The agony was unbearable.

But the loneliness was worse.

No one came for me. I was left to rot in the cell with no food or water, but then a heavy rain started, causing rivulets to run in through the window and down my wall. I was able to cup my hands and fill my palms with water to quench my parched throat, at least.

Another full mark came and went, and the rain, once the answer to my prayer, slowly spilled across the floor, soaking the pile of hay that was my bed. A simple spell would have easily kept the water at bay, but each attempt drained me a little more. With the rain came a cold chill, and the shakes followed.

Sleep was my friend, for when I slept, the pain and hunger faded away. When I opened my eyes, I was greeted by the black, beady ones of Gobbersnot. He was alive, and he'd found me! His face was still swollen, and he sported a long cut along his cheek, but otherwise he seemed perfectly normal—for him, at least. He patted my head and then moved to my shackles, trying to gnaw them off, but to no avail. Obviously not wanting to leave my side again, he curled up and placed his head in my lap like a dog. Together we would wait until the end came.

A crevice by the wall slowly filled with water, and with the barest moonlight trickling in, it created a reflection. An idea came then.

Maybe I could call for help.

But I needed blood. Nudging the goblin, I explained what I needed him to do and prayed he would use self-control and not bite a full digit off. If my plan worked, the loss of a finger may be a price I was willing to pay.

Biting my lip, I held out my finger. Gobbersnot opened his mouth, and I stared at those sharp, pointy teeth. They closed around my finger, and I felt the needlelike jabs into my skin. He must have taken it clean off, for the pain hurt so great.

A slight sucking followed, Gobbersnot slurping and licking at my wound. I let him feed as payment for serving, but only a few seconds. I pulled my hand away and sighed in relief to see that all of my fingers were there, though one had a ring of cuts around it and blood trickled down.

I moved to the reflective pool, knowing I must hurry; the moon was still rising, and I would soon lose what little light I had left. It wasn't a deep cut despite the pain of all those teeth, but it would be enough. Holding my finger out, I released three drops into the pool and whispered the incantation to call my sisters.

As soon as the first magical word crossed my lips, the chains burned into my skin and I cried out, but I fought through the pain to finish it. The smell of burnt flesh reached my nose, and I knew I would pass out soon. Collapsing to the ground, I turned my head and hoped one of them could hear me.

"Sisters," I whispered, but I knew it wouldn't be loud enough. They were probably sleeping.

"Sisters! Help me!" I tried again louder, but the shackles absorbed my magic and I was fading fast.

A shadow appeared in the puddle as one of my sisters answered my call, but I couldn't make out who it was. If they looked, all they would see was the roof of my cell.

Please let it be Aura. I dug deep inside myself and tore down the wall I had spent a lifetime building up, for I hadn't the energy to speak or tell anyone what had happened.

"H-Help," I began, but the pain took over and I passed out.

CHAPTER TWENTY-EIGHT

Hours turned into days, and my mind struggled with what had transpired. Did my sisters get my message? Was I going to spend the rest of my remaining days in the pit?

No food came other than what Gobbersnot had been able to pilfer for me. Most of the time, what he came back with was raw and dead animals, my stomach churning at the sight. Sometimes he would find an apple or slice of bread, but then he disappeared and didn't come back, and I worried he had abandoned me, or he was dead. Water was available when I had the energy to drink from the puddle in the corner, but it hadn't rained in days, and my supply was slowing drying up. The hunger pains had already stopped, signaling that my time would be limited.

What good was my gift, my powers when I hadn't been able to save anyone, least of all me? I was going to die here. There wasn't any doubt.

But I didn't want to go down without a fight.

A door creaked open, and steps sounded from down the hall. Allemar appeared outside the cell after a moment. "Here you are. I've been looking for you." He smiled widely, showing many of his back molars, but his face looked pained, awkward, and his enthusiasm didn't match his persona.

Sprawled out along the cold floor, I tried to focus on him, but he wavered in and out like a spyglass adjusting. I knew those signs, or knew how to look for them.

"Eden?" I murmured. "Is it really you?"

The glamour faded and my glorious sister Eden kneeled beside me, reaching between the bars to grasp my cold hand. "Yes, I've come for you."

My body began to spasm—no, not spasms but great heaving sobs. "The b-bands." I raised my wrists, and she looked aghast.

"What is this?"

"Allemar, he did this. Beware of Allemar."

"Don't worry, Rosalie. We will get him, and they will pay for what they've done to you. They will all pay." Her normally sweet voice was hard like steel; her eyes even had a glint of danger about them.

Backing up, Eden raised her hands to the door, and she began to work out the enchantment around the cell. As delirious and tired as I was, I panicked as she began to mumble her thoughts on the counterspell.

"No, Lochni will blow us to smithereens. Use Lochen," I corrected

Eden shook her head. "Yes, that's right. Sorry." She quickly corrected her formula, and with a piece of chalk began to draw symbols over the ground. Eden still needed to visually see her spells; she couldn't imagine them in the air and hold them like me.

Though she was the weakest when it came to spells and would frequently get them mixed up and end up entangled in a mess, she was still the one who I would have chosen to come. No one could beat Eden when it came to glamour, and when sneaking into a castle, she was the best choice.

"How's it look?" she asked nervously, tucking a stray

blonde hair behind her ear. Even now, during an escape, she needed my help.

Pulling myself up to a kneeling position, I took her piece of chalk and corrected one letter. "It will do," I encouraged.

She gave me a grin as I moved to the back of the cell; my legs wobbled underneath me, and I clutched the stone wall for support. I didn't look, just turned my head as she muttered the spell and the cell door blasted inward. Wind and debris hit me, and I looked to my right and saw part of the door had shattered and was now embedded into the stone two inches from my face.

"Oops!" Eden gasped, and I gave her a disapproving look.

"What good is it to kill me during the rescue?" I chastised. "Remember, visualize, control, and release."

"Yes, Rosalie. I'll do better next time I sneak into a palace and break you out of prison," Eden said sarcastically, but her eyes were twinkling, betraying her jubilant emotions. She came to me and wrapped my arm around her shoulder, then helped me out of the cell.

I sighed. "You better." Turning, I pulled her into a hug and cried.

"Hey, hey." She patted my back and ran her hand down my hair. "You've taken care of us for so long. Now it's my turn to take care of you." Eden's hand glowed as she touched my forehead. My whole body tingled with warmth as she healed my smaller wounds. The anti-magic bands prevented her from healing my wrists, so she focused on other areas. I could feel my strength slowly returning and with it—my vengeance.

I was reluctant to let her go but knew we needed to get moving. The blast probably alerted the guards. "That's enough, Eden. Save your power. This battle is far from over."

"What's that?" Eden stepped back, clearly startled, and looked down at the goblin who had joined our group hug. His green arm had wrapped around her knee. Eden laughed. "You have a redcap as a familiar? How did you manage that?"

Looking down from above at Gobbersnot's bald head, I saw what Eden had immediately noticed—a faint red stain along his skull. Redcaps were known for soaking their hat in the blood of their enemies and wearing it. Well, mine must have been a little defective, for he liked to wear women's clothes and soak himself in perfume. To each his own.

With each step up the stone stairs, my calves and leg muscles screamed. I must have been down here longer than I thought, but each searing, painful step only goaded me further. My anger built, fueling me as we came to a trapdoor.

Eden waited, her ear pressed close as she listened. When all was quiet, she lifted the trapdoor and crawled through before reaching down to assist me. When I followed her out into the round tower, she carefully closed the trapdoor in the black-stained floor.

"Where are we?" I asked.

Eden held her finger to her lips and whispered, "We're in the sorcerer's rooms. That's why it took me so long to find you. I spent days searching the palace."

"Days?" I said in surprise.

"Mmm," she murmured. "I've been working as a servant in the kitchen, a maid, and a soldier. Finally it was a young man in robes who led me here."

Stepping back, I could see the dark-stained floor and the symbols painted in white, the sacrificial symbols for power. My heart raced in horror as I saw the extra chains strategically placed around the symbol on the floor. The reason for the dark color was because the floor was stained with blood. Allemar was supplementing his power with human lives, and blood was the key. I felt sick to my stomach at the death weighing heavily in the room, being very careful to not touch any of the dried blood for I feared I would go crazy with their deaths. It must have been hundreds, or thousands.

My mouth filled with bile, and I dared not share my discovery with Eden. She was too pure to deal with the darkness that was Allemar.

A quick glance around the room showed shelves of books, plus jars of dried bat wings, chicken feet, and what looked like decanters of blood. All ingredients for the dark arts. I shivered, then rushed over to look among the paperwork and books, searching for the spell to release my bonds. "Help me, Eden."

The two of us ruffled through his papers and pulled every book off his shelf, looking for hidden compartments or anything that seemed like a spell. Gobbersnot also helped—running through the shelves, he opened each bottle and ate all of the contents, even the bat wings and slugs.

"I'm not finding anything," Eden cried out.

Discouragement poured down on me, and I knew the answer couldn't be found here.

"You need the counterspell," a dry voice said from above.

We turned toward the stairs, and who should be coming down from the upper level but my brother, wearing blue apprentice robes. Which meant he hadn't fully completed his studies. The more levels he passed, the darker the robes he could wear. It also signaled his power level, and I knew without a doubt that I was stronger than him. My mother didn't believe in the dark arts, despite what the world viewed us as, but we knew among ourselves where we stood.

"Give it to me, Aspen," I said, moving away from Eden to the center of the room. If it came down to a physical fight, I was stronger than my sister, though I wasn't sure if I could hold him off for long.

"No," he said smugly, moving to stand a few feet in front of me. He had also gained his height from our father, and though he was younger, he was still a few inches taller than me. I decided to test my theory and took a confident step toward him, watching as he subconsciously backed up.

I grinned. He was scared of me, which I could use to my advantage.

"Why not?" I taunted. "Because otherwise you wouldn't be stronger than me. You can only beat me if my powers are bound."

"That's not true!"

"It is. I'm more powerful than your master. He couldn't even kill the queen or princess of Baist. Two measly women. No, wait." I pointed to myself. "Make that three."

"You're wrong. Allemar is one of the most powerful sorcerers in the known kingdoms. He said I could be just as strong or even surpass him one day, even you."

"If that's true, then why hide behind his magic? Remove my bonds and show me what you've learned, little brother. Show me how powerful you really are."

The gauntlet was thrown; there was nothing else I could do but hope he took the bait.

He watched me warily. Based on my bare feet and my soiled and torn dress—my hair probably didn't fare much better —if ever I looked like I was downtrodden and weak, it was now.

He swore under his breath and held up his hands. Silently, his fingers began to weave in the air, what I assumed was the counterspell, and my nimble eyes followed it like a hawk, memorizing it. Immediately the manacles fell from my wrists, and my arms felt like they were floating without the weights. Once the air hit my wounds, I sucked in my breath and held it from the ache.

I could hear my mother's voice.

"Use it, Rosalie. Use the pain."

And I did.

Aspen's mouth worked, and like Eden, I could see him begin to form a spell. He was no match for me.

In a weakened state, I was still a mighty force to be reckoned with, and I didn't give Aspen a chance to fight me. With a flick of my wrist, I flung him across the room into the workbench, knocking him out cold.

"Whoa!" Eden squeaked. "Remind me never to get on your bad side."

"Let's go!" I snapped, angered at how quickly I had defeated my brother. It shouldn't have been this easy. It should never have come to this.

We left Allemar's workroom and came into a long hall. His rooms were actually an old armory tower and were quite a distance from the main palace living quarters. Eden turned, grabbing my sleeve and trying to lead me out the side door and to freedom. Gobbersnot waddled out after us, holding a bag filled with what I could only assume were more dead things.

"No." I shrugged her off. "I'm not finished."

"Rosalie, you are in no shape to fight. Let's go now. Fight another day."

"Not until I bring the kingdom of Florin to its knees," I vowed. My words held power, and I could feel the powers of the moon and stars listening in, hearing my plea.

"Uh-oh," Eden murmured. "The ice queen is back."

"And she's livid," I seethed.

Storming into the throne room, I expected to confront the king, but the room was empty. So was the study. In fact, very few people or servants were around, and the ones I did find were quickly packing their belongings.

"What's going on?" Eden asked, grabbing a maid by her elbow.

"They're here," she said, fear filling her voice, but didn't elaborate.

"Who is?" I questioned, but the servant grabbed her bundle of clothes and ran.

A retinue of guards jogged past us in full armor, swords drawn, and headed out into the courtyard. As I searched the palace for the king, we continued to run across soldiers preparing for war and servants preparing to flee.

"He's not here," I said once I'd searched the king's personal study off his suite.

"Rosalie," Eden called, waving me over to the window.

I followed and could see the great mass of soldiers lining up in the courtyard two stories below us. Archers were in place along the wall, waiting. Not once in our search did I even think to look outside.

But that wasn't where Eden was pointing. She directed my gaze out past the palace walls to the hills beyond.

The field was covered with blue specks of moving flowers— no, not flowers. Soldiers in blue uniforms marching across the field. It was Baist!

"What are they doing here?" I muttered, but my heart soared. If the army was here, that meant Xander was probably down on that field as well. Had he come for me?

Then I remembered what he'd said. Baist wasn't as large a kingdom as Florin; their armies had nowhere near the strength or the magical artillery at their disposal.

"No!" I gasped when I realized what this could mean. They would be slaughtered.

Running out of the king's room, I stumbled down the stairs, Eden on my heels as we barged out the front doors and into the midst of chaos. As frenzied as the inside of the palace was, this was worse. How had I not heard the trumpets blaring, the troop leaders shouting orders, and the chainmail as soldiers ran to prepare for war? I had become tunnel-visioned in my desperation for justice.

Out of the corner of my eye, I saw a group of servants carrying large potato sacks between two outbuildings; from their fearful glances at one another, I knew they were escaping. *They must know of a hidden exit.* Motioning to Eden that we follow, we used glamour on our clothes and quickly blended into the mass of servants.

I was right; they headed down into a cellar and rolled a keg away from the wall to reveal a hidden tunnel. One of the girls held out a torch to the first woman and she ran ahead, lighting the way for the others to follow. I grabbed Eden's hand and we followed the lead girl through a twisting cave. Just when I thought there wouldn't be an end, I saw daylight.

The servant girl stopped at the door and tried to push it open, but it wouldn't budge.

"It's locked from the outside!" she cried out fearfully.

"Eden." I motioned for my sister to step forward.

"*Lochen.*" The lock fell off, and we pushed on the door, but it was still latched. Furious at another stumbling block in my escape, I raised my hands and blasted the door right off the hinges.

"Stars above!" Eden whispered at the power I carelessly displayed, but I didn't have time to dillydally; people I cared about could very well be hurt if I didn't get going.

The tunnel dumped us into a small field west of the palace near the woods. The rest of the group ran for the tree line while I turned to Eden. "Please find Prince Xander. Bring him through the tunnels and meet me in the throne room."

"Rosalie," Eden warned as I struggled up the hill. "Dear sister, you're not in any shape to fight."

"And neither is Baist."

Cresting the summit of the hill, I froze and my heart plummeted at the sheer mass of Florin's army, easily five times that of Baist. From the palace window, they were sloped downward, hiding their numbers, but from my position I could see it would be hopeless. It looked like Baist's army would be swallowed in a sea of red.

"You are the only one I trust. Go, hurry!" I pushed Eden forward. "I believe in you." It was a dangerous mission I was asking of her, but I knew she could use her magic to protect her and make it across the field toward Prince Xander.

Retracing my steps, I made it back to the hidden tunnel. I had to use mage light to light my way until I was back in the courtyard.

Where are you, Allemar? He was the one I needed to find, the one I needed to get answers from, even if it meant I would have to torture him.

As I searched the halls, I could feel the subtle underlay of magic converging on one wall.

Here. There's something hidden here.

Running my palms up the wall, I closed my eyes and felt the waves of magic—glamour, to be exact. Trusting my instincts, I reached forward, and even though I only saw a wall, I brought my hand down until my fingertips brushed the cold handle of a door.

I smiled. *You will not be able to hide from me for long.*

Turning the handle, I pulled the door open. Before I could focus my eyes and look inside, I was thrust into the darkness from behind. Falling, I tried to brace myself, but the door closed, cutting out the light just as I landed on someone.

"Sorr—" I began but stopped when my head fell back, my mouth open as I watched King Basil loom over me. He reached for my heart, his finger touching my chest over my paisley vest.

"What are you doing, my liege!" My voice was deeper, from years and age. My chest constricted and my heart beat picked up, racing uncontrollably as a pressure squeezed it. The king wavered before my eyes, the pressure slowly building in my chest until it burst and the pain stopped.

Trapped in the closet, so close to the body, I relived Peder's death over and over, each time worse than the last.

The vision was debilitating, and I collapsed onto the ground. Peder's death wasn't swift, and I was paralyzed as he struggled to breathe, his lungs filling with blood, slowly suffocating him. It was worse than death, being this close yet unable to escape the confines of the cupboard and the vision.

It could very well be the end of me, if it weren't for Magda, who opened the door and crouched next to me.

Magda was surrounded by light, a halo illuminating her as she pulled me from the confines of the cupboard. Her fingers dug into my shoulders, her eyes frantic and wild.

I was no longer touching the body, so Peder's death vision had ceased, and I was able to get my wits about me and sit up. Magda looked behind me into the closet, and I turned and saw Peder's crumpled body. "What did you see?" she asked, her face one of desperation.

"What do you mean?" I asked. She couldn't possibly understand my gifts.

"Peder, how did he die?" She gripped my shoulders, turning me to look at her, her eyes glassy with tears. "I know you can see their deaths, see how they died." Her bottom lip quivered, her shoulders shaking.

"You did it as a child with our son, Renard. Don't you remember? I had tucked you into bed myself and gone to check on Renard, but he had gone missing. We searched all through the night, but to no avail. The next morning I found you shivering in bed, drenched and covered in mud, crying out that Renard was sleeping under the dock."

I shuddered but couldn't remember any of this. But if she remembered, it had to be true. "I'm sorry."

"No!" she admonished. "You told me where he was, even who he was with, and we were able to question the other children. We learned it was an accident, that he had fallen off the dock hit his head and drowned.

"Now tell me, Rosalie," Magda cried out in almost hysterics, tears pooling down her face. "Who killed my Peder? I know you can. Just tell me, please." She was becoming hysterical, unhinged, and I knew then that she was the one who had pushed me into the cupboard.

"You've known all along what I can do."

"Like mother, like daughter." Her eyes wild, she couldn't stop staring at the still form of her husband lying in the cupboard. "I told your mother what you had done. She told me of her blood curse and how she has to take small doses of wolfsbane to keep from traveling and answering the call of the dying. But over time, the body will build up an immunity. It was a secret we had to hide from your father." She brought her hands to her mouth and poured out her heart. "I've done nothing other than what His Majesty has asked all these years. Have served loyally. I don't understand how this could happen to my husband. Now tell me who did this to him!" she screamed at me.

"I don't know," I said, pulling away from her. Her fingernails left deep red scratches on my arm.

"Yes, you do, but you won't tell me," she wailed and flung herself on the floor. "Please, I need answers."

Calmly, I closed the cupboard. Once the latch clicked, the glamour was back in place. How had she known it was there when I had almost missed it? What other secrets was she hiding?

"I did see who murdered Peder, but what I see is not always the truth. You have to believe me on that. But I will make sure they pay."

Once the door of the hidden cupboard had closed and she could no longer see Peder's lifeless form, Magda had become still. Now she moved away, as if she had forgotten what secrets were held within and her own hysterics that had overcome her only moments before.

"Peder? Have you seen Peder? And Renard hasn't come home for dinner, and I made his favorite pork pie." Magda smiled calmly and turned, going down the hallway in search of her dead husband and son.

My heart was breaking in two, her husband's death having destroyed her. The woman had taken care of me for years, and all she had to show for it was the loss of her loved ones—Renard, then me, and now Peder.

I stormed into the throne room and decided it was time for him to know I was done playing hide-and-seek. Wind picked up around me, moving the tapestries on the wall and making the torches flicker as I sent the command out.

Come. I am here.

I waited for the reply.

A few moments passed, and then my father came out from behind the golden throne and sat down on the red cushioned chair.

We stared at each other from across the hall. Even though he wore the face of my father, I knew it was a lie. It was a mask he was preparing to don permanently.

It was true. I did see who had killed Magda's husband, and the reason behind his sudden and unreasonable death.

"The face does not suit you. In fact, it ages you quite a bit."

The king disregarded my taunt. "It suits me just fine, and I don't have any plan of giving it up. Not yet anyway."

"It is not your throne," I hissed.

"Who's to say otherwise?" the king said calmly as he

gestured to the empty room. "The personal servants, the royal guard, the staff?"

"All—"

"Dead," he sneered. "Their sacrifice will not go in vain, and I will attain new ones."

"Why?" I asked.

"Why not? I was bored. The king was easily manipulated, greedy in his quest for land, blind to his dwindling staff and troops, all who died when they questioned me. Now I will finish what I started."

"What is that?"

"Revenge on the kingdoms."

"Get in line," I snapped.

"Oh, that's right. Your mother has her own agenda as well. Tell her I send greetings. She'll remember me. They all do. We could pool our resources together and enact vengeance at once."

"I don't think so," I snarled. How dare he pretend to know our story. He was a fool. Just another power-hungry mage who had meddled in too many lives and must be stopped.

"King Basil of Florin," a masculine voice called out, and I turned to see Xander in full armor being escorted into the throne room by Eden. "I've come to you with my own demands. For years you've threatened us with war over the death of your wife. Well, now I have brought the war to you."

My heart fluttered at the sight of him, drinking him in. He seemed taller in his armor, dangerous, his blue ceremonial robe flowing out along the floor behind him. But his eyes had shadows under them, and I wondered if he had been sleeping well.

Xander's hand rested on his blade, his eyes locked on mine. I could see the question hiding there, and the hurt, but I looked away. He may easily be able to forget the betrayal but not me. I was the one imprisoned and brought here in a cage.

"How did you get past my troops?" King Basil roared.

Xander smirked. "I walked right through the front gates."

"Impossible. The guards were—" His eyes fell on my sister, then back to me and sneered. "Oh, I see. Another one? Two of Eville's daughters here?"

Eden clasped her hands demurely in front of her and smiled.

"Well, then it will hurt Lorelai all the more when she hears the news that I've killed two of her brats."

"King Basil—" Xander started.

"That's not the king," I cut in. "It's Allemar. He was the one who tried to poison your mother with wolfsbane and kill your sister with the adder. He's nothing more than an imposter."

Eden inhaled in awe. "To do that, he would need to have a personal belonging."

I closed my eyes and thought back to Peder's death vision, how Allemar was leaning over the real king, working away at something on his hand.

"He did. He took my father's ring," I answered.

"Then where's the real king?" Xander asked.

"Dead. You'll find his body hidden under the floor of the cupboard where Peder's body is. All because Peder saw you shift into the king, didn't he?" I directed the question to the sorcerer.

"He always was a nosy servant. He should have been one of the first I sacrificed instead of the last, but I needed their life energy to supplement my power as I traveled through that magic-barren land of Baist."

"And why my father?" I hissed.

Allemar sighed. "Because the puppet wanted to be his own

master. We can't have that now, can we? I needed to cut his strings."

"Hard to make a king go to war over the loss of his wife and child if we're both alive still," I said.

Xander looked to me, his amber eyes sparkling less. "You knew, didn't you?"

"I knew the night I healed Queen Anya that she was hiding her real identity. I just didn't know from whom or why until now."

"If you knew, then why didn't you say anything to me?" he cried out. "I have been holding on to this secret for years, the burden of keeping our countries from war."

"Hello? Newcomer here. What secret?" Eden asked.

Queen Anya walked into the room on the arm of King Gerald, her face full and glowing, her skin radiant.

"That I am the long-lost queen of Florin," she called out loudly. "Hello, Allemar." She looked right into the sorcerer's eyes as she called him out. "I'm surprised I didn't recognize your stench from the moment you entered the kingdom. But again, you never show your true face to anyone, do you?"

"We meet again, Queen Hyacinth. What, do you not approve of the form of your old husband? How about this one." Allemar grinned down at us from a different physical body, one I had never seen before. Gone was his beard, his hair was a golden blond, skin tan, and he almost sparkled like a god.

"And still alive, no matter how many times you have tried to kill me," she growled, her back stiffening, her face a mask of hatred.

A moment of pride ran through me, and I understood more about myself. I was right when I smelled the wolfsbane in her blood and identified the blood curse, but I didn't know what it was until now. She was my mother and was cursed with the death seeker gift, so, like me, she took small amounts of wolfs-bane to keep from traveling during our dreams.

Xander growled, but his stepmother stepped up in challenge.

"No more, Allemar," Anya yelled. "You've had your claws dug into Florin for years. Now it's time to feel mine." Her hands sparked with power, but she was untrained. Anya sent a bolt of power directly at Allemar, but he deflected it easily, like swatting away a gnat.

"How pitiful." He chuckled, then waved his hand, tossing her into the golden thrones. I heard a sickening crack, and she cried out and fell across the red cushions her body still. A wail of grief came from King Gerald, who rushed to her side and cradled his beloved queen. Her face wasn't shining, and a trickle of blood came from her mouth. She looked to be sleeping, but I feared the worst.

"So long, Queen Hyacinth!" Allemar taunted as Aspen walked past.

"Wait, Mother's here?" Aspen yelled. "She's alive?"

Allemar's cackled and pointed to her still form. "Not for long." He beckoned with his finger, and a lone man came from behind the curtain. His hair was gone on one side of his head, and his body had been burned, but there was no mistaking his stride and confident smirk.

It was Gaven, the burned remains of the enchanted brack-enbeast skin draped over one shoulder.

"Kill them," Allemar commanded Gaven, who took a wary glance at Xander and the queen, "and I will give you an even greater predator fur to hunt with."

"With pleasure," he said firmly.

Gaven's body contorted as he moved forward, pulling his cloak over his head as he shifted. With the crack of his bones breaking and reshifting, and his teeth popping out of his gums, he howled in pain. His fur only grew in patches along his skin, and only one horn sprouted from his malformed head. Saliva dripped from the deformed brackenbeast's lips as it stepped down the stairs to the marble floor.

He turned and roared at Xander. The beast's thick lips pulled back, revealing yellow teeth over black gums. He snarled and took a step toward King Gerald, raking his claws along the wall, leaving deep furrows.

"Father, go!" Xander screamed, his body stretching, the armor plates falling from his broad shoulders. I couldn't look away as my amber-eyed prince turned into a copper- and gray-furred werewolf. His coat rippled as he lunged, but when the brackenbeast swung, Xander torqued his body midair, dodging the claws and latching his strong jaws onto the beast's wrist. I heard the bones snap, and Gaven howled in fury. His left hand gouged, clawed, and ripped at Xander's wolf's head as he tried to dislodge the jaw.

King Gerald joined the fight then, his mighty arms lifting his sword over his head, yelling as he brought it down straight toward the beast's. Red-rimmed eyes turned and the bracken-beast grabbed the sword with his claw midair, the blade not even piercing his skin.

"What the—" King Gerald cried out, but he was flung backward as the beast swung Xander's wolf into him, trying to dislodge the steel trap of teeth that still gripped his arm.

Xander held on for dear life; if he let go, it was over. His back paws came up and dug at the brackenbeast's stomach, leaving bloody scratches all along his torso.

I smelled the magic before I saw it, and so did Eden. We turned and searched the room, finding Aspen standing over the still form of his mother, his hands weaving a spell in the air. Eden and I shared the same horrified look. He was trying to summon a magical beast, one only the strongest of magic users could, and I knew he didn't have the talent nor strength.

"No, Aspen," I warned, but it was too late. He hadn't time for a full conjure, and a vortex opened up in the sky above Gaven and Xander. Lightning spilled out of the hole, singeing the floor and columns and catching the curtains on fire.

"Do something, Rosalie." Eden pushed me forward. "You're the only one strong enough."

With the brackenbeast distracted and Aspen having opened a portal in an attempt to pull something through, I knew I needed to end this, but I couldn't. I felt the death vision pull, and I couldn't fight it.

"R-Rosalie." My mother coughed, and I closed my eyes, letting myself be pulled through the air to appear next to her. When I opened my eyes, I could still see myself standing across the room near Eden, frozen in time. But this time I was awake, next to my mother, kneeling by her side and holding her hand as her blood soaked into my dress.

"My darling," she whispered, and everything around us stilled until only she was there as she shared her death vision with me. "I'm sorry I didn't recognize you, for I truly thought you were dead. Allemar wanted to use you, and your father didn't love you and bartered you away. I was selfish and foolish and tried to run away with you. I'm sorry I was robbed of my time with you. If I knew you were still alive, I would never have given up looking. I even planted an imperial rosebush in remembrance of you. My darling Rose."

I reached for her to try and heal her, but my hands passed through.

"It's no use," she whispered. "I'm already too far gone. You are here to hear my truth and not interfere. Please, take care of him."

"Who?" I asked.

"Your brother, Aspen. It was my fault. I abandoned him to Allemar and your father's machinations. He didn't have anyone who truly loved him. And your half sister, Ameline, will need you after I'm gone. And Xander, he will need your love and strength if he is to rule, for I believe he will bring his kingdom into the future. Accept what others cannot, if you would but show him the way. I love you, dear daughter. I always have and always will."

She released a soft sigh, and I knew she had passed on. There was a loud sucking, and I moved through the air and once again was in my own body, my hands covered with Anya's blood. This was the first time I had stayed awake to speak with the departed, and it was heartbreaking. This was my gift, and one I vowed to learn to use to help others.

With blood on my hands and time moving at a normal speed again, I came to my senses. I looked up and saw Xander's wolf on the ground, his mouth still clamped around the brackenbeast's arm.

"Stop!" I roared, using magic to amplify my voice. Gaven in his beast form paused his killing blow and looked over at me, and I shuddered when I could almost hear his thoughts. Gaven's blood was coursing with excitement because he held Xander's life in his hands. Even now, he had access to Xander's throat, showing me how he could rip it out so easily.

"This has gone on long enough. I will stop you," I declared.

A thunderous roar came from above, and we all looked up, distracted by the sound. *A daemon—Aspen tried to summon a daemon?* My blood went cold. *Where in the kingdoms did he open this portal, and how did he even learn of such beasts?*

Allemar's laugh echoed through the room. He seemed to be enjoying the magical battle between siblings and beasts. I could tell he didn't think any of Eville's daughters were strong enough to stop them.

275

"Rosalie!" Eden called out. I could not hesitate a second time. Lorelai was right—feelings made one weak. There could be no mercy.

Let go! I sent the command to Xander, but he growled in response as he fought my compulsion. They had fallen to the floor, Xander trapped beneath the larger beast, who was taking great pleasure in slowly ripping him to shreds.

A whine followed, and I could feel his pain as my own.

Let go, my love. You've done enough. I'll handle it from here.

I could see Xander's hesitation. If he released his hold, he would be pinned and even more vulnerable, but Xander's wolf did as I'd said, and a triumphant snarl came from the bracken-beast. Xander whined, his tongue hanging out of his mouth as he watched the beast go for his throat.

Having struggled to access power in a magic-barren land had fine-tuned my abilities. I had learned to pull water from a rock. Now close to a ley line and without the bands holding me back, magic rushed to me willingly, flowing like a mighty ocean. With a flick of my wrist, I slammed Gaven against the wall, freeing Xander.

I didn't hesitate this time when I called forth the magic. "*Incendium!*" I cried out, sending not a fire but an incinerating spell, the same one I had used on the adder. I didn't release, didn't look away or flinch, until the brackenbeast was nothing more than a large pile of ash.

I waited for the shift and the pull of the world to reject me for my merciless killing. I had upset the balance and killed unnecessarily. There would be repercussions. But when I didn't feel the turmoil, I wondered if I had finally crossed a line and feared for my soul.

"Eden, stop Aspen," I ordered.

She used a blast of wind and sent Aspen flying into a wall, causing him to black out. Once he lost his concentration, the summoning portal began to close, but it was too slow. A dark being made of burning embers could be seen approaching the portal.

Allemar stood up, and I knew this was going to be a battle between the two of us. I wasn't sure if I would survive it.

"Eden, I need a snare," I whispered so only she could hear.

"What?" She began to panic, eyes as wide as saucers. "No, no, no. Please, not me."

"Do it!" I demanded.

Eden patted her dress, reaching inside her pocket for a piece of chalk. She quickly weaved an invisibility spell around her, then shimmered as she disappeared. It wasn't a strong spell, because I could see her fading in and out as she began to sketch sigils on the floor in front of the portal, but I hoped it would be enough.

Allemar sent a bolt of lightning toward me, but with a wave of my hand, I reversed it and shot it right back at him. He ducked, and the lightning incinerated the top of the golden throne.

"Impressive," he said. "Just think how powerful you would have been if I trained you instead of your mother."

Xander tried to come to my aid, but with a shake of my head, I stopped him in his tracks. He looked angry, but I didn't have time for his interference. He disobeyed and moved to strike, but I quickly cast a holding spell and forced his boots to stick to the marble.

As I moved, I passed a candelabra and waved my arms, compelling the flame to grow like a dragon and attack Allemar from behind. He turned and smothered the fiery dragon until nothing but a puff of smoke remained.

I cast my eyes to the symbols and saw that, in her haste, Eden had drawn the wrong character for snare and instead wrote "hare." A roar came from the portal, and I could smell the sulfur from the daemon as it approached. Keeping my teeth together, I gritted out the correction and attacked Allemar again, hoping to distract him from Eden's work. I could see her invisibility spell was wavering.

"This is child's play." Allemar yawned, and I circled the room, putting him closer to Eden and in front of the portal. "I would have thought this would be more of a challenge. I'm bored. Let's end this, shall we? What the—"

He'd noticed the waning invisibility spell and saw Eden just as she finished the snare and crawled away.

Using the distraction, I blasted him backward. He fought the attack as his feet crossed into the spelled circle, but when he tried to move, he was trapped inside.

"Oh, this is more like it!" He laughed and looked down at the trap. "This is what I expected from a daughter of Eville." His face turned critical as he took in the work. "Although, if you wanted to hold me longer, you shouldn't have used this character." He pointed to her mistake.

"Oh, come on!" Eden whined as even her enemy began to criticize her spells.

"It won't hold me forever." Allemar grinned evilly.

"I don't need forever. Just a few seconds," I said. Closing my eyes, I quickly weaved the same spell my brother had used, but backward, activating the spell to bind his powers, similar to what he had done to me with the enchanted shackles. He tried to send a spell my way, but nothing happened. He was powerless.

Sending a blast of power at him, I pushed him through the portal to the other side into who knew where. Gritting my teeth, I sent all of my energy into it, envisioning a thread of light weaving stitches back and forth over the opening and pulling the portal closed, but I didn't think it would be enough.

The smell of sulfur and smoke billowed out, and I heard

the groan of the daemon as it approached the portal opening. Eden came and placed her hand over mine, and I felt a surge of strength. Another hand touched mine, and I looked over and saw Anya's ghost, her face pale, shining pure. She whispered, "You can do it."

I could. I had to.

Xander came up from behind me—his boots abandoned and still stuck to the floor across the room—and wrapped his arms around me. "I believe in you," he told me.

I would do this. I had people I loved who needed my protection. They pooled their magic into mine, and I channeled it, watching as the blue color of my sister's magic weaved into my red one. My mother's was white, and even Xander had a faint line of power. Together they strengthened my own.

"Ahhhhhhh!" I screamed as I pulled on the layers of power I had weaved over the opening. Allemar rushed toward the closing portal to escape the grasp of the daemon, his face a mask of hatred, his hands glowing purple with dark magic. His spell broke through the portal just as it closed, hitting me square in the chest.

I was blasted backward and crashed into the stone steps. All I remembered was the pain that racked my ribs and the burning sensation that ran up my arm and face. I coughed and blood splattered the white marble floor.

Eden's face hovered over mine, tears streaming down her face, her hands glowing with power as she tried to heal the damage that I believed was inescapable. I knew what was happening, had seen it one too many times before.

I was dying.

Xander was there, pulling me close, his mouth moving, but I heard nothing as he shifted in and out of focus, my own death vision coming to an end.

CHAPTER TWENTY-NINE

V oices murmured softly like the crashing of ocean waves,
slowly bringing me out of my slumber. Light streamed in
through the window, warming my eyelids; the scent of lavender
soothed my battered soul. My eyes flickered open as I saw the
bundle of dried lavender lying by my head, and I knew there
would be another bundle tucked under my pillow, with probably a satchel of other herbs under my mattress. Eden was
reading out loud, and Meri was splayed across the bottom of my
bed. I was home. In the tower.

"The stars have blessed us with your return," Eden whispered when she noticed I had awoken. She leaned forward and
brushed a strand of hair out of my face. "We feared we had lost
you." She tried not to look, but I saw her quick glance down to
my hands and the anguish she was hiding there.

I looked down, finding my hands braced with splints and
wrapped in gauze. I felt like a toy doll, unable to move. Sighing,
I lay back down on the pillow, sore that something as strenuous
as lifting my head had exhausted me.

"What happened?" My voice was hoarse from disuse.

"You've been asleep for a very long time," Eden said.
"Days."

"You did what you had to do," Mother Eville added from

the stairwell as she came to sit next to my bed and patted my arm.

"You knew," I accused her. "You knew all along who I was, who Xander and Queen Anya really were."

"Yes, I knew. For I was the one who brewed the potion to help Queen Anya—I mean your mother, Hyacinth, conceive a son. You were only four when I met you and saw your affinity for magic. You wouldn't remember me, but I remembered you. You in your room on the rug, turning the pages of books with only your mind. Oh, how it terrified your mother. She feared Allemar would use you for evil. It was her idea that I bargain your life for the son, that I take you and raise you as my own."

I played with a string on my quilt as I pondered the enormity of what she was saying. It was the opposite of what my father had told me.

"The night your brother was born. I came and stole you away as promised. Your mother, weakened, tried to escape through the mountain pass into Baist, and it just so happened that King Gerald and his young son were hunting a werewolf that was terrorizing the town of Celia. As they were coming out of the pass, the very wolf they were hunting attacked them. Young Xander was mortally wounded. Your mother with her death seeker gift was pulled to them as he lay dying, and she tried to help them.

"Luck would have it that I stumbled upon them, the dying prince, the distraught runaway queen, and the panicked king. Fates were smiling down on me that night. You were fast asleep, so I glamoured you to look like a bundle of sticks on my back, and then I kneeled beside the prince and bargained for his life and your future. Your mother saw me without you and fainted, thinking I had eaten or fed her daughter to the were-wolf itself." Mother Eville chuckled in glee.

I frowned, putting myself in the distraught queen's shoes.

What would I have thought to see the woman who had stolen my child hours later childless? I probably would have thought the same thing and hated her for it.

Mother Eville sighed and tapped her hand against her thigh, looking at me as she continued her tale. "I saved young Prince Xander's life, but there was nothing I could do against the werewolf's bite, for he was too far gone. King Gerald has never forgiven me for that. He refuses to believe the beast he was hunting was anything more than a normal wolf, that it was I who placed the monstrous curse on him." She looked out the window, her eyes taking on a shine, and I briefly wondered if she was tearing up. "As for your mother, it did not take long for the king to fall in love with his secret runaway. She dyed her hair, married the king, and together they had Ameline, who is your half sister."

"I never suspected she was my real mother," I said.

"Nor should you have! That woman fainted when she learned her stepson was to be married to one of my daughters, never even suspecting it could be her own child. Now tell me, daughter, did Queen Anya ever recognize you?" she asked smugly.

I shook my head. "Not until the end."

"That's because you were truly mine, dear child. It was better that I raise you to your full potential."

"So that's how you arranged our marriage. You demanded his life if you saved it."

"Yes. I was in a magnanimous mood, and I not only saved the prince's life but created wards around the palace. As long as Xander stayed within them, he would never succumb to the werewolf change. But if he strayed past them—" She shrugged.

"Thereby almost forcing him to be a prisoner within the palace. You should have told me," I said as I thought back to our time on the road, how Xander would disappear at night and return come morning. He said it was for my own safety, but he was trying to protect everyone from himself.

"It wouldn't have done anything but cloud your judgment and make you weak. Your birth mother was not an innocent. Neither King Gerald nor King Basil understand the value of children and instead barter them like cattle." Mother Eville's hands shook in anger. Her normally quiet demeanor was unraveling like a cat batting at a ball of yarn. "Daughters are not to be tossed aside for boys. We are valuable," she hissed, and I understood that there was an underlying backstory I did not know and may never uncover.

"Yet you meddled in the affairs of not one but two kingdoms. You're just like them. You bargained me away, forced me to wed a stranger, someone who loathed me. He could have murdered me in my sleep."

Mother Eville scoffed. "Nonsense, you are much too powerful for that."

"Xander bartered me for his kingdom."

"No, King Gerald did that. I don't know if you heard, but he is heartbroken over his wife's death and has abdicated his throne to Xander. You are now queen of not only Baist but Florin, since you are the eldest child," Mother Eville said smugly.

"What of my brother, Aspen?"

Her smile faded. "He disappeared. Last we heard he got on board one of the merchant vessel ships, the Arotas, and took out to sea. But did you not hear me, child? You, my daughter, are queen. I have arranged that." She placed her hand across her chest. "I dealt out a worthy punishment upon two kingdoms and at the same time have made my daughter queen of both." She was as proud as a peacock, and yet I looked out the tower window and knew I wanted nothing to do with this place. Nor did I want Baist or Florin, not when I couldn't have their prince's love.

"He hates me," I whispered.

"And yet you've grown to love him." Lady Eville's eyes twinkled with knowledge.

"I don't love him," I said angrily, not sure if I was trying to convince myself or her.

"You tell yourself that, but yet the proof of your love grows strong." She glanced at my midsection, but I ignored her.

"That's not true, for I made my own bargain with the prince of Baist," I whispered, dropping my bandaged hands across my stomach protectively.

Lady Eville's brows furrowed. "What is this?" She was not pleased.

"A bargain that undoes everything you have worked so hard for," I snapped, tears sliding down my cheeks.

"What have you done, my daughter?" Her voice became quiet, her body still, and I knew her anger was reaching a boiling point. The quieter she became, the angrier she was.

"I'm leaving," I whispered. "His country is safe, and I will now go quietly into the night and live out the rest of my days."

She sucked in her breath so hard that I heard it whistle across her teeth. "No, I can't believe that's what he wanted!"

"Yes, it is!" I held up my hands and began to pull at the white bandages. "Look at me. I'm hideous." When I had unwrapped one red and scarred hand, I worked furiously on the second and then saw the damage that was done. Angry red lines ran up my arms. Pulling my dress away, I confirmed the spell Allemar had cast had left permanent scars across my whole body, creating a pattern that was very unbecoming. My body was hideous.

Scared, I reached for my face and called out for a mirror. Eden, who had retreated to the hall while we talked, brought a small handheld one to me. My hands screamed as I forced my muscles to grip the handle, the mirror shaking uncontrollably. Taking a deep breath, I brought it up to my face, but Lady Eville placed her hand over the mirror.

"Listen to me, daughter. You are still beautiful. This means nothing."

Hearing her reassuring words only filled me with dread. I gathered my courage, lifted the mirror, and wanted to cry out at the stranger looking back at me.

"I'm repulsive," I cried, as my face was not spared. One bright red scar touched my face, trailing from my forehead across my eye and down to my chin. My finger shook as I traced it, and tears fell freely. I prayed the mirror lied, but yet it only spoke truth. I was hideous, beastly. I angrily tossed the mirror across the room, where it landed on a padded chair. I was furious that it hadn't broken on contact like my heart.

"Has he seen me like this?" I asked.

"Not since that day," Eden answered. "I did everything I could to save you, then had to call Mother and Lorn. Prince Xander was not happy when we whisked you away to our tower to take care of you. King Gerald and Prince Xander stayed behind to deal with stately matters."

"That's right." He would have to deal with becoming the new king of Florin and burying Queen Anya. They wouldn't have time to visit me, and I wasn't sure if he even would now. He had what he wanted—freedom from Florin, freedom from me. He could now marry Yasmin.

"Well, we can take you back now that you're fully recovered." Lady Eville lifted her hand and was probably about to snap her fingers to open my trunks and begin packing.

"Yes, let's pack," I said, pulling myself into a sitting position, although I had no desire to return to either kingdoms. "But I need you to do something for me, Eden."

"Anything, dear sister," she said.

"I need you to deliver something to the prince for me."

CHAPTER THIRTY

The days had come and gone, and with each passing season, I had grown comfortable in my new way of life. I had to stop taking wolfsbane and became accustomed to using my death seeker gifts. Now unhindered by drugs, I traveled from town to town and frequently found myself helping solve unexplained deaths.

In Vearin, a cow was found dead in a valley, and two farmers almost came to blows blaming each other for its murder, but it turned out to be nothing more than an accident. In another town, a young child had died of what everyone believed to be natural causes but was actually poisoned by the wicked stepmother.

In the beginning, I was helping solve the crime after the death. But then I accepted my gift and it changed, and I started to save lives. My gift came full circle when my death vision brought me to a young boy who had fallen into the lake and couldn't swim.

I was paralyzed in the vision, unable to move, but then I broke through the magic barrier and instead of watching, I was able to jump in and pull the little boy out. Drenched and shivering, I carried him out of the river and passed him to his crying mother. I couldn't help but think of young Renard and Magda.

I couldn't save them in the past, but I could help those in the future. The mother turned to thank me, but I was gone, pulled back from the death vision and into my bed, my mattress soaked in water and covered in weeds. It didn't matter. I went to sleep with a smile on my face.

But when it became too hard to travel, I chose to settle in Celia—maybe because I wanted to be near a place where we had shared a few happy memories together.

It wasn't so bad being a hedge witch. I moved into the same cottage Xander had taken me when I was injured by the arrow. I used all of my power to keep it protected, and the more I dug deep into the land searching for magic, the more it came. First it was like a little seedling, but the more I used it, the more it grew until it became a fountain. I wasn't sure, but I believed I was witnessing the birth of a new ley line, right through the land of Baist and under my cottage.

This was exciting, because it meant I could use magic and not be plagued with headaches or have to take to using stored magic from sacrifices like Allemar.

A few days a week, I would travel into town with my charms and sell them at my stall, earning enough to make a decent living. The people of Baist were hungry for the basic necessities that were readily available in other kingdoms: matches that would never get wet, stones that would always stay warm and could be used as bed warmers, candles with enchanted wicks that wouldn't blow out with a strong wind, jugs that could keep milk cold for hours. All of them were simple spells that I had easily mastered as a child and took very little energy to conjure into an item.

When the magic would fade, the villagers would return the item, and I would recharge it for them for free. The scar across my face had lightened, no longer an angry red but a silvery white like a spiderweb. It still made people uncomfortable to look directly at me, however, so I took to wearing my dark hair over one side of my face.

At first the villagers were frightened of me, and I could feel myself getting angry, hardening my heart toward them, but then something miraculous happened and they accepted me as one of them.

The time was drawing near. I had heard the rumors in town about the new princess's sudden disappearance. How I left as suddenly as I appeared. Prince Xander has had plenty of time to declare me officially dead. I found myself making more trips into the village to hear news, waiting on pins and needles for the new marriage banns to go out where he would announce his engagement to Yasmin. Of course, with each passing day I had darker thoughts, a shorter temper and was very irritable. I was even barking at Lucinda, one of my best customers, who was having issues with one of my lighting charms.

"Well, have you tried turning it off and on again?" I snapped, rubbing my knuckles into the small of my back.

"Rosa," she said calmly, using the name I had adopted with my new lifestyle. "Maybe you should head home early and put your feet up."

"I don't have time to put my feet up. I have to work hard to prepare for the coming months when I can't make it into town as often."

"Well, you know you can always send me a message through the mirror and someone will get it to me," Lucinda said, pointing over to the newly installed mirror vendor two stalls down from me.

"How? When?"

"Just yesterday. I'm surprised you didn't notice the hammering and construction. The prince has ordered one in every town in Baist and Florin. I'm not sure if I trust it yet, but

I'm excited to receive my first message. The prince is here to give a demonstration on how they work. Promise me you'll be the first to message me?" She patted her hair, which was neatly pulled back into a bun.

"What? The prince—here?" I craned my neck, searching for his tall, dark form among the crowd. The market had been busier than usual, and sure enough, I hadn't noticed the royal guards coming in two by two. I instantly recognized Xander leading the troop, though his face seemed more worn and tired, his chin unshaven.

"I need to go," I said while I hastily tried to tie up the tablecloth with all of my charms. "If anyone needs me, tell them I'll be back in a few weeks, or send them to my cottage."

"Is something the matter, dear?" Lucinda asked, holding my bag as I dumped my possessions inside.

"No, nothing. I'm just needed at home."

"Don't you want to stay and meet the prince?"

"No, I definitely do not," I snapped out a little too harshly, instantly regretting it. Taking the bag from her, I pulled the hood of my cloak over my face and kept my head down as I tried to shuffle through the crowd that was already gathering.

He's here! I was an idiot for not paying closer attention. I couldn't let him see me like this. There was no way I could answer his questions; he would feel betrayed.

Trying to make a hasty retreat, I didn't notice the horse-drawn wagon before I stepped out into the street.

"Whoa!" the driver cried out too late.

Turning, I saw the horses and grabbed my stomach.

Strong hands pulled me out of the way of the horses. My hood fell back, and I looked up at my savior in surprise.

"Rosalie?" Xander said in shock as he stared deep into my eyes, but I quickly turned my head to the side, refusing to look at him.

His hands were like iron bands on my arm that tightened when he looked down. His jaw clenched, and his eyes turned dark and foreboding.

I didn't wait, just pushed him away, running as fast as I could toward the woods while pulling my hood up to cover my raven hair, but I couldn't run far. Soon, I was out of breath and stopped by a creek. I sat on a rock and waited, tears running down my face. I could use my magic to disguise my scent and trail, but that wouldn't be fair. He was a wolf, and he would find me, especially now that he had seen what I had stolen from him.

I was scared of Xander's wrath, for I had sinned greatly against him, and there was nothing I could do to seek his forgiveness.

The snap of a twig alerted me to his presence, and I waited, sitting on the rock and soaking my feet in the water, the cold easing the swelling. Another twig snapped, and when I looked up, there he was, staring at me from across the creek. Xander's wolf had indeed followed my scent. His ears were back, his nose sniffed the air, and his amber eyes bored into mine accusingly. His lips curled, and I heard his bark of admonishment.

Ignoring him seemed the best option, so I continued to look at the water until I felt the change in the air as the wolf shifted into my copper-haired prince. He stepped through the creek and stood before me, his boots now in the running water next to my bare feet.

"You swore a blood oath," Xander said angrily.

"I did what you asked," I replied humbly. "Your kingdom is saved. I kept my end of the bargain and left, leaving you free to wed another."

"Rosalie, that's not what I meant." His voice was filled with emotion as he kneeled on the embankment and reached for my hands. Grasping them between his, he put one on my protruding stomach and felt for the life within. At Xander's touch, my baby kicked back in excitement, and fear took hold of me.

"You promised me that you would not take my firstborn child." His hand balled into a fist so tight his knuckles were white, and he became very still. I was afraid of him and what I had done.

"I swear I didn't know," I cried out, keeping my face low. "Not until weeks after I'd had already left."

"Goodness, woman, I thought something had happened to you. I searched high and low for you. Your mother refused to tell me where you were and accused me of losing you."

"You looked for me?" I gasped.

"I have spent the last few months installing those stupid mirror centers in every city and town I visited, just in case you sent word to me. Look." He pulled out a small mirror in a case. "I even keep one on me at all times, in the hopes you would ream me out like before. But nothing. You dropped off the face of the known kingdoms."

"I was only following our agreement, Xander."

"That's Prince Xander to you."

His words hurt and felt like stones in my stomach as I corrected myself. "Prince Xander."

He reached into his vest pocket and pulled out the chess piece king. "Then you had the gall to have your sister send me this. That's when I knew what you had done. That you had abandoned me."

"No, you abandoned me. Traded me for Earlsgaarde—er, Allemar to save your kingdom. You're holding the wrong piece, my lord. We should have used a pawn instead of a king," I said bitterly.

"This is what I think of our bargain." Xander stood and tested the weight of the chess piece before chucking it into the creek bed. It slowly sank to the bottom, leaving only rings upon the surface.

The tears were flowing freely now. "Where did you go? You could have stopped Tipper from arresting me, sending me to Florin."

"I didn't know until it was too late. You ran away from me, and I needed time to cool off. When I had calmed down and returned to the manor, I learned you had left with Earlsgaarde. Tipper said you went with him willingly, that you admitted to murdering all those people."

"That was a lie."

"I know that now. Pru was the one who told me the truth. I was a fool to believe the woman I loved was a monster. She couldn't have done those things, and I was ready to risk everything to get her back."

"You love me?" Tears welled up in my eyes.

Xander reached up beneath the hood to touch my face, but I shuddered, pulling back. "You cursed me, Rosalie, to marry for love. I should be angry, furious even, if I hadn't already started falling for you hard."

"I thought you hated me."

"No, I hated how much I thought about you."

"You couldn't possibly, because you didn't know me."

"Rosalie, I've known since the night I kissed you that you were mine." He grinned. "I just needed time to come to terms with the fact that my enemy, the woman I married, was also the woman I loved. The woman I needed more than the air I breathe." He leaned forward, pressing his face into the crook of my neck, and took a deep breath. "Remember, I knew the night I saved you from the thieves, who you were."

"But why play along?"

"Because I didn't like how fast I was falling for you. It was as if you really did put a spell on me, and I hated it. I hated myself and took it out on you."

His admission made me laugh, and I hit him in the shoulder. Xander pulled out the rose pin I had lost and attached it to my cloak.

"You were right about one thing," I whispered, my hands shaking as I gripped the edge of the hood, preparing to reveal myself and have him go running away in horror. "I am as hideous as a beast." I pulled the hood back, my dark hair still covering my face, but I struggled to look at him. I couldn't meet his gaze in case his face turned to revulsion. I couldn't bear it.

What had I done?

Xander's hands reached for my cheek, pulling me closer. His left hand brushed my dark hair away from my face, revealing the small white scar that marred my beauty. I closed my eyes, not willing to see his reaction. He gasped, and I shuddered, a tear squeezing out between my lashes to slide down my cheek.

His thumb brushed it away, and his warm breath lingered on my cheek as his lips claimed mine. My eyes opened in surprise and my lips parted as Xander kissed me, his hand on the back of my neck, pulling me in closer. How could I have forgotten his kisses? I missed him so. Reaching for him, I gripped his vest, my breathing becoming ragged.

He broke the kiss first, and his eyes searched my face, truly seeing me, and what I saw there did not make me pull away. All I saw was an outpouring of unconditional love.

"Beast? No. All I see is my darling beauty," he whispered huskily, then left a trail of kisses along my scar before claiming my lips again. "Please come home with me."

It was painful to pull away from those kisses, for they were powerful like a drug. "Hmm, have you not remarried yet?"

His breathing was as ragged as mine. "What? Why, when I

have a wife already, one who, when crossed, could scorch the kingdom? I would be a fool to leave you."

My hands went to my face, and I turned away in horror. "No, I can't be your queen when I look like this. The people already fear me. I couldn't take it to be stared at and called any more names."

Xander grabbed my wrists, pulling my hands from my face. "Rosalie, those are your battle wounds, earned when you saved our kingdom from a great and terrible beast. If the people cannot see past your outside, then they can leave and go to Sion for all I care. I want you as my queen. No one else will do. I want my wife and child to come home."

Pregnancy had made me an emotional wreck. My nose was red and stuffy, my face puffed up from the tears that never seemed to end.

"And where is home?" I sniffed, wiping at my nose. "Florin or Baist?"

"Whichever you choose, or neither. I would freely give up both and live with you in this village if that is your wish. I will become your house husband and tend to you as a doting husband and father."

"But the country—"

"I'm sure father could be persuaded to take the throne again until Ameline is old enough to ascend to the throne and have children of her own."

"Ameline," I whispered, my heart hurting. I wanted to see her, my half sister.

I swallowed. "What if we lived for half a year at each court, until my brother can be found?"

"Aspen?" Xander said. "He was in league with Allemar. He's gone."

"Yes, but I believe he was being used by Allemar. He did try to redeem himself in the end."

"By almost killing all of us. If it weren't for him, you wouldn't have the scars." Xander gently touched my hands and traced his fingers up my arms.

"If it weren't for him... if he hadn't opened that portal, I don't know if I would have been able to stop Allemar. I still don't know if I did. I believe he's still out there, waiting to come back as anyone, anywhere."

"I would hate to be him, then." Xander snorted.

"Why?"

"Because you have six other sisters, Rosalie. Six vengeful sisters who are extremely angry at what he's done to you. He better hope he doesn't meet any of the others."

I took comfort in what Xander said but couldn't let go of the nagging feeling that we would meet again. Allemar knew Mother Eville, and she knew him. I began to wonder if there was a bigger game at play here between the two, and my sisters and I were nothing more than pawns in their ruthless plan. But first he would have to come back across the plane from where I sent him, and that could take months of storing his power and strength.

"I can't come with you."

"Why not?" His brows furrowed.

"Because I can't go back to the way things were."

"Silly woman, don't you understand why I've crossed the kingdoms searching for you? I'm ready for a change, a different future, one where magic is acceptable."

"Why?" I waited, needing to hear the words I never thought he would say.

"It's because I love you."

"Say it again," I whispered, needing to hear it a second time, cementing it into my memory.

"Rosalie, never again will I keep you hidden from the

world. I want you by my side for all eternity. You and our child."

Xander wrapped his arms around me, my very large belly coming between us. He looked down and frowned. "Hey, you."

I grinned as the once notorious prince, feared for his temper, cooed to our child.

A grumbling came from the grass, and Gobbersnot crawled up into my lap wearing my baby's christening dress. He cuddled against my big belly, giving the prince a wide, toothy grin.

"That's one ugly baby." Xander laughed.

Gobbersnot puckered up and made a kissing face at Xander, who looked repulsed.

"Don't worry, he grows on you," I said. "And he makes a great guard dog."

Xander grinned. "I'm sure between a wolf, witch, and goblin, our child will have a completely normal upbringing."

I couldn't hold back my laughter.

"Thank you, Rosalie," Xander said, his eyes misty as he leaned in and pressed his forehead to mine.

"For what?" I asked softly.

"For loving me despite my curse. For proving that even a beast deserves a chance at love," he whispered, claiming my lips.

"I love you too. Always and forever," I promised.

Continue the
Daughters of Eville Series

Of Glass and Glamour
Of Sea and Song

www.chandahahn.com

ABOUT THE AUTHOR

Chanda Hahn is a NYT & USA Today Bestselling author of The Unfortunate Fairy Tale series. She uses her experience as a children's pastor, children's librarian and bookseller to write compelling and popular fiction for teens. She was born in Seattle, WA, grew up in Nebraska, and currently resides in Waukesha, WI, with her husband and their twin children; Aiden and Ashley.

Visit Chanda Hahn's website to learn more about her other forthcoming books.
www.chandahahn.com

Printed in Great Britain
by Amazon